ONE MAN'S PRINCESS

NICOLE BURNHAM

One Man's Princess

By Nicole Burnham

Copyright © 2017 by Nicole Burnham

Cover design by Patricia Schmitt

Edition: May 2022

ISBN: 978-1-941828-13-7 (paperback)

ISBN: 978-1-941828-12-0 (ebook)

For more information or to subscribe to Nicole's newsletter, visit nicoleburnham.com.

For Suzanne Marion
For your resilience, your optimism, and most of all, for your wicked sense of humor.

CHAPTER 1

Lina Cornaro could—and for all she knew, did—talk lingerie in her sleep. Price points and profit margins. Fabric content. Sex appeal.

She was damned good at her job. However, she needed the three women and two men seated at the glass-topped conference table fifteen floors above New York's Sixth Avenue to believe it as powerfully as she did. It'd become the most important thing in her life.

Lina circled the table and clicked to a screen that pictured Isola's new table display. She kept her tone engaging. "We've all seen exclusive boutiques where only associates handle the merchandise or visited high-end stores where shoppers feel they're under a microscope if they dare run their fingertips over a garment or read a price tag. At Isola, we take the opposite approach. Our displays invite shoppers not only to look, but to touch."

She plucked a pair of lace panties with high-cut leg openings from the table, then gave the rich aquamarine fabric at the waistband a light tug to show its resiliency. The Mirabeau store managers leaned forward, which brought her a swell of reassurance. From the moment she'd started speaking, Lina suspected more than one listened to the cadence of her voice rather than the content of her presentation. Examined her gestures as she moved around the room. Discreetly studied her features. Attempted to determine what she had and hadn't inherited from her biological father, as if it were proof of…something.

Then again, maybe none of them followed the European tabloids and her concerns were unfounded.

"When a woman feels the stretch of our lace panties, she'll realize they're strong enough to hold up to her daily activities, yet will lie softly against her skin without rolling or pinching. A man whose thumb glides over the lace of a bra cup crafted in our Italian factory will recognize the artistry of it. He'll know it's worthy of the woman whose body it graces."

That drew smiles from the group, though not as many as when Lina made a similar presentation to a London retailer in January, shortly before her life was upended…first privately, and then publicly.

"Our work is beautiful to behold, but it's the tactile experience that proves Isola is the perfect marriage of aesthetics and engineering, and that it's excellent quality for the price. During next week's launch event, the sales team at each of your stores should encourage shoppers to hold our lingerie. Allow them to experience Isola's trifecta of style, comfort, and durability. To understand that while it appears delicate, it's exceptionally strong. They'll pull these pieces from their lingerie drawers day after day, knowing they can wear them with confidence in any situation. It's what differentiates Isola from the competition and will make it a rousing success at your stores."

She clicked to the final screen, closing her presentation by emphasizing the upward sales trend at her shop in Milan and early sales figures from the London retailer before taking questions.

Ten minutes later, having left the store managers with gift bags, Lina took the elevator to the ground floor. Alone at last, she allowed her smile to slip. The Mirabeau staff had been gracious, professional, and enthusiastic. No one mentioned the fact that, following her mother's death, Lina had been publicly outed as the illegitimate daughter of Sarcaccia's very popular—and very married—King Carlo. None of the administrative assistants or other staff gave her awkward looks or whispered as she'd walked by their desks.

She rolled her shoulders, suddenly aware of how much stress she'd carried in anticipation of today's meeting.

Ever since the king's press conference six weeks ago, when the monarch broadcast their relationship to the world, Lina had kept her head down and worked, determined to stay out of the public eye and let the royal family handle questions about the king's scandalous affair. She'd kept her business humming, using her extensive To Do lists as a shield against the grief of losing her mother to a long, painful battle with liver disease. So far, that tactic had worked, at least as far as the public's interest in her was concerned.

The elevator slowed to a stop. Lina straightened and resumed her professional demeanor. She'd take today as a sign to get over her paranoia. New celebrity scandals occurred daily. The world would eventually forget—or it simply wouldn't care—that while he was a teenager, a famous king had an improper relationship with his private tutor and that he'd continued that relationship through the early months of marriage to his equally famous wife, and that Lina and her siblings were the result. If she kept on her current path, Lina would be defined by her professional accomplishments and her kindness toward others, rather than by a man she'd never met. Or, worse, by the nature of her mother's long-ago relationship with that man.

And if she truly believed that, there was a bridge not far from her current location any New Yorker would be happy to sell to her.

She nodded to the security guard manning the lobby desk, tightened the belt on her camel-colored coat, then pushed through the revolving door and stepped into the chill, uncharacteristic in its bite for mid-June. Despite the penetrating wind and gloomy skies, pedestrians clogged the sidewalk, starting the weekend early. A man wearing a sandwich board stood near the curb, pushing cards touting a comedy show into the hands of skeptical tourists. The scent of an unseen hot dog cart teased Lina's nose. A woman walked by holding a little girl's hand while the girl licked white frosting from the top of a cupcake. Beyond the horde, taxis and bicycle messengers hummed along Sixth Avenue.

The scene instantly put Lina at ease. Manhattan was a world away from Lina's home in Milan, but she loved it here. The noise, the lights, even the rumble of the subway beneath her feet as she passed over the sidewalk grates. She'd lived on cheap food in a tiny, overheated Chelsea flat with ramshackle furniture while attending design school here, but they'd been the most wonderful four years of her life. She'd worked hard and dreamed big.

Her forced smile turned to a full-fledged grin. After placing a limited selection of Isola lingerie with the London retailer, she'd been presented the opportunity to gain more attention for her line by hosting a reception at London Fashion Week in February. She'd blown it by withdrawing at the last minute. Not that she'd have made a different decision, given her situation at the time, but with this second chance— a contract for a trial run selling Isola merchandise in five locations of Mirabeau, New York's most elegant department store—she planned to grab the brass ring and hold on tight. Maybe, someday, one of those billboards in Times Square would advertise Isola. When that happened, she just might stand in the middle of Times Square and open a bottle of champagne in celebration, crowds and traffic be damned, and toast her younger self.

A couple in their twenties passed close enough for Lina to overhear their analysis of a Broadway musical, giving her another dose of nostalgia. Tempting as it was to nab a last-minute single ticket to a show, her favorite New York indulgence, tonight Lina planned a luxurious soak in the claw-footed tub of her late mother's condo. She'd earned it after the long flight from Milan, followed by this afternoon's department store presentation. There wouldn't be time for relaxation next week, when she was scheduled to visit each of the five Mirabeau locations for the launch. Then, on Thursday night, she'd thank all those who worked on Isola's New York campaign with a cocktail reception at Cooper Hewitt, home of the Smithsonian Design Museum. She'd work from the condo on Friday, then fly to Milan on Saturday…and a flat that didn't have a tub.

Once Lina and her brothers sold their mother's condo, that piece of heaven would be lost forever. The theater could wait.

Lina pivoted in the direction of the subway entrance, keeping close to the building to avoid the crowd, but stopped short when a burly man wielding a massive camera blocked her path.

A feminine, upper-class British voice called from her right, "Ms. Cornaro, do you remain committed to appear at Mirabeau next week when your line makes its American debut?"

She hazarded a glance in the direction of the voice. A rail-thin redhead in a stylish navy coat repeated the question, then took a stutter-step forward when people knocked into her from behind. Within seconds, Lina was surrounded by reporters, each jockeying for position with microphones and cameras and shouted questions.

"When did you learn about your mother and King Carlo?"

Cameras clicked away. The photographer who first blocked her path moved so close she could touch his lens.

"Have you met the king? Do you have a relationship?"

"Does the king approve of your career?"

"Have you met your half-siblings? What have they said about your mother?"

"It's been reported that Princess Sophia ordered lingerie from your Milan boutique last year. Can you confirm that?"

The last was asked in Sarcaccian-accented Italian. Lina had successfully avoided the European tabloids for weeks now, even going so far as to stay in a short-term rental in April when they'd surrounded her Milan flat for several days following the royal press conference. How had the gutter scum found her in New York?

Despite the fight-or-flight instinct that made her want to take action, she locked a polite expression in place, looped her handbag more securely on her arm, and sidestepped the burly cameraman. She refused to answer their questions, but she wouldn't duck her head and run, either. Lina's mother taught her the skills necessary to guard one's privacy while enjoying a robust career, even if her mother's motives in doing so hadn't been pure.

"Excuse me." She narrowed her gaze at the reporters standing behind the cameraman. None of them moved. Cameras clicked with the rapidity of machine gun fire. So many questions were shouted she couldn't pick out which speakers asked what. Not that she cared. The words *falsified* and *deplorable* cutting through the din were enough to steel her resolve.

She stood taller, straightened her shoulders. "Please allow me to pass. I have an appointment."

"You heard her. Move."

The gravelly voice coming from behind her held an undisguised threat. The last—the only—time she'd heard that voice speak in that tone, it'd been directed at her. The specific words being, "Get out and leave me alone. Don't ever come back."

Those words had broken her heart.

Before Lina could look over her shoulder, a few of the reporters shifted. A strong, protective hand went to her lower back, propelling her through the gap.

"She has a bodyguard?" someone asked.

"Apparently."

"No, that's Ivo Zanardi."

"Who?"

"The Formula One driver. The one who wrecked during preseason testing." The hissed identification came from the reporter with the Sarcaccian accent. "Quick, get a shot."

Once again, the reporters surged toward her.

"How do you know Lina?"

"Are you a fan of Isola, Ivo?"

"Do you plan to race at all this season? Will you rejoin Ferrari?"

One voice rose over the others. "Ivo, are you and Lina together?"

Lina caught her toe on the sidewalk and nearly tripped. The casual use of first names was bad enough, as if these strangers knew her socially. But with such personal questions…how deep into her background had these trolls scrounged? If they knew about her relationship with Ivo, why hadn't it already been reported?

Maybe they didn't know and were fishing.

"Don't answer." The warning came close to her ear. She couldn't see Ivo, not without wrenching her neck, but she could feel his presence. She could even smell him. The scent of his skin was burned into her memory after cozy evenings spent watching movies on the sofa in her Milan flat and long nights making love in hotel rooms as he traveled throughout Europe to race.

And oh, that voice. The gritty timbre of Ivo's voice captivated her the moment they'd met.

"Our relationship is private. If you don't move, I'll call the police and have you moved."

"It's a public sidewalk!"

Ivo extended an arm to split the crowd, then directed her toward the curb. The light changed at the end of the block, sending a rush of cars their direction. Ivo flagged a taxi and opened the door for her. Lina slid inside and started to give the driver the address to her mother's condo, but Ivo slid in behind her, forcing her to the far side of the seat.

He gave an address a few blocks north. "Sorry for the short drive. I'll tip well."

The driver shrugged, then pulled away from the curb.

"If anyone follows, I'd be obliged if you'd lose them." To Lina, he said, "Do you really have an appointment?"

"What?"

"You told the reporters—"

"Oh. No."

"Good."

At the next intersection, the driver slowed for a yellow light, then dashed through at the last second and made a quick left onto the next street, throwing Lina against the seat, then toward Ivo before she could plant her palm to steady herself. Midway up the block, the driver cut through a hotel's valet tunnel to emerge on a one-way street heading the opposite direction.

"Well done."

The cabbie angled his head to acknowledge Ivo's compliment, then drove to the address Ivo provided. Lina remained silent. Not only had he overridden her planned destination, she had so many questions, she wasn't sure which to ask first. The last time she'd seen Ivo, in February, he'd been in bandages, in pain, and—when told he faced weeks, not days, in the hospital—as angry as an injured bull staring down a matador.

Ivo paid the driver and a doorman approached to open her door and help her from the cab. Lina didn't move. Instead, she folded her arms and stated the obvious. "This is the Park Hyatt."

"I'm staying here."

"I'm staying at my mother's condo."

Ivo twisted in the seat, giving Lina her first full view of him. He was every bit as coolly intimidating as she remembered. He wore faded black jeans, a T-shirt the color of stainless steel, and a leather jacket that molded to his wiry torso as if it were custom-made. A day's worth of stubble dotted his dark skin, which was out of character for him. Rather than make him appear tired or disheveled, it added to his air of danger.

He slid one arm along the back of the seat and gave her a long, assessing look before his flat, jet-black brows raised a notch. "You think they haven't found her place?"

They hadn't this morning. Then again, they hadn't been outside Mirabeau when she'd arrived.

"I don't know. Even if they have, it's a private building with a keyed entry." Reporters couldn't touch her once she crossed the threshold.

His eyes bored holes in her. "Come inside. Let's talk. Then you can do as you please."

Her jaw tightened. She could do as she pleased anyway. She nearly pointed it out, but an uncharacteristic twitch of his hand against his denim-clad leg made her pause. Ivo was a lot of things; nervous had never been one of them. She pretended not to see, gave a curt nod, then allowed the doorman to assist her from the cab and followed Ivo through the lobby to the elevator.

They'd been together a little over two years, though most of their face-to-face time came during Ivo's short winter off-season. During the other nine-plus months each year, she'd join him on occasion at his hotel on Grand Prix weekends. In rare instances, they'd even spend a weeknight together when he could break away from the grind of the circuit and she wasn't traveling for her own career. It was a lot of time, if one ticked off months on the calendar, and yet very little. It was the reason they'd agreed to remain casual. Uncommitted. He'd hurt her that day in the hospital, but she'd allowed it by opening her heart when that wasn't the plan.

He'd extricated her from a group of hungry paparazzi faster than she could've done on her own. It was reasonable to give him the benefit of the doubt.

Though—if she were honest with herself—she said yes to satisfy her own curiosity.

She said yes because she'd never refused an invitation from Ivo Zanardi.

CHAPTER 2

Ivo propped a shoulder against the side of the elevator, his attention riveted on the lights that ticked off the floors. Lina stayed to the opposite side of the carriage, her shoulders relaxed and expression placid. He didn't buy her casual act, nor did he suspect she bought his.

Last time—hell, every time—he and Lina stood in hotel elevator together, they'd been on their way to a shared room. One where they'd ordered room service. Debated and laughed over in-room movies. Enjoyed the bed. Enjoyed the shower. Enjoyed the bed some more.

On the few occasions they'd been together prerace, they'd even sprawled across the sheets and slept.

Lina remembered it all. He'd bet last season's Monaco Grand Prix title it was on her mind right now. Whether she thought of those times with fondness or regret, that he couldn't determine.

He couldn't determine anything about Lina. He wasn't sure he'd ever truly known her. After seeing her face and name all over the news and the Internet these past weeks, with each story claiming new information about her background, he was damn sick and tired of wondering.

The elevator stopped with a bounce that jarred Ivo's healing spine. He released a long, silent breath, cursed himself for overdoing it at yesterday's physical therapy session, then braced the door with one arm and gave Lina the room number, allowing her to lead the way.

Big mistake. Watching her familiar walk made him ache.

He curled his fingers into a fist against his hip. From the moment he'd first witnessed that walk, Lina had drawn his attention. He'd been behind her, almost as close as he was now, as they navigated the looping line through passport control at Heathrow early one December morning. He was connecting through after a promotional appearance in Toronto; he learned later that she'd attended a design seminar in New York. Her hair had been up in a loose bun, but several tendrils had escaped to dance along the back of her neck. The strap of her handbag dug into her shoulder and a wisp had been caught beneath it. He'd wondered if it pulled.

If she'd been his wife or girlfriend, he'd have lifted the bag and fixed it for her.

Instead, he'd looked away, watching the slow progress of the zigzagging line that would carry them through the screening area. In front of them, on the other side of the nylon divider, a mother clutching Chinese passports pushed a restless child in a stroller while she toted an infant in a front pack. He'd felt a pang of sympathy for her. When the toddler started to squawk, Lina wiggled her fingers at the little girl, then played an impromptu game of peekaboo, settling the child and earning a grateful smile from the mother. A few minutes later, as the mother and children passed them again, Lina withdrew a small box from her handbag. In a voice soft enough to keep the toddler from hearing, she explained to the mother that it was a promotional item she'd been handed at a conference, a chain puzzle suitable for small children, and that the toddler was welcome to have it. The mother hadn't appeared to understand everything Lina said, but as she'd inspected the box, her appreciation was clear.

Ivo had been smitten.

A half hour later, he'd spied Lina in the waiting area for his flight to Milan. He'd taken the empty seat beside hers and told her she'd been great with the little girl. She'd given him a quiet thank you and he'd thought that'd be the end of it. He'd closed his eyes to wait for the boarding call and hadn't spoken to her again.

When she was seated beside him on the plane, they'd shared a quick smile, but didn't speak. He'd leaned back in his seat to read while she opened her computer and answered email. But an hour later, when they both selected the chicken marsala, the flight attendant apologized and stated that there was only one left. Ivo insisted Lina take the chicken, claiming that he'd be fine with the beef stroganoff.

It didn't take Lina long to figure out he wasn't a fan of beef stroganoff, despite his effort to fake it. They'd chatted for the rest of the flight. First, about the horrible line, then about their families. He'd discovered that she'd been raised in Italy, as he had, though neither had been part of a traditional Italian family and each had spoken English at home. He'd told her about his Nigerian mother—only briefly mentioning that he had an Italian father—while she'd spoken highly of her late stepfather, an American named Jack Cornaro, and described her mother, a woman from a small farming village on the Mediterranean island of Sarcaccia, in glowing terms.

Both steered clear of discussing their careers. She'd said she had a fashion job, then abruptly changed the subject. He'd been happy to let her. He'd been burned too many times by women infatuated with what they perceived to be the glamorous life of a F1 driver to tell anyone what he did for a living, assuming they didn't recognize him before they approached him. When they disembarked, rather than asking for Lina's number, he'd made the last-second decision to give her his, sensing that she'd be more comfortable with the control in her hands.

When she'd called and asked if he'd be interested in attending an outdoor concert in Milan, he'd been floored. They'd enjoyed the music, then talked late into the night as they shared gelato, strolled the cobblestoned streets of the town center, and watched tourists gape at the architecture of the illuminated Duomo. He'd walked her home, then given her a soft kiss on each cheek before watching her enter the exterior door to her flat.

It wasn't until later, on their third date, that Lina confessed that her fashion job was as the owner and chief designer of a high-end lingerie line and explained that she hadn't elaborated because she didn't trust the motives of men who asked her out after they learned what she did. When he told her about his profession, she admitted she'd looked him up after their first date went well, but knew nothing about F1 other than the fact it seemed fast, loud, and extremely risky.

They'd laughed over that. Bonded over the nature of their out-of-the-ordinary careers. Discovered they each preferred life with a limited number of deeper friendships to numerous relationships maintained over social media. They'd lingered over dinner. Found a park bench in the city center and enjoyed the emerging stars and night air, followed by long kisses that had grown increasingly passionate. He'd left for Abu Dhabi the next day, the first stop on a string of off-season promotional events and awards galas, but returned to Milan two weeks later for a dinner date that never made it to dinner, though it ended with a glorious breakfast in bed.

She'd walked to the kitchen naked to refill his coffee that morning. And oh, how he'd loved that particular walk.

"This way?" she asked when they reached the short hallway leading to the suites, then turned at his nod. He shoved down the memory as he followed her the last few paces. Stargazing with Lina on that warm Italian evening seemed a lifetime away.

He keyed into the room, once again holding the door and allowing her to precede him. He remained near the door, giving her space to survey the room. She took in the stone flooring, the sumptuous area rugs, and the king-sized bed with its crisp white pillows before her attention shifted to the seating area, which contained a sleek modern sofa and two chairs on either side of a low coffee table. Housekeeping had left the curtains open, showcasing the view of Carnegie Hall's elegant roof, but Lina's gaze breezed past it to the window treatments themselves before she scanned the subtle texture of the wallpaper and the understated artwork. He knew she approved of the decor when her eyes didn't stop on any one element, the way they had when she'd noticed the damaged blind at his hospital window.

He waited until the door was closed to speak. "I owe you an apology."

Lina grimaced, then set her handbag on a desk that stood opposite the seating area. She kept the strap threaded between her fingers. "I thought I'd compliment your room, maybe mention the view or the fact this place is three times the size of your flat in Milan. Or I'd give you a chance to explain what you were doing outside Mirabeau's corporate office. But all right. Why do you believe you owe me an apology?"

He removed his leather jacket. Rather than toss it on the bed, he fished a hanger from the closet. He held out a second hanger, but Lina shook her head.

Not staying long, then.

He gave her a quick head-to-toe perusal. She'd lost weight since he'd last seen her. She walked everywhere and kept a healthy diet out of habit, but when work put her under pressure, Lina nibbled rather than ate. She didn't appear gaunt, though, thank God. Given the strain she had to be under since her mother's death and King Carlo's press conference, he'd wondered about her health. And worried. When they'd dated, they'd avoided the public eye, unwilling to subject their relationship to scrutiny. Once, when she'd waited to leave his hotel in order to avoid the F1 press, she'd noted that she preferred to keep her press interaction limited to the fashion industry and focused on her products rather than on her personal life. "Why invite stress?" she'd asked.

Now the spotlight was on her personal life whether she wanted it there or not.

"It was wrong of me to throw you out of my hospital room. I'm sorry."

Her expression was carefully bland. "I thought you were going to apologize for shoving me into a taxi and driving the opposite direction I planned to go."

"That was for your own safety. I didn't want those vultures following you. My behavior at the hospital, however, was out of line. I regret it."

"Apology accepted."

He jerked. "That's it?"

"You said it. You were wrong. I'm over it." She gave a dismissive wave. "Well, I'm not over-over it. What you did was…let's call it a shock. But you were frustrated and in pain and it happened a long time ago. I've moved on. I have other priorities. So yes, apology accepted."

"It wasn't that long ago." Only a few months. He moved closer. "Though it probably feels like it, given all that's happened in your life. Care to talk about it?"

"No. Not unless you mean what's happening to me with work. That is going spectacularly."

He heard the unsaid *now* at the end of her sentence.

"It would have gone well sooner if not for me."

Her hand returned to the top of her purse. "That wasn't your fault."

"I heard that you gave up London Fashion Week to stay at the hospital while I was unconscious."

"That was my choice."

And with that choice, she'd changed the nature of their relationship. They both knew it.

They'd agreed from their first night together they'd keep things relaxed. Commitment meant responsibility to another human being, and their careers made that extraordinarily difficult. It wasn't long before he'd wanted more—and suspected she had, too—but given that their time together was largely limited to weekend encounters, neither had been brave enough to broach the topic. A discussion of logistics— who'd give up what in order to deepen their relationship—risked the loss of what they had. When Lina made the decision to stay with him during his hospitalization—to be responsible for him—she'd done with her actions what neither of them had done in words. He'd awakened and responded with a sound rejection.

Finally, he said, "You didn't choose to take care of an ass. Especially given that you took time away from work and had to get a waiver from my mother to have access to my room."

"Ivo, I told you, apology accepted." Her tight smile relaxed a fraction. "You look much better than the last time I saw you. Ready to move forward. I'm glad."

There was a definite period at the end of her statement. He didn't miss that her gaze flicked to the room's art deco clock.

He resisted the urge to put a hand to the underside of his jaw, where a raised, purplish-black burn scar remained. This wasn't going the way he'd envisioned. He hoped to find Lina at Mirabeau and take her to a nearby restaurant. Somewhere they'd have privacy, but where she wouldn't feel cornered. He'd grovel for a while, Lina would hear him out, and she'd reluctantly forgive him. She'd ask about his recovery, maybe about his plans to race. If he were really lucky, she'd tell him she'd missed him as much as he'd missed her. That she'd wished he'd been by her side when the news of her paternity broke in the press. That she owed him an apology, as well. She'd confess the reasons she'd kept her entire life a secret from him. She'd realize why he'd been so damned angry. Why it should all be in the past.

After that, he'd make sure she knew he was here for her now. He'd kiss her—probably not anything more, but a man could dream—and they'd move toward reconciliation. A new start. A better, braver start.

It was a long shot at best, but he'd always defied the odds.

"Let's discuss something else." He gestured toward the sofa. When she hesitated, he added, "It's safe. I won't bite." Unless she wanted that.

"I shouldn't stay."

"You can stay long enough to convince those reporters you aren't coming home."

Her brows drew together. "What makes you think they're at my mother's condo?"

"An educated guess, given how many were outside the Mirabeau office. Assuming the property is in your family name, it wouldn't take much research to find it."

"It's in a trust."

"More challenging, then." But not impossible.

The edges of her mouth twitched as she weighed her options, then she moved to the sofa. Rather than sit beside her, he chose one of the armchairs to grant her space.

"Why were you there?" she asked. "At Mirabeau's office?"

You.

He stretched his legs in an effort to project calm. "Mirabeau is hosting a charity fashion show for UNICEF next week. It will be my first public appearance since the accident, so the organizers expect both fashion and sports reporters to cover it. I attended a planning session this afternoon and heard you were meeting with a team of Mirabeau's store managers. I decided to catch you on the way out of the building if I could."

He'd supported UNICEF from the moment he'd earned his first racing paycheck. Once he became a familiar face on the circuit, he regularly fielded calls from his UNICEF contact asking if he'd contribute autographed items for one of their auctions or make an event appearance. He'd deferred since his accident, but when he'd seen a brief business piece announcing Isola's launch at Mirabeau during the same week as the UNICEF fashion show, he'd been the one to make a phone call.

It wasn't much of a plan, but approaching her in a location where they were both scheduled was easier than showing up at the door of her Milan flat or at her boutique, either of which risked revealing their private relationship to the press.

She didn't hide her skepticism. "You heard? How?"

"I asked. They answered." Fine. He'd admit it.

"You saw the Isola press release." At his nod, she continued, "Still, it doesn't make sense that the fashion show organizers would know I was in the building for a private business meeting. Why would they care?"

"The Isola launch is the talk of the company. Like it or not, you're a big draw right now."

She frowned at that. "Did you know the reporters were waiting?"

"No." Nor had he expected them to be so aggressive. He was used to dealing with the press at Formula One events, when dozens of sports reporters would swarm the drivers to ask about tactics or various turning points in the race, hoping to get information ahead of the standard post-race press conference. But rarely was Ivo approached on city streets by anyone other than fans hoping for a photo or autograph. Never by people who worked for gossip rags. He'd been careful to keep his private life devoid of anything that'd interest them.

"I'm sure you were an added bonus for them once you were recognized." She let out a self-deprecating laugh. "I bet they found someone at Mirabeau to confirm my presence. I'd hoped the Mirabeau employees would think twice before talking to European tabloids. I suppose that's too much to expect of fashion people. Promoting new lines to the press is habit."

"Equivalent to expecting them never to wear black." He couldn't help but lean toward her. When she met his gaze, he said, "Congratulations, by the way. Placing Isola at Mirabeau is a coup."

"A temporary coup." She shifted on the sofa, recrossing her legs. It made him want to slide a hand up her thigh, as he'd done so many times before. To tease the sensitive skin on her knee where it peeked out from the hem of her skirt, which itself was just visible beneath the hem of her coat. She always squirmed with pleasure when he feathered his fingertips around her knee.

First she needed to act as if she planned to stay longer than another minute. He forced his attention to her face. "Why temporary?"

"It's a trial run at a few locations. Whether Isola joins the store's permanent collection depends on sales. We redesigned our store displays to appeal to Mirabeau's demographic and we're hosting a reception at the Smithsonian Design Museum on Thursday to thank those involved and extend press coverage of the launch. After that, our success depends on Mirabeau's sales staff. I'm optimistic."

"What about Fall Fashion Week?"

"There have been some last-minute opportunities to get on the calendar. Seems that the fact I'm related to royalty and I design lingerie is scandalous, and scandal means press coverage. Hence charity show organizers aware of the fact I'm in town." She waved a hand as if she should have seen it coming. "Even so, there isn't time to do a show, not the way I'd want it done. It would also be a huge expense. The museum reception and redesigned displays are enough of a financial gamble right now. The Milan store is doing well and I want to keep it that way. Better not to risk the entire enterprise by overspending to grow."

That was his Lina. Deliberate, thoughtful. A planner. A big picture person.

"Still, you must be expanding. How many people work for you now?"

"Including the retail staff in Milan, I'm up to fifteen. If Mirabeau offers a long-term contract" —she stretched to tap her knuckles on the coffee table's wood top— "I'd need to hire more at the factory. I'd also need to make my website person full-time and add one more person to marketing. Unfortunately, the reporters this morning could throw a wrench in the works."

"You don't believe all publicity is good publicity."

"Not when the focus is on my mother and her history with King Carlo, rather than the product." Her lips twisted. "You heard the questions they were asking. They weren't talking about Isola. Their goal is to sell magazines, not lace bras or seamless panties."

"They did ask if I'm a fan." He couldn't stop his mouth from curving into a smile. "I didn't answer, but you know my taste."

She started to say something, then stopped as if mentally checking herself. "Isola can't be what you wanted to discuss."

A siren echoed from the street below, drawing their attention to the window. Rain spotted the thick glass.

"Take off your coat and scarf and stay. It's hard to talk when you look like you want to bolt."

"What do you want, Ivo?"

He looked at her coat. Waited. Thunder rolled overhead, then rain hit the windows with enough force to become audible.

She rolled her eyes, her expression easily translating to, *nothing else comes off, so don't even think about it.* She stood and unwrapped her scarf, then draped it over the desk chair and added her coat.

In her black suit and cream-colored blouse, she looked like a lawyer ready to negotiate. It wasn't an improvement over the coat.

"Well?"

He folded his hands and braced his elbows on his thighs once she resumed her place on the sofa. "I planned a lot more than a simple, 'I'm sorry.' Not only do I owe you an apology for my behavior, I wanted to tell you that I'm sorry about your mother. I know how much she meant to you."

Pain narrowed her eyes and puckered her forehead before her gaze dropped to a spot on the coffee table. In a surprisingly clear voice, she replied, "Thank you."

"Her death may have been expected, but that doesn't make it less agonizing. The aftermath with King Carlo and his public announcement must've made it a hundred times worse. When I was finally released from the hospital and heard the news—"

She flinched. "Ivo, no."

"Look, there's no elegant way to say this, but it has to be said. I made a huge mistake. Because of it, I wasn't there when you most needed a shoulder to lean on. It was inexcusable."

Suffering, the kind born of a soul-deep ache, rolled off her in waves, despite her stoic posture. He waited until she raised her chin before he added, "Lina, I'm here for you now. You might not be willing to admit it, but you need me."

Her expression went dark. "Ivo, don't—"

"You need to trust me."

CHAPTER 3

A DOZEN sharp reactions fought for dominance at the tip of Lina's tongue. None had yet claimed victory when Ivo added, "Before that happens, I have a request."

She folded her hands in her lap and willed herself to remain calm, at least on the outside. "A request. In exchange for what, comforting me? Giving me that shoulder to lean on? Has it occurred to you that I *don't* need you?"

"Like you didn't need me outside Mirabeau today?"

"I'd have been fine. I'm tougher than you think."

He extended a hand, palm out, conceding the point as if it were never in doubt. "I didn't intend to start an argument. I'm attempting to deliver a proper apology. However, I'm hoping you can find it within yourself to apologize, too."

She managed to keep her expression even and her eyes locked with his, rather than do what her instincts told her, which was to grab her coat and leave. She certainly wasn't going to apologize to him, not when he was the one to end things after she'd sacrificed so much to stay at his bedside, and willingly. But she knew Ivo well enough to know he'd follow her into the hall if she didn't hear him out.

"What I said to you in my hospital room in San Rimini was wrong.

But did you ever wonder *why* I said it?" His voice softened. "You knew how I felt about you. It would've taken a hell of a lot more than physical pain to cause that outburst."

She didn't have a response. She knew they had fantastic sex. That they enjoyed each other's company and shared the same taste in movies. That they preferred to spend their leisure time in quiet pursuits, outdoors if possible, rather than attend parties that meant elbow-to-elbow crowds and noise. That they shared a hatred of licorice, a passion for stargazing, and each frequently dropped money into the open guitar or saxophone cases of sidewalk buskers.

But she didn't know how he'd felt. They'd never discussed their feelings beyond expressing how much they were enjoying a particular day or activity. Not until he'd tossed her from his room with a "don't ever come back."

That had been definitive.

"Lina, I was falling in love with you. I thought—I'd hoped—that you were falling in love with me. Don't you think we owe it to each other to clear the air, to see if we're stronger together or apart? If we're stronger apart, then we'll end on a better note than the hospital. But I'm gambling that we're stronger together."

Lina's anger dissolved in the face of Ivo's earnest expression, despite her desire to hold on to its protection as tightly as a free climber who'd wedged her fingers between the gaps in a sheer rock face. It'd be so easy to collapse into Ivo's arms. To lay her head on his shoulder as he wished, to forget that terrible afternoon in San Rimini. To once again say yes to an invitation from the most compelling man she'd ever known. To hope that he'd had the same feelings for her that she'd developed for him. To give him the trust he wanted.

But if her experience with her mother had taught her anything, it was that misplaced trust would come back to bite her. Hard.

"I know this comes out of the blue, but I've been thinking of you from the moment you left the hospital." Ivo rounded the coffee table to sit beside her, placing his hands over hers. She was too shocked to pull away and too unsure of her own reaction to meet his gaze. Instead, she studied his rough knuckles, the smooth, black skin along his wrists, and the breadth of his palms as they enveloped her hands.

With one word, a single yes, those palms would cup her cheeks. He'd pull her mouth to his and kiss her senseless. He'd make love to her now and continue their conversation later, knowing she'd be more agreeable. Because damn, after sex with Ivo, what woman wouldn't be?

She swallowed hard and forced herself to straighten. "I don't know what to say."

"Then don't. I want to earn your trust." His thumb ran over the top of hers, then paused and asked, "Have you had anyone since we last saw each other?"

Stunned, she was about tell him it was none of his business, but he clarified, "I mean anyone you could talk to. About work. About me. About everything else that's happened."

Oh, he knew how to pull her emotional strings. She drew a breath to the depths of her lungs, then slowly released it in an attempt to settle herself before meeting his gaze. "You mean what my mother did to King Carlo?"

His expression was grim, his nod nearly imperceptible.

"I've talked to Rocco. A little to Enzo. We aren't together often." Besides, Rocco had his own career keeping him busy and Enzo, her twin, had never been the type to discuss feelings.

"I assume your mother was still living with Rocco when she passed away."

She nodded. "He handled the funeral."

Lina would have done it—God knew having Teresa Cornaro move in with Rocco and his wife, Justine, nearly wrecked their marriage— but Rocco had a sizable guest suite in his Dubrovnik villa and connections in the medical community Lina and Enzo didn't. If anyone could've saved their mother's life, it would have been Rocco.

And if her mother had been living with Lina in Milan, how would Lina have handled Ivo's accident? Not that she had *handled* it. Staying at the hospital had blown up in her face. Which brought her back to Ivo's question of why.

His hands tightened around hers, drawing her to the present. "Was the funeral in Croatia?"

Lina nodded again. "Not long after she was diagnosed, she told us she'd purchased a plot in a cemetery in Dubrovnik and asked that we scatter Jack's ashes with her, since we hadn't done that yet. We told her not to jump to conclusions about her odds of survival, but she told us it gave her peace of mind knowing we'd honor her wishes. Thankfully, the end—the painful part—was quick."

March had passed in a blur. Lina was still reeling from the experience in Ivo's hospital room and was digging out at work after her extended absence when Rocco called to let her know their mother had taken a sudden turn for the worse. Her liver was failing. She had days, maybe only hours, to live. Lina had taken the next flight to Dubrovnik. Enzo, Lina's twin brother, arrived two hours after she did. Their mother had been in and out of consciousness those last few days. Still, she'd had enough moments of lucidity to hold Lina's hand and tell all three of her children how much she loved them.

She didn't tell them the truth about her relationship with their biological father, despite knowing they'd learn of it after her death. Croatian probate law had seen to that, requiring her mother's original birth certificate be presented in order to process the estate. She'd gone in relative peace, leaving her children to face hell alone.

In the months since the funeral, Lina had kept a tight rein on her control. She'd focused on work and told herself to keep a cool head for the sake of her employees, who'd already picked up the slack while she'd cared for Ivo in San Rimini.

Above all, she refused to acknowledge the truth: she spent every free moment at Isola for her own sanity. Because what woman could learn that a mother she'd loved, the woman who'd run behind her laughing and cheering when Lina learned to ride a bike, who'd taught her to make mouth-watering lasagna, and who'd encouraged her to pursue design school when the odds of making a living weren't great, had been lying to her children her entire life?

Oh, not about their biological father's identity. That information they'd always known. Rather, Teresa Cornaro lied about the nature of her relationship to that man. Misled her children and Jack Cornaro about the circumstances surrounding its beginning and its demise. Even the birthdate on her passport had been a lie. Thinking of it now left a hollow pit in Lina's stomach, one that couldn't be filled.

"I saw that Rocco attended King Carlo's press conference. You and Enzo didn't go."

"No." She held in a sigh and extracted her hands from Ivo's. "It isn't necessary talk about this."

"I suspect you haven't talked to anyone about it."

"Let me clarify: I don't want to talk about this." She didn't hide the warning in her voice.

"Don't you trust anyone?"

"I trusted you and you threw me out of your hospital room."

"Bullshit." The word was low, as if he fought to conceal anger that had been set to a long, slow burn. "There was more to it and you know it, Lina. You didn't trust me at all. Two years together, and you never once introduced me to your brothers or mother. I know what your family means you. I heard the adoration in your voice every time you mentioned them. I attributed it to my career and yours, to the distance, and to the fact we had such limited time together we only wanted to spend it with each other. Then I thought, well, maybe it was because I hadn't introduced you to my mother yet. But when you kept leaving my hospital room to take phone calls, even when you knew you weren't bothering me, I started to wonder. Then, that last afternoon, while you were in the hallway on yet another call that you didn't want me to hear, it occurred to me that you always ignored the phone when I was at your flat and your mother called."

"Ivo—"

"No. I need to finish." A harsh laugh escaped him as he ran a hand over his head. "You see, in that moment it occurred to me that the reason I hadn't met them had nothing to do with logistics. You didn't want us to meet. I know we were keeping things relaxed, but that hurt. I didn't know if it was because I somehow embarrassed you, or because you had zero investment in the relationship, or what. I'm not as close to my mother as you are to your family, but my mother certainly knew you existed. That at some point, you might meet." Lina watched as Ivo's jaw worked. In a quieter voice, he said, "That's when I lost my temper and threw you out. But my assumption was wrong, wasn't it? When I heard about King Carlo's press conference, I discovered that the truth was even worse. Your secrecy was about trust. You were afraid if I met your family, I'd discover your paternity and that I'd share it with the world. It made me furious. Beyond furious."

"You're way off base." Temper rose in her like a white-hot ball. As if on cue, thunder cracked outside the window, drawing her attention.

How had she gotten into this mess? She should be in a warm bath right now, easing her muscles while she inhaled lavender- and lemon-scented steam. Thinking about the Mirabeau launch. Not debating the past with a man who'd kicked her to the curb—a man for whom she'd sacrificed so much—and who now had the audacity to ask her for an apology.

"Then clear it up for me, Lina. I'm over my fury, which is why I'm making an effort to see things from your perspective and understand why you kept the truth from me, why you didn't trust me. But it's still damned difficult."

She gritted her teeth. "From the time I was little, I've known King Carlo is my biological father. My mother felt we should know. She also stressed the importance of keeping it quiet. She was certain that if it became public, it would change our lives. I honored her wish, despite the fact I never thought his having illegitimate children was as big a deal as she did. Lots of famous people—even royalty—do, and no one cares. I didn't know there was more to it."

When Ivo remained silent, she forged ahead. "As far as I was concerned—as far as I'm concerned now—Jack Cornaro was my father. My Papa. I was a toddler when my mother married him and I have no relationship with King Carlo. Never met him, never cared to. If I'd have introduced you to my mother or to Rocco or Enzo, that's all you would have learned. I wasn't afraid you'd discover the identity of my biological father and tell the press. My family never talked about him and he's never mattered to me. As for the rest…I had no idea until she died. I wasn't hiding anything from you, because I didn't know."

He stared at her, his eyes flat in a way she'd never witnessed. After a painful minute, Ivo pushed off the sofa to pace the room. He had something to say, but Lina waited as he mulled over exactly how he wanted to say it. Finally, he stopped pacing and planted his hands on the back of one of the chairs. "So are you telling me that my first assumption was correct? After all our weekends together. After all you told me about them. They didn't know about me, did they? Neither did anyone who works for you. That's why you took your calls outside my room."

He flexed his fingers and adopted a quieter tone. "I overheard one call, you know. When you thought I was asleep, you answered the phone in the room. As you walked to the hallway, you told the caller you were with a sick friend. It didn't occur to me until now that you didn't say who. You didn't say where." His cool demeanor didn't mask the hurt and anger in his dark eyes, and Ivo wasn't a man prone to bruised feelings. "I'm right, aren't I?"

"Yes." Much as she wanted to erase his pain, she wouldn't lie to him. "I thought it was best for us at the time. It certainly wasn't because I was embarrassed or didn't have feelings for you. If that'd been the case, do you think I'd have been at the hospital?"

"Then why the big secret?"

"I didn't know where our relationship was going. I didn't want to deal with my mother's fears until I absolutely had to."

Angry at herself and feeling hemmed in by Ivo, she went to the window. It only deepened her sense of confinement. Gray, brutal clouds sat low enough in the sky to skim the tops of the buildings. Soon, the view across the street would be obscured.

She turned toward Ivo, hoping to make him understand. "In the year before your accident, my brother Rocco's marriage fell apart. Justine was having an incredible season on the slopes and it was becoming harder and harder for him to keep a low profile as her husband. You know how it is on the World Cup circuit—it's not that different from what you do—reporters are always talking to family members waiting at the finish line, asking personal questions. King Carlo is a huge alpine skiing fan and attends at least one event each season. My mother was paranoid about what could happen if Rocco and Carlo appeared at same venue and anyone noticed the resemblance. She was on Rocco all the time about it, yet insisted he keep the reason from Justine. It caused a huge strain on their relationship. When my mother moved in with Rocco at the same time Justine was forced to take time off for a broken leg, it was a disaster. Justine left him."

Ivo considered that, then braced his hands on top of his head. "Rocco looks just like King Carlo's oldest sons. It's astonishing."

"I'd call it disconcerting, but I'll accept astonishing." She leaned against the window and flattened her hands on the sill. "I look like my mother and nothing like King Carlo or his other children. But if I'd introduced you to my mother, a Formula One driver who gets even more press than Justine—" She waved off the thought. "I didn't have the strength to tolerate what Rocco and Justine had endured. I didn't want to fight with her when she was terminally ill. Of course, I thought my mother's biggest fear was having our paternity identified, not that it'd come out that she was ten years older than any of us knew. And twelve years older than Carlo, rather than two. I had no idea that my silence—my complete lack of a backbone—helped to hide a predator."

There. She'd said the words she'd held deep inside her for months.

Teresa Cornaro, the woman she'd loved more than anyone in the world, was a predator.

Lina hadn't believed it at first. She'd firmly believed there was a mistake when Rocco gathered the paperwork necessary to put their mother's estate through probate and the date on their mother's birth certificate didn't match any of the other documents. Nor did it match Rocco, Enzo, and Lina's own knowledge of their mother's birthdate.

A call to the Sarcaccian village where their mother was born shattered that illusion. Lina had been repulsed, sick, hurt…devastated. It wasn't simply the age difference. Plenty of people could overlook that, given that Carlo was seventeen at the time. It was that Teresa was in a position of authority and schemed to take advantage of him.

"You had to have been in shock."

Her glance at Ivo told him it was an understatement. Thinking about it made her chest tight; talking about it felt as if air might never enter her body again.

"All our lives, our mother led us to believe she had a youthful, once-in-a-lifetime romance with the crown prince she'd been tutoring for his college entrance exams. That they'd kept their affair a secret due to the fact she came from a Sarcaccian farming village, rather than the aristocracy. She told us she'd been nineteen and Carlo seventeen when Rocco was born. That she left her position at the palace to hide the pregnancy because it'd be such a scandal in those days if anyone learned that the crown prince fathered an illegitimate child, especially at such a young age. She even told us he'd promised her they'd marry someday, when he was out of college and out from under his father's thumb."

Lina's throat constricted with the heat of tears. She willed the sensation away. "Imagine discovering after her death that she was twenty-nine and so desperate to be queen—to have that wealth and adoration—that she got pregnant on purpose. And then learning that she used Rocco to manipulate Carlo into her bed to get pregnant again. That second time was after his arranged marriage to Fabrizia. What kind of sick person *does* that?"

A flash of lightning drew her gaze to the street. Those remaining on the sidewalk hid under the cover of umbrellas and hoods angled to shelter their faces from the pelting rain. It'd turned into a nasty evening.

"I'm stunned no one discovered it."

"You and the rest of the world." Lina allowed her gaze to follow a bright plaid umbrella until it disappeared from view under an awning, using the moment to temper her fury. "After she left her palace job, my mother worked as a civil servant in Sarcaccia. Doing what, I don't know, but she apparently had the access necessary to forge a passport for herself. Other than the original copy of her birth certificate—the one we had to produce from the village where she was born when her estate went into probate—her paperwork showed her to be ten years younger."

Lina finally looked at Ivo. "She wasn't the person I thought I knew.

She was diabolical…there's no other word for it. She preyed on a teenager and manipulated him for years. Used his status and his children against him until he finally called her bluff. When he did, she carried through on her threat to leave Sarcaccia and deny him access to us." She shook her head. "When she met Jack Cornaro, she gave him the sob story version of events and Papa bought it, hook, line, and sinker. Kept her secret all his life. Could you imagine marrying a woman with three little children? He did, and he treated us as his own. He loved her that much. How could she have been so evil? How could she have done this to him?"

"And to you."

"And to me."

"When the only face you saw was that of a caring wife and mother."

She'd been so stupid to believe it all. To trust. Lina pushed off the windowsill and closed her eyes, attempting to regain her equilibrium. "The story that she and Carlo couldn't be together because of their difference in status—because he couldn't stand up to his father and say no to an arranged marriage to Fabrizia—it fit the person she pretended to be. Maternal and virtuous, like a movie heroine. Like a true queen. We hated Carlo Barrali for it. Hated the entire Barrali family our entire lives. My mother fostered that hate because she didn't want us anywhere near them. To protect *her*, not to protect us."

Her jaw shook and she quickly pressed her lips together to stop it. She would not give in.

There was a brush at her cheek. She opened her eyes to see Ivo studying her. Moisture glistened on his thumb. "It's all right to be angry with her, Lina. It's also all right to be heartbroken and sad, not for Jack Cornaro or for your brothers, but for yourself. Criminal or not, you loved your mother."

"It wasn't real. She lied about everything."

"Yes, she did. But that doesn't mean your feelings weren't real. The longer you force yourself *not* to feel—the more you shove everything deep inside because you're horrified by your mother's actions—the worse it will hurt. You'll never get beyond it."

Tears started flowing in earnest, which made her want to curse. She hated crying. She hated anything that sounded like pop psychology, even if it was her truth. "There's no getting beyond what she did, especially when she's not here to answer for it."

"It's perfectly appropriate mourn her death. No matter what she did before you were born, you loved her. It's all right to love her still."

Ivo's fingers grazed her cheek once more. It was the barest of contact. It shouldn't have mattered.

His dark eyes searched hers with understanding rather than pity, and Lina leaned into him.

CHAPTER 4

ALMOST IMMEDIATELY, she backed off. She would not lose it. Not with Ivo, not now, not when their relationship was in tatters. She pressed against his chest and shook her head. "I can't."

"You can."

Then his arms came around her, holding her in place. Her entire being seemed to exhale in relief. Not because she mourned her mother —she wasn't there yet—but because Ivo acknowledged her loss when the rest of the world could not, and he did it with respect.

He guided her to the sofa and drew her cheek to his shoulder. A huge, all-encompassing sob threatened, but she stifled it, instead taking comfort in the worn fabric of his cotton T-shirt and the expanse of lean muscle beneath it. In the protective manner in which he held her, in the pressure of his jaw pressing to the top of her head. In the familiar, masculine scent she'd so loved awakening to when they'd shared a bed.

She wrapped her arms around his waist. As always, it felt like holding a warm chunk of granite. People underestimated Ivo when they met him. His mixed Italian and Nigerian heritage made him diffi-cult to stereotype. They saw his lean build, his height—a couple inches shy of six feet, which was typical for a driver—and his gracious, wide-lipped smile and didn't think of him as powerful. But a simple hug or a glimpse of his bare torso and a person's opinion would change. Every bit of him was wiry, corded muscle. Within five minutes of speaking to him, it was obvious his interior was the same as the exterior. Ivo Zanardi was efficient, determined, and capable. The perfect man to put behind the wheel in a difficult situation. Or have guarding your back.

"You're one of the toughest people I've met in my entire life," he murmured into her hair. "You will survive this. You'll be stronger for it. But you don't have to be strong today."

It was what she needed to hear. What she needed to *feel*. Hot tears seeped from the corners of her eyes.

He tightened his hold. In that moment, she forgave him everything. She'd missed him terribly. She hadn't wanted to admit it, hadn't wanted to perceive herself as weak. But it was the truth. And she was as much to blame for the situation as Ivo.

Several minutes later, when she could breathe evenly again, she said, "I'm sorry."

A quiet laugh shook his chest. "You're not holding me that tight. Though if you'd like—"

"No." She raised her head to look at him, needing him to be serious. "You were right. I shouldn't have kept your existence a secret from my family. It was unfair to you."

He traced her cheekbone with an index finger. A smile flitted across his face before he dropped his hand to his lap. "You did it out of self-preservation and love for your family. I'm glad I understand it now." He changed position to face her directly. "You're forgiven, though I hope you can forgive me, too. And not just say it, but believe it. I should have asked about my suspicions rather than lose my temper. I know better than that."

"Because a head injury, burns, and severe inflammation around your spine ensure you're in your usual controlled frame of mind."

"You forgot the collapsed lungs."

"And two collapsed lungs."

Lina's phone vibrated deep in the side pocket of her handbag. It was likely Tomasina, her assistant in Milan, hoping for a report on the Mirabeau meeting before she went to sleep.

"You need to get that?"

She shook her head, but the spell between them was broken. She leaned back to run her pinkies beneath her lashes.

"You look fine."

She doubted it—she'd be surprised if there weren't black smudges under her eyes—but thanked him.

A long roll of thunder shook the building. "I should go."

At the same time, he said, "Stay for dinner. I'll order room service."

She hesitated. Awkwardness settled between them. "I have spread-sheets to review in the morning. They need to be handled before the Mirabeau launch. And I need time to decompress so I'm able to sleep."

"You need to eat." Ivo stood and strode past the bed to push open the bathroom door. "You always said the one thing missing in your flat is a bathtub. Whenever you stayed in my hotel rooms at events, you used the tub. This one is glorious."

"Ivo, I'm not taking a bath."

"You'll do a better job on your spreadsheets if you get a good night's sleep, and you'll get a better night's sleep if you're relaxed and fed. Decompress here."

He crooked his finger. She huffed and went to look, fully intending to give him a polite smile, thank him for the offer, and decline.

Then she saw it.

Instead, it was Ivo who gave a polite smile. "Does salmon sound good?"

Her neck, back, and calf muscles begged to be in the tub he'd revealed: an elegant, deep, white beauty with nickel fixtures that sparkled with cleanliness. An array of high-end bath products rested on an ebony shelf at one end. On a wall nearby, a fluffy white robe hung from a hook, defying her to walk away. Better—or worse—yet, the entire space smelled of lavender and vanilla.

She opened her mouth. Closed it again. She'd never indulged in a bath this sublime.

She felt rather than saw his amusement before he said, "I'll order the salmon."

HALF AN HOUR LATER, Lina stepped from the bathroom wrapped in a hotel robe and glanced toward the entry hall. "Are we alone? I thought I heard room service arrive."

"We are and you did."

Ivo tried to keep his hunger from showing on his face. Not for the food, though it smelled delicious, but for Lina. Whenever she'd taken a bath during his race weekends, she'd emerged from the bathroom with damp, tousled hair and a freshly scrubbed face. She'd update him on Isola, then he'd rehash his practice run or qualifying race with her, a discussion that helped him wind down from the adrenaline rush of the course. Afterward, it took little effort to convince her to drop the robe and join him in bed. They'd make love, then fall asleep with the day's stress gone. That wasn't happening this time. Instead, her hair was dry, piled on her head to keep it out of the water, and her makeup remained perfectly in place. She'd even touched up a spot at the edge of her left eye where she'd smeared her mascara earlier. A firm knot held her robe in place.

He still couldn't believe Lina had cried. In all the time they'd known each other, she'd never shed a tear. Even when he'd awakened after his accident and asked where he was, her eyes had brightened, but no tears had fallen as she'd explained the situation.

Then again, he'd been unconscious for nearly three days before he awoke to see her sleeping in a chair at his bedside, her phone balanced precariously on one knee, her head propped on one fist. Was it wrong to want to believe she'd cried in the interim? Not that he wanted to worry her, but once in a while it felt good to be worried about. To feel loved.

He mentally kicked himself at that thought. *Love.* He'd flat-out told her he'd been falling in love with her. What had possessed him? Or to say he'd hoped she was falling in love with him? They didn't have that luxury. Not then. Not now. Their relationship was supposed to be easy. Accommodating of their careers. Sexy fun on a catch-as-catch-can basis. She'd taken the step toward more by staying with him at the hospital. But that wasn't a declaration of love.

Was he that desperate to have her in his life again?

Yes.

He'd chased her all the way to New York without analyzing how he felt; he'd only known he wanted her. He should thank the heavens she hadn't interrogated him about what he'd meant when he'd made his pronouncement—in fact, she hadn't seemed affected by his words at all—because love wasn't an emotion he could define. He'd only known how angry he was when he threw her out of hospital and how rotten he'd felt afterward.

At least he'd said *falling in love* instead of *in love*.

He'd gone on to tell her he'd missed her—which was true—and she'd told him she didn't know what to say before he'd changed the topic to how she'd handled the past few months. Then the emotions had come tumbling out of her. Now he wasn't sure what he felt. Or where to go from here.

He eyed her head to toe and directed the question to her. "How do you feel?"

"Wrinkly. Better." She checked the tie at her waist before rolling her shoulders. "I didn't realize how tight my muscles were. Even my calves needed a stretch."

He removed the utensils and napkins from the tray that room service left on the desk, setting them on the coffee table beside the plates he'd already arranged. "I ordered a bottle of water and a bottle of Chardonnay that sounded like it'd pair well with the fish."

"That'll be good for relaxing, too." Her eyes widened as she surveyed the spread. "This looks decadent. Give me a minute. I'll be right back."

He wanted to tell her she didn't have to dress, but didn't trust himself to keep desire from his voice. He poured both the water and the wine, then removed the cover from her plate as she emerged from the bathroom with her dark blond hair loose, wearing her skirt and blouse and carrying her suit jacket over one arm. She set the jacket near her coat, then took a seat in one of the armchairs.

"Unfortunately, there isn't a proper dining table."

She leaned forward and inhaled the lemon and spice scent of the salmon. "This more than makes up for it. Thank you."

He raised his glass. He wanted to toast a fresh start, but given the fact she'd changed out of the robe, he settled on, "To my favorite hotel dinner companion. And to Isola's successful launch in New York."

"And to your health. It's good to see you looking like yourself again."

He smiled at that, then took a deep drink. They stuck to current topics—upcoming movies, a recent earthquake in central Italy, the news that a British billionaire purchased an American baseball team—until a far-off flash of lightning reminded Ivo of the late hour. Lina's mind must've taken the same course, because she said, "I think the F train runs through the station around the corner."

"It does, but you're not taking the subway to your mother's."

"It's perfectly safe and I won't melt. With this weather, it'll take a lot longer to get a taxi or a ride share service." A genuine smile lifted her cheeks. "Besides, I love taking the subway."

"In that case, I'm going with you."

"I'll be perfectly fine."

"What if there are reporters at your mother's?"

"I'll walk past them and go inside."

He blotted his lips and set the napkin beside his plate, which he'd scraped clean. He'd been hungrier than he'd thought. Lina's plate, on the other hand, held half her meal and she'd had only sips of her wine.

Her tearful moment might be over, but she remained unsettled. He'd ensure she made it safely home, at least. "It'll be good for me to get out of the hotel and get some fresh air."

"Fresh air? On the subway? During a thunderstorm?"

He couldn't help but be warmed by the amusement in her eyes. "There's the part where we walk to the station and then to your moth-er's. And sure, why not? It's part of being in New York. Experiencing all the sights and sounds and smells."

"The smell of tired, rain-soaked bodies crammed onto a subway platform is an experience. Not one I thought you'd want, though."

"First, a Manhattan subway doesn't compare to what it smells like inside a racing suit at the end of the day. Second, you left Mirabeau at the peak of the evening rush. The storm has pushed everyone indoors since then. It shouldn't be that crowded." He gestured toward the window, in the direction of the nearest station. "I can handle it."

He expected her to argue. When she shrugged and started clearing their dishes, he knew he'd made the right call.

Fifteen minutes later, during a break in the storm, they made their way to the station and walked to the downtown platform. As Ivo had predicted, the station was relatively quiet. Several commuters stood near the track. Most focused on their phone screens, while others rummaged through their bags or stood aloof, listening to books or music through headphones.

"Where's your mother's place?"

"Greenwich Village. Walking distance from the West Fourth stop." Her expression turned inquisitive. "You offered to escort me and you don't know?"

"It's never come up." He traveled regularly to major cities in Europe and the Middle East, but with America behind the curve on Formula One racing—so to speak—New York wasn't familiar to him. "I've only been here once before and I didn't know you then."

A light frown creased her forehead. "Guess I didn't realize that. What brought you the first time?"

"The Formula One owners were negotiating a television deal for the U.S. market five years ago and wanted drivers from the top teams to speak about the sport. I'd just signed my deal with Scuderia Ferrari, so they brought me. Figured I'd be enthusiastic."

"You do radiate enthusiasm when you talk racing."

"Given the commitment required, I should." A wash of air blew past them as an uptown train departed, billowing the bottom of her coat. When it was quiet again, he said, "It bothers me when drivers either take their position for granted or act with indifference, especially when they speak in public. If they're burned out, they should take time away from it. For the risks we take and the number of people whose livelihood depends on our performance, it's selfish to stay in the car just for the money. A driver should have a passion for it. They should also exhibit genuine gratitude for those who support the sport."

Lina looked as if she were about to say something, but the groan of metal on metal announced the arrival of their train. They scanned the cars as the train slowed and approached a section with available seats. They remained silent for ride, listening to the conversations taking place around them and the slow clack-roll-clack of the tracks. While Lina scanned the headlines of a newspaper left behind on an adjoining seat, Ivo studied her. Her posture was perfect, as always, but exhaustion showed in the loose way her fingers covered her handbag, which tilted sideways in her lap.

She'd needed that bath. Too bad she wouldn't have considered crawling straight from the bath into his bed. He'd have slept on the sofa without complaint if it meant she'd get a good night's rest. She needed to sleep away thoughts of her mother, of the reporters, and of their hospital argument so she could face the upcoming week with renewed energy.

At the station, a fine mist shrouded the top of the exit stairs. Ivo cast a look of apology at Lina. "I should've grabbed an umbrella from the concierge. It looks wetter than when we left the hotel."

"I told you, I won't melt."

She smiled, but it didn't quite reach her eyes. When they reached the street, she indicated they should walk northeast. Two blocks later, he said, "You're quiet."

"Tired."

"Understandable. This is more than that."

Even walking beside her with only the streetlights for illumination, he caught her expression of surprise. "You know me too well."

"If that were true, I'd know what's bothering you."

She gave him a playful smack on the arm as they reached an intersection and were compelled to wait for the light. "I'm not bothered. Just…preoccupied."

"But not with work."

"I'm always preoccupied with work. But in this case, I was thinking about what you said on the platform about your passion for racing. You didn't answer that reporter's question about racing again this season."

"I was focused on getting you away from them."

The light changed and Lina leaped off the curb—heels and all—to clear a puddle at the edge of the crosswalk. "Do you have an answer to the question?"

"Not one for public consumption." He waited until they were across the street and away from other pedestrians to elaborate. Even then, he kept his voice low. Speaking of his future felt like daring the universe to ruin his plans.

"I estimate I'm two or three weeks away from medical clearance, which puts me into July. The season ends in November. Much as I want to race, I think my best move is to spend those months in the simulator and on the test track. I need to focus on getting my body and my reflexes into peak condition so I can start fresh in late January. That's when Pirelli will want to conduct wet tire testing at the track in San Rimini. If all goes well for me—for the team—I should be good to go for preseason testing in late February or early March."

He'd already filled a notebook with his training goals for the summer and fall. With luck and hard work, he'd be as fit as he was before the accident. He'd need to be.

She remained quiet for a few beats, then said, "So the short answer to the reporters' questions is yes."

"You can't be surprised."

"Not at all. It's who you are. I didn't expect you'd start at the same track where you crashed."

"I'd start in the simulator. You'd be shocked at how realistic it is."

She made a face as they rounded a corner onto a residential street. Rain dripped from trees planted at intervals along the sidewalk. Otherwise, all was still. "You know what I mean. Don't you want your return to be somewhere else?"

"What happened in San Rimini was a fluke. Wet tire testing is part of the job." Just as facing one's demons with an even temperament was part of the job. "But I appreciate the concern. I promise, you won't have to go to the hospital in San Rimini ever again. Though if I ever were to get hurt, it's one of the best facilities in the world for—"

"Don't you dare!"

She swiped at his arm, but he caught her wrist and held it. "I'm barely out of the hospital and you're trying to injure me? Shame on you, Lina Cornaro. Where's the logic in trying to injure me because I was injured?"

"You drive the logic out of me sometimes."

"You need the logic driven out of you sometimes. You think too much."

She stopped walking and angled her body to face him. "This from the man who's likely planned his comeback down to the day. How many workouts have you scheduled? Appointments with trainers and sports psychologists? You're a fine one to lecture me about logic and thinking too much."

He still held her wrist aloft. One by one, her fingers curled. She worried about him. Cared for him. He could see it in the gorgeous, gold-flecked depths of her eyes. He wanted her so badly he ached with it. More, even, than before the accident.

Déjà vu washed through him. How many times had he held her wrist like this, then held her gaze while he kissed the pale skin where her veins fanned at the base of her palm? It drove her mad. Drove *him* mad.

Her eyes drifted closed. She tipped her face skyward and puffed out a breath in exasperation.

"What are you doing, Ivo?"

"I scared you." He paused, waiting for her to open her eyes before he added, "I'm sorry for that, too."

"The doctors didn't know if you'd survive those first twenty-four hours. You know that, don't you?"

Gently, he released her wrist. "I'm resilient. I'm also more likely to be hit crossing the street here in Manhattan than I am to get in another wreck on the course. I'm very good at what I do."

"One of the best in the world."

He heard in her voice that she knew it to be the truth. That truth didn't reassure her.

A siren blasted nearby, then an emergency vehicle crossed at a nearby intersection, its red and blue lights flashing. After it passed, Ivo put a hand to her waist to urge her to continue along the sidewalk. "Let's get you home. The rain's picking up again."

"We're here. Mom's condo is on the third floor. Better yet, no paparazzi in sight." Her gaze went to the stairs behind him, which led to a tall set of black doors on a whitewashed brick building. "Thank you for walking me home. It was good to see you again."

Disappointment shot through him at the realization their time was at its end.

One side of her mouth lifted. "I should also thank you for the bath and the ugly cry. Not what I'd planned for the day, and I'm trying hard not to be embarrassed, but I do feel better."

He couldn't help but return her lopsided grin. "If you call that an ugly cry, you've never really cried. That being said, I feel better, too. We needed to clear the air."

"I don't usually appreciate the risks you take, but I'm grateful for that one."

She slipped her hand into the side pocket of her handbag and withdrew a set of keys. When she raised her head, a drop of rain landed below her right eye, clinging to her skin rather than rolling away.

He brushed away the raindrop. Stilled as her lips parted and her breath warmed the damp hairs where his wrist extended from the cuff of his jacket.

In that instant, he knew he couldn't let her go.

CHAPTER 5

Ivo captured her chin between his thumb and forefinger and bent to kiss her.

Lina froze for a split second, her brain attempting to process the myriad sensations hitting her at once: the cool rain against her cheeks and forehead, the pull of her handbag on her forearm, the pressure of Ivo's thumb at her chin, then the slow-motion sensation of Ivo closing the distance between them and the warmth of his lips moving softly across hers.

The clink of her keys hitting the pavement.

Ivo smiled against her mouth. Then his hands cradled her head, firm, possessive, and fast, holding her in place. His mouth did the opposite, moving against hers in a gentle exploration, still asking her permission. The combined effect was intoxicating, making her want to spin him around and push him backward, flat against the nearest wall, so she could position her body as close to his as was humanly possible.

Ivo knew exactly what he was doing. Even the first time he'd kissed her on a secluded park bench in Milan, he'd waited for the perfect moment. He always made her want more.

His lips brushed hers again. She refrained from pushing him

against the building, but she did lean in. Even without kissing him back, it was all the invitation he needed.

He opened his mouth ever-so-slightly against hers. Paused, waited.

Lina sighed and returned his kiss. Once. Tenderly. Then she dug her fingers into the fabric of his T-shirt just above where his dark jeans rode his hip bones and kissed him again, despite knowing where the second kiss would lead.

A low, satisfied sound rose from deep within him and he pulled her body tighter against his. The familiar scent of him, the press of his torso against hers, the rock-hardness of his thigh framing her leg…all of it made her want to groan aloud in the middle of the sidewalk as she slid her hands under his open jacket to his waist.

His chest rose against hers, then fell before he eased his mouth from hers. In a voice barely indistinguishable from a growl, he said, "Invite me inside."

"Come inside."

She should think about it, but the time for thinking was past. She couldn't get the words out fast enough.

He swooped to retrieve her keys from the sidewalk, then pressed them into her palm as she climbed the stairs. They were up the three flights faster than she thought possible, yet it seemed to take forever. With each step, she was aware of Ivo's presence behind her, of his eyes on her, of the burning need that welled within her. When she bobbled the key at her mother's door, Ivo moved behind her, put a hand to the small of her back, then pressed a kiss to the side of her neck.

"That help you concentrate?"

"No." Especially when Mrs. Metzger, the neighbor across the hall, likely put her eye to the peephole the minute she heard footsteps in the stairwell.

Lina turned the knob, finally having released the lock, then entered, only to have Ivo pause to remove the keys she'd left dangling in the door.

Obviously her brain wasn't functioning.

He kicked the door closed, then tossed the keys toward a basket on the entry table as he strode toward her. Less than a second after her keys hit the rattan, he took her handbag. He dropped it to the floor, then his mouth met hers, this time with fervor banked from long, frustrating months apart.

He was all heat and power and desire. He buckled her knees, even as her hands went to his face.

Part of her wanted to savor the moment, to map the contour of his lower lip, the curve of his ear, the wide bridge of his nose. To memorize the way his adept fingers undid each of her coat's buttons and its belt, then slid the garment from her shoulders. To enjoy the dips and curves of muscle as she ran her hands over his chest, his abs, his back.

To be grateful for those muscles, which had protected him as his car flew through the air and slammed into the track wall, twisting into fiery pieces.

But she couldn't. Desire consumed her. All she could think of was removing his jacket, freeing him from his shirt, and having his skin against hers as soon as possible.

An image flashed through her mind of Ivo lying in his hospital bed, silent and still, the day after the accident. Deep horror had gripped her as the doctor explained about collapsed lungs and scans of his spine, then about velocity and g-forces and impact. Internal bleeding…somewhere. About the fact Ivo likely would have died if he hadn't been in such phenomenal shape and that it would help in his recovery. The doctor's words had gone in one ear and out the other as she'd watched Ivo's chest and face for movement, searching for signs of life, fearing each monitored beat of his heart might be his last. Praying inwardly for him to hold on, to stay strong.

He cupped her rear and lifted her against him. "Where?"

She spun him toward the short hallway and the guest room where she always stayed. "Left. Second door."

Seconds later, the back of her knee connected with the suitcase she'd left near the bed. She gave it a hard kick so it toppled out of the way, then toed her shoes in the same direction. Ivo's leather jacket dropped to the floor. His hands went to her sides, his thumbs stroking upward with the ideal amount of pressure to make her crave more. His mouth grazed her temple before he lavished attention on the delicate spot below her ear. She arched in response. She'd forgotten how well they fit. How incredible it felt to have his breath warm her skin, his powerful body entwined with hers.

No, she hadn't forgotten. She'd tried to forget. She'd buried the memory of this exquisite sensation in the deepest recesses of her mind, knowing it'd only cause pain to remember.

"I missed this." Enough light filtered through the gap in the curtains to reveal intense need in his dark gaze. "I missed you."

That look was her complete undoing. In that instant, she understood what the last few months could have been if she'd been open with him.

"I missed you, too." She closed her eyes. "So much."

This time, his kiss was savage. She responded equally, craving the taste of him, the skillful thrust of his tongue, the low sound that resonated from deep in his chest. She wanted all of him, with no hesitation, no filters.

Her skin burned. She broke contact for the moment it took to pull his shirt over his head, then his mouth was on hers again. She freed the snap at the top of his jeans, needing to see him before her, hot and willing and gloriously naked.

"Ah, Lina, I—" Whatever he wanted to say was lost as he kissed her cheeks, then moved to her neck and collarbone, nipping and sucking his way along her skin, making her moan with the pleasure of it. Her head fell back and she gripped his shoulders, allowing him to unbutton her blouse for more access. Then his mouth closed over the lace of her bra, drawing both fabric and nipple into his mouth. The friction sent damp heat between her legs in a rush so dizzying she feared she'd tumble backward.

His hands cupped her backside again, holding her fast against his thigh as he moved to capture her other nipple with his teeth and tongue. "Someone," he said between torturous strokes, "designed a beautiful, sexy bra that fits you to perfection, but I want to see you out of it."

"I want to see you first."

"Mmm. We'll see about that."

He lavished attention on her breasts until she writhed from the sweet agony of it, then he smiled at her, his grin wolfish before he eased both blouse and bra from her shoulders and laid her on the bed. She watched, lips parted, as he removed his jeans and underwear and kicked them away. She didn't miss the grimace of pain as his foot connected with something on the floor, but before she could comment, he moved to the bed. His forearms bracketed her shoulders, his skin heated hers, and the weight of his hard body as he slowly lowered his torso to hers made Lina's heart thunder in her ears.

Rising to press her lips to his, she was met with a slow, soft, romantic kiss. His hands threaded through her hair, holding her in place. He withdrew and she opened her eyes to catch a raw, turbulent expression cross his face, a look completely out of character for the Ivo she knew, a man capable of controlling every aspect of himself, both mental and physical. This was bare. Needful. Untamed. Then it was gone, shuttered as he closed his eyes and moved to torture her collarbone.

"I'm going to make love to you all night," he murmured. "But only if you let me lead. I need to protect my back. But I promise, it will be slow. It will be deep. It will be agonizing. And it will be perfect. And you will crave it again and again and again."

"I don't want you to hurt—"

"Shh." He dropped a lingering kiss at her temple, then with certainty in his tone, he vowed, "This will hurt in all the best ways."

She sighed her agreement and felt his smile of victory as he dragged his lips along her cheek. He held himself above her, worshipping her with his mouth for long, agonizing moments, then slowly allowed his full weight to sink onto her.

Oh, yes, she'd missed this.

His teeth tugged at her ear, then he whispered, "I'll keep you safe, Lina. You're always safe with me."

Tomorrow, she knew that statement would scare her, given that his career was demonstrably unsafe. Tonight, however, his words only made her want to wrap herself around him and hold him fast.

With one hand to the outside of her leg, he raised her knee, fitting her hips to his. His fingers brushed over her skin in long, sinful strokes before he moved to kiss the inside of her thigh.

She squeezed her eyes shut against the exquisite sensation. Stars danced against her eyelids as he made love to her with his tongue and his teeth.

"Holy, oh…Ivo…yes, there—"

Heat shot through her core in a wave so powerful she thought she'd combust, then a cry tore from deep in her throat as the fire raced along the surface of her skin. She called his name, reaching for him, needing him inside her, wanting to kiss him, to hold his face in her hands, to show him how bone-deep her craving for him had become. To make him want her as she wanted him.

His fingers threaded with hers and he raised them over her head before he kissed her deeply. She could feel the ironlike thickness of him against her leg and ached to touch him, but he held her fast.

"If you do, it'll be over sooner than we'd like," he growled. "That's not going to happen."

She shifted her hips, opening to him. "Please."

He kissed her again. Moved to hold both her hands in one of his, then caressed her breast, teasing her nipple first with his fingers, then with his mouth. He grew even harder against her, and she breathed an expletive, begging him to move to where she really wanted him.

He ignored her pleas, continuing the slow, passionate plunder of her breast, then giving the other equal time.

Finally, when she thought she could take no more, he gave her a brief kiss, then sucked her lower lip between his teeth. His lower body changed position and she raised her hips in encouragement.

He whispered, "Are you still on—"

"Yes." No concerns of pregnancy.

His knuckles grazed her stomach, then he parted her with his fingers, exerting upward pressure with his thumb that made her gasp before he slid inside her in one smooth stroke, filling her, making her skin tingle from head to toe at the deliciousness of it. His thumb moved between them, rolling over the most intimate part of her. As if she'd received an electric shock, her legs jerked in response.

"Oh, Ivo, yes, yes, yes."

He did it again, sending another hot current through her before he buried both hands in her hair and sank even deeper. "You are so damned beautiful."

She clutched at his shoulders, then his rear, forcing herself to let him set the pace as he drove into her. It was a battle not to grip him harder. She ached to give as good as she got, to push him to his back and ride him as if her life depended on it. He thrust into her again, then again, the rhythm as pure and exquisite as time itself. A feral noise escaped him before he uttered her name on an exhale. Sweat beaded his forehead and he met her gaze with wild eyes, full of heat and desire and an emotion she couldn't name.

It was the sexiest thing she'd ever seen.

A knot built within her, twisting tighter and tighter, until her nerve endings screamed for release. Ivo hitched his elbow under her knee, raising her leg to gain even deeper access. Arching against the onslaught, scared of what she'd discover as she approached her limit, she raced toward it nevertheless.

"Not yet, Lina. Hold on."

In agony, she dug her fingers into the hard muscle of his backside. He cursed, then put his mouth to her shoulder and nipped at her. Again and again he plunged into her, driving her to the edge, then drawing her back to reality before shifting to hurtle her forward yet again.

Her lips parted as she neared delirium. There was nothing in her world but Ivo. His hands, his scent, his breath at her neck and temple. The delicious, painful things he did to her body.

"I'm dying—"

"Now."

Everything within her unfurled at once, the release both sweet and ferocious in its intensity. Her head fell into the pillow, her hips driving against Ivo as he continued his torture for one, two, three more excruciating strokes before he tensed, shuddered, then came apart in her arms.

She held him fast, her hands splayed across the muscles of his upper back. Her pulse thrummed in her throat while Ivo's chest rose and fell against hers.

Rapture. Nirvana. Bliss. Whatever one called it, Lina experienced it with Ivo Zanardi.

CHAPTER 6

I WAS FALLING in love with you. I thought—I'd hoped—that you were falling in love with me....

Lina resisted the urge to trace the arch of Ivo's brow as he slept beside her. Early morning light filtered into the room from the transom over her bedroom door. She'd opened the shades in the living room when she'd arrived in New York yesterday, but hadn't thought to close them before she and Ivo fell asleep.

She pressed her cheek deeper into her pillow, watching Ivo as she considered what he'd said at the hotel last night. The sheet stopped in the middle of his torso, giving her an up-close view of his chest, the solid line of his collarbone, the dips of muscle at his shoulders, and the thick slash of the one eyebrow that wasn't buried in the bedding. His chin was tucked and he had at least two days' beard growth, preventing her from seeing the burn marks left behind after the fire lapped the narrow gap between his racing suit and his helmet. His heavy, even breathing assured her that he was sleeping comfortably. In the hospital, he'd only slept like this when sedated. Once he'd regained consciousness and started arguing against medication, that was rare.

She wrapped her fingers in the sheets and said a prayer of thanks that Ivo was healthy again.

She'd feared for him during those first harrowing days when the matter of his survival was touch and go. Then when it was clear he'd recover but the question of how much and how quickly couldn't be answered, she'd ached for him. Ivo was a competitor. A scrappy, against-all-odds driver who defied the judgment of the sport's power brokers and prognosticators to become a success. But when the battle was against his own body and doctors offered little reassurance, she wasn't sure how Ivo would fare. Particularly when she'd stood in the hall outside his room and overheard the doctor urging him to click his morphine button when he needed a respite from the pain.

Disconnect it, Ivo had snapped. *I don't need it anymore.*

There's no valor in pain.

There'd been a grunt from Ivo that would have driven a lesser doctor from the room. Then:

Withdrawal will add to the time it takes me to get back in the driver's seat. I need to compete as soon as possible. That is my singular goal. Not comfort.

The dose is controlled. It can help with inflammation. I'll leave it connected should your decision change.

Don't bother.

The doctor left the button connected and within reach for nearly a week, but Ivo remained firm. He never touched it.

To see him sleeping like this gave her hope, far more than she'd had when their elevator jerked as it'd reached his hotel floor and she'd seen his quick grimace. More, even, than late last night, when he'd moved her to the edge of the bed for a second round of lovemaking, but in a position more protective of his back.

Ivo was a fighter. She admired him for his grit and independence. After his kindness, they were the first qualities that'd attracted her.

A surge of emotion made her eyes fill. He was a kind man. She knew it deep in her heart. It's how he'd known she'd feel conflicted about her mother, how he'd known to offer condolences over her death. Heartfelt condolences, rather than the mumbled platitudes she'd heard from friends and colleagues who weren't sure how to react after her mother's story hit the news. It was how Lina knew Ivo told the truth when he claimed the words he'd said in the hospital had come from a place of emotional distress, not cruelty.

Carefully, so she wouldn't disturb him, she blotted moisture from the edge of her eye and stifled a sigh.

He'd also claimed he was falling in love with her.

It seemed impossible; had she missed the signs?

Another, more pressing question filled her mind as she regarded him: had she been falling in love with him? After so long together, she should have known. She hadn't. Certainly she was attracted to him. Yes, they had mind-blowing sex. She'd thought of him often when they were apart. When he was far away—whether at a prerace meeting in Canada or speaking to the media at a promotional event in Abu Dhabi —she'd craved his smiles, missed his voice, and wondered about his opinion on the latest episode of their favorite tv drama. When they were together, she reveled in the sound of his masculine laughter. She enjoyed the simple nearness of him and her heart leaped whenever she caught a mischievous glint in his eye.

But love? She'd avoided that issue entirely.

They both had.

With their careers, the time they'd spent apart, and—for her—the drama taking place at Rocco's house in the months before everything fell to pieces, it'd been easy to do. But now Lina needed to figure out how she felt about the man lying beside her. After last night, he'd want to know where she stood. Would she be there to support him during the remainder of his recovery? Or when he climbed into the car? And if she did, what did that mean for her and her company, given the media scrutiny she was under? She and Ivo wouldn't be able to keep their relationship quiet, as they had before.

Everything would change.

Lina's mother urged her, from a young age, to pursue a career and rely on herself rather than a partner. Believing her mother had been wronged by a partner, Lina had taken that advice to heart. The challenge made her happy. Fulfilled.

On the other hand, that mindset created a layer of insulation around her heart. It kept her from having to trust.

Once more, she fought the compulsion to touch his face. Lying in a warm bed, a few hours post-lovemaking, wasn't the time to assess her feelings with clarity. Waking up beside such a breathtaking, dynamic man, who wouldn't love him? Who wouldn't trust him? Her mind was a tangle.

"You're thinking again."

The whispered words hit her like a sonic boom. "How'd you know I was awake?"

"I have ears." His thick lashes parted and he gave her a sultry smile. "Your breathing slowed and you were trying to keep still instead of curling up like you do when you're asleep. A quiet Lina is usually a thinking Lina."

He scooted so the sheet was higher on his body, then flicked it to ensure she was covered. "Don't have morning-after thoughts. At the very least, save them for after breakfast and coffee."

She frowned. "I don't think there's food in the house. I haven't been here for months. Neither have Rocco or Enzo."

"We're in New York. We can order whatever we want." He skimmed the contour of her hip with one hand. "In fact, I noticed a grocery at the corner with a 'we deliver' sign when we came from the subway. I bet we could get coffee, eggs, milk, and bread. Maybe some tomatoes and cheese. While you shower, I'll make something delicious."

It sounded decadent. Lina was no slouch in the kitchen, but neither was Ivo. She'd loved the rare occasions when he'd stayed at her flat and they'd enjoyed breakfast together, especially when he did the cooking.

"Please tell me you're not thinking of spreadsheets."

She shimmied closer to him. "No, but I did hear my phone vibrate earlier. I suspect that's what woke me."

"I heard it, but was hoping you hadn't." He flattened his palm against her hip and looked at her with desire in his eyes. "I had other plans in mind before you look at the phone or spreadsheets."

"It's early."

"There's a rule against morning sex?"

"When your back needs a rest, I'd say so."

"My muscles are warm and loose now. Perfect timing."

An hour later, after he proved just what his muscles could do, Lina slipped into a robe and hummed to herself while Ivo stepped into the shower in the adjacent bathroom.

The apartment wasn't large, but it was comfortable. It boasted high ceilings, two bedrooms that were spacious by New York standards, and a spa-like bathroom that'd been created from two smaller ones. A compact but airy living room with its original fireplace made the perfect spot for morning coffee or evening relaxation. A modern kitchen situated at one end of the living room completed the space. More than the layout, though, it was the art that made the apartment special. Jack Cornaro had collected a range of paintings and sculptures over his lifetime—some valuable, some strictly sentimental, all beautiful—and this apartment had served as the repository. Each corner and wall held a piece she'd come to enjoy. Thinking of the stories behind them made her feel as if Papa were still here, ready to share his opinion on world events or deliver one of his awful knock-knock jokes.

She ran her fingers over an alabaster jar from Egypt, then settled into one of the room's plush chairs to listen to her phone messages. As she'd guessed, Tomasina had called the night before. Lina wrote her assistant a quick email summarizing her meeting with Mirabeau and thanking Tomasina for the time she'd spent listening to Lina perfect her presentation. After that, Lina confirmed an order from one of her suppliers and answered questions sent from the manager of her Milan boutique. The water stopped in the bathroom as she sent the last message. She stretched to set the phone on a side table when a message from her older brother, Rocco, lit her screen.

F asked for your number. Haven't responded.

She frowned. F? She didn't know an F. What the—?

Oh. *F.* Lina's throat constricted. Fabrizia.

As in Queen Fabrizia, King Carlo's wife. And, for Lina's entire life, the woman Teresa Cornaro had demonized to her children for stealing away Carlo. Given what Lina had learned about her mother in recent weeks, she wasn't convinced Fabrizia was the devil Teresa made her out to be, but the popular queen wasn't someone Lina wanted to know.

What in the world could that woman want with her?

She set the phone on the table face down, her sense of peace shattered.

Unfortunately, leaving the phone on the table didn't clear its message from Lina's mind, nor did firmly massaging her temples.

Fabrizia had a talent for appearing where she wasn't wanted.

The day of Teresa's funeral, Fabrizia showed up at Rocco's front door in disguise after he'd refused to take her calls. Unwilling to leave her waiting on the street where she might be recognized, Rocco allowed the famed royal inside, then listened while Fabrizia explained that her security team inadvertently discovered his wife, Justine, was under threat. He'd thanked the queen for the information and asked her to leave, but it'd been the start of a tentative relationship between the two and the first step toward a reconciliation between Rocco and Carlo.

Lina wasn't willing to take those steps. When Rocco was a toddler, he met Carlo and had vague memories of the king's visits. Lina had no such bond, nor did she want one….and that was the only reason she could conceive for Fabrizia's request. A biological link to Sarcaccia's king wasn't enough to justify placing herself in the crosshairs of the tabloids on a permanent basis, let alone enough to justify enduring a conversation with a man whom her mother wronged so terribly.

What could she possibly say to King Carlo? Maybe: *I'm sorry my mother manipulated you and that I exist as a result.*

Or, perhaps: *I don't need you to step in and act as a father to me. First, because I'm an adult, and second, because that job belonged to the wonderful American my mother married.*

Neither approach appealed. Nor could she undo the past. On the other hand, she couldn't leave Rocco hanging. She retrieved her phone before Ivo exited the bathroom.

F has resources. If she wants my number, she knows how to find it.

Rocco's answer was instantaneous.

She's taking the polite path and asking.

Lina grumbled at the screen. Mother once claimed that the queen had a spy network that rivaled MI6 and the CIA, and that Fabrizia was wily enough to know how to use that network for maximum effect. She'd proven as much by making that surprise visit to Rocco's without attracting attention, a difficult task when she was one of the most-watched women in Europe, if not the world.

Fabrizia was wrong to put Rocco in this position.

Give it to her if you wish, but tell her not to expect a response. Hope all is well with you and Justine.

There. That should keep Rocco on good terms with both King Carlo and Queen Fabrizia, yet wouldn't compel Lina to have a relationship with either of the Barralis.

We're planning an August trip to Rome. Could visit Milan if you're free and can tolerate us.

That, at least, was good news. Lina told him that'd be great, then set down her phone. She had always liked Justine, who was the perfect yang to Rocco's yin. It'd be delightful to see the two of them happy, the way they were when they first married. Maybe when Justine retired from competitive skiing, they'd make Lina an aunt. One could hope.

"Hope what?" Ivo emerged from the bathroom in his underwear, a towel draped over his shoulders.

She hadn't realized she'd said it aloud. "Rocco and Justine are visiting Rome in August. They may make a side trip to Milan." The dream of a little niece or nephew didn't need to be shared. Given what happened last night, Ivo might misinterpret her enthusiasm as a craving for her own children, though at the moment Isola was her baby. With the tenuous state of his own career, the last thing Ivo could possibly want would be a pregnant girlfriend or a colicky infant.

That was leaving aside the whole question of their relationship status.

He wiped his ear with the towel and raised a brow. "I'll hope for that, too. Seeing Rocco always puts you in a good frame of mind."

She stood. "If you're done, I'll shower. I'm caught up on calls."

"Go ahead. I'll try the grocery and see what I can whip up."

She couldn't resist kissing the damp skin of his shoulder as she passed him. Yes, Ivo Zanardi was her dream man. But love…love was a difficult question. She wished she had the answer.

CHAPTER 7

IT DIDN'T ESCAPE Ivo's notice that Lina ate every bite of her breakfast. It wasn't proof she was at peace or that she considered their relationship status solid, but it was a start.

He refilled each of their mugs, then carried the empty coffeepot to the sink to give it a rinse. With his back to Lina, he asked, "After spreadsheets, what's on your agenda today?"

"More phone calls. I'm planning an early dinner with Papa's sister, Pippi. I don't see the American side of the family very often, so we make an effort whenever I'm here."

"Pippi?" He smiled at the name. "She lives in Manhattan?"

"Hoboken. That's why dinner is early. She's taking the train here, we'll eat, then she needs to get home. She's in charge of the town's arts and music festival and there's a meeting tonight at eight."

He flipped the coffeepot to drip dry, then retrieved their empty plates and flatware. Lina moved to help, but he waved her to her seat and told her to enjoy her coffee.

"Will it be an easy visit or a tough one, given what's happened since your mother passed away?" Lina's aunt Pippi could be angry, disheartened, or both about the lies her late sister-in-law told.

Lina took a long sip of her drink, then adjusted her position in the chair. "I'm not sure. We didn't discuss it when I called to tell her I'd be here. Aunt Pippi's a lot like Papa, though. Laid-back, rolls with the punches. When we planned dinner, she sounded the same as always, so I'm hoping for the best."

"As long as there's no media."

"As long as." She aimed a look at the window. "When you went downstairs to meet the grocery delivery, was there—"

"No one." He located a box of soap under the sink, then started loading the dishwasher. "Either they haven't figured out the condo's location or they assume you're staying at a hotel."

Relief washed over her face. "With any luck, I won't have to deal with them again."

"Not in private, at least. I suspect they'll be at Mirabeau for your launch events."

"I suspect you're right." The corner of her mouth quirked. "I'm making appearances at five locations this week. Monday I'll take the train north to launch at the White Plains store, then Tuesday's the big day. I'll be at the flagship store near Central Park in the morning, then the SoHo store from late afternoon through the evening rush hour."

"You'll be busy. And visible."

"Especially Tuesday." She ran a hand over her hair, which still held moisture from her shower. "As long as the tabloid types are outside Mirabeau rather than inside, it should be fine. Now that I know they're around, I'll be prepared. I should have been prepared yesterday. I've dealt with the media for business, but it's entirely different than…this."

He set the flatware rack in the dishwasher, then located a roll of paper towels to tackle the counter. It'd been a while since he'd cooked for her, let alone cleaned. Lina often insisted on doing her share. Yet he'd always enjoyed the rhythm of tidying a kitchen. It helped clear his mind. He glanced at Lina, noted the frown crisscrossing her forehead, then continued his task.

Ignoring the question of how she planned to prepare, he said, "I understand what a shock it was to discover your mother's true involvement with King Carlo. What I don't understand is why you chose to go public. King Carlo's press conference was broadcast around the world.

Every news outlet in Europe covered it and the discussion went on for weeks."

Lina wrapped her hands around the outside of her mug, savoring its heat. "Justine and Rocco were separated when my mother died. The day of my mother's funeral, Fabrizia appeared on Rocco's doorstep to warn him that Justine was in danger. You can imagine his reaction to that. He had a lot of questions aside from the threat to Justine. Rocco demanded to know why the royal family had been watching him and how the queen even knew about our mother's death, but Fabrizia was cagey. Later, when we verified our mother's birth certificate and realized what it had to mean—" Lina moved deeper into the chair, then shrugged. "We realized then that the queen was afraid of my mother's past coming to light and what it'd mean for her family."

"It was more complex than three illegitimate children."

Lina nodded. "Enzo, Rocco, and I got together at Rocco's to discuss what, if anything, we should do. Our mother left each of us letters explaining herself—she knew we'd discover her real birthdate during probate—but we didn't know what to believe…what parts of her story were true, what parts weren't, and what other secrets might be lurking. It left us all unsettled. We decided to ask King Carlo for his side of the story."

"This took place while I was still in the hospital?"

"Yes." She kept her attention on her coffee rather than meeting his gaze. He could only imagine the emotional turmoil she'd suffered. First, when he'd acted so callously. Then, from her mother's death and deceit.

"Rocco arranged to meet King Carlo at a cabin outside Dubrovnik. The king confirmed most of what our mother admitted in the letters— her true age, that she'd manipulated him, that she left Sarcaccia after Enzo and I were born—and he clarified other points. Carlo made the trip in the middle of the night, but a reporter spotted his plane on the return to Sarcaccia. At an event the next day, the king was asked about it. He put them off, but knew they'd investigate. He called Rocco to warn him."

"Rocco knew their connection would be discovered."

"The king thought it better to host a press conference to reveal the information on his terms, rather than allow the press to dig up the truth and shape the story for their own purposes. Rocco agreed."

"He attended. You didn't." Rocco had taken a spot in the rear of the room, offering his support to the king. It didn't take long for the press to ferret out his identity.

"We dealt with the situation in different ways." She rolled her mug in her palms, then downed the last of the coffee. "Enzo and I wanted nothing to do with the press conference. A few hours beforehand, I checked into a short-term rental under a pseudonym and stayed away from my flat and the office. I couldn't reconcile the mother I knew with the woman being portrayed in the press. Staying out of sight allowed me to tune out the noise and focus on work. Smartest decision I could have made both for my mental health and for Isola."

He eyed her empty mug in a silent offer to start another pot of coffee. She shook her head, so he finished wiping the kitchen counter and took the seat opposite hers. "Pouring your energy into work is convenient emotional compensation."

"Compensation or not, the work had to be done. It's what you would've done, too."

"True." Experience taught him that work buffered a person from pain, from confusion, or from having to fully experience rejection from someone you believed incapable of it. He immersed himself most in work when he felt the skepticism of F1 pundits or his mother's disapproval of his career choices. At the end of the day, that's what Teresa Cornaro had done, as well: rejected Lina by refusing to share her deepest self. Whether Lina fully realized it or not, what left her bereft was the knowledge that her mother didn't love her enough to trust Lina with her secrets during her lifetime. Even in death, Teresa had only come clean because she'd been forced to do so.

"But you believe you can deal with the press now, in a manner that'll protect your mental health and Isola?"

"I don't have a choice. Not if I want Isola to thrive, and I do. A lot of people are counting on me. Frankly, *I'm* counting on me. But I need to be prepared. This has been my dream for as long as I can remember and I don't want what my mother did to take away that dream."

That he could understand. However, he owed it to her to make it easier. She'd already given up her dream once, and it was to stand by his side in a hospital room. "Perhaps you could take a cue from King Carlo. Guide the direction of the press yourself. As sensational as the coverage has been, it would've been far worse if Carlo hadn't called the press conference and given his version of events. It gave the press a focus."

One side of her mouth hooked into an endearing smile. "I doubt a press conference would do me any good."

"I wasn't thinking a press conference." He took her empty mug and set it on the side table, then pulled her hands into both of his. "You need to decide what story you want them to cover."

"Isola." Amusement flickered in her eyes. "Lingerie with the trifecta of style, comfort, and durability."

He admired her ability to see the humor in the situation. "You know the tabloids won't print that, even if the fashion press does. But you can give them a story that provides the sensationalism they crave. One that will draw attention away from your mother and steer them in a more positive direction."

He waited, then saw the understanding in her gaze. "You?"

"The story about your mother and King Carlo has stayed front and center this long because royal scandals sell. Until another royal scandal comes along, they'll pursue you to feed that sales beast. You can't control the demand for royal gossip, but perhaps you can use my celebrity to move the reporters' focus from your mother's choices to yours."

The strategy had formed while he'd cleaned her kitchen, but her words about Carlo and the press conference cemented it. He gave her hands a squeeze. "I've worked hard over the years to maintain a good reputation with the press, because the way I interact with them reflects on the entire F1 industry. But the longer I've stayed out of sight, the more speculation there's been about the extent of my injuries and whether I can race again. We can make those factors work for both of us."

"How?"

"If I'm in attendance at one of your events, I'm bound to be recognized. It'd be easy to stay in the background and decline to answer questions, but drop the offhanded comment that you're the steady hand who keeps me sane. The person who nursed me through my crisis. You heard the reporter outside Mirabeau ask about our relationship. He may have been guessing, but his question will make the others curious. They'll figure out sooner or later that we're involved. This way, the revelation comes in the most positive light possible, one that explains why you missed London Fashion Week."

The tight set of her shoulders eased. "You really think that'd work?

He nodded, instinct telling him he was on the right track. "At another event, I might mention how professional you are, how you care for your employees, how much pride you take in your work. It will speak to your brand and—without saying it in so many words—it'll show you to be everything the press portrayed your mother not to be. At the same time, my presence proves I'm healthy enough to be out and about. Win-win."

She looked at their hands, then met his gaze and smiled. "That's very kind of you, but it's unnecessary, and I suspect the press would see through it. Besides, you don't need me to prove you're healthy. You have the UNICEF show."

"Not until the end of the week. If I appear at your events in the meantime, it helps us both. You'd be amazed at how subtly I can leak information to reporters." He lifted one shoulder, then let it drop. "Perhaps it'll draw more attention to the UNICEF show. In which case, triple win."

Her fingers flexed in his, but she didn't pull away. "That's a big commitment."

More than appearing at Isola events, she meant. It'd put their relationship in the spotlight.

"You're not ready to make that kind of commitment. I understand completely." How he managed to say the words as breezily as he did was a miracle.

It wasn't his sudden disappointment so much as the weight of it that shocked him. Much as he enjoyed spending time with Lina, he wasn't ready for a commitment. Not the type that meant daily good night calls or ensuring she always had milk in the fridge. Racing encompassed unpredictable days at the track and long stretches away from home.

The fact she wasn't ready for that should be a relief. So why did it cause heaviness in his chest?

"It's not what you think," she said. "It's…more than anything, I want this week to be about the product. About the people who work for me and the quality of the fabrics my suppliers produce. I want to see women discover lingerie that actually fits and feels good. That makes them feel sexy and confident. Then, when they've worn Isola for a few weeks and know it's everything they'd hoped, I want those women to come back for more and bring their friends."

He admired her passion. "You're afraid having me at Mirabeau will detract from that."

"No, not afraid." She freed one of her hands to cup his cheek. Eyes of deep honey searched his, then she smiled. "Your idea's a good one. This is more about being deliberate in my decisions. I had a plan in place, one formulated over several months. The past twenty-four hours have been intense and unexpected, both personally and professionally. I need to take this one step at a time."

He leaned forward to give her a soft, slow, tender kiss, one that signaled he wouldn't push the issue. "See how your appearance in White Plains goes. In the meantime, remember what it is you do and do well."

"Design lingerie?"

"Exactly. Given your mother's history, some reporters might go for a sleazy angle and ask leading questions. Don't fall into that trap. Focus on your strengths. Your brand's strengths. Be classy. Own what you do. I know it'll work out, because I know you." He gave her a final quick kiss, then stood.

She leaned back and looked at him in surprise. "You're leaving?"

"You have spreadsheets and Pippi. I have my own plans." He didn't bother to hide the heat in his gaze as he promised, "I won't be far away."

TWO HOURS after Ivo returned to his hotel, Lina's phone dinged. She finished making a notation, then rose from the barstool and stretched. The logical side of her knew she'd have to give serious thought to Ivo and their relationship soon. On the other hand, the physical aftermath of a glorious bath and hours of lovemaking—followed by a decadent breakfast—meant her mind and muscles were in a state of total relaxation. The stress of the last few months had fallen away, giving her a charge that'd fueled her entire day.

Leaving her computer and notes spread across the kitchen counter, she crossed to the seating area and retrieved her phone, her heart thrumming in anticipation of a note from Ivo. She clicked a button to pull up the message, then wished she hadn't.

I am visiting New York tomorrow and would enjoy the pleasure of your company for a private tea. I hope 2pm will suit. - QF

No, it did not "suit."

Lina set the phone on the kitchen counter and resumed work, though regaining her previous level of concentration proved impossible. After finishing her review of the spreadsheets, she read an industry article Tomasina had forwarded to her, then answered a message from the head buyer at a Frankfurt department store. Lina had been courting the Frankfurt store for several months and had high hopes of landing a contract there soon.

First, she needed the Mirabeau launch to go well. She'd felt buoyed by Ivo's pep talk encouraging her to focus on her strengths. Somehow, a simple text from Fabrizia plunged her right back into a sea of tension.

Her phone pinged again, this time with a message from Aunt Pippi confirming their dinner reservation. As soon as Lina answered, another message appeared on the screen.

My apologies. I should have included the location. The room is reserved under the name Maria Rossi. I look forward to meeting you. - QF

A map appeared with the name and address of a coffee shop only two blocks away, one Lina had patronized on earlier trips to New York. At that time of day, even the main seating area would be quiet. No one would notice the presence of Maria Rossi—the Italian-language equivalent of Jane Doe—in the private room at the rear of the shop.

Lina drummed her fingers on the countertop and stifled a curse. The woman hadn't arranged this on the fly. She had a purpose, one she hadn't shared with Rocco or he'd have told her.

Instead of answering, Lina verified that the appropriate stock had arrived at each of the Mirabeau locations for the launch, then slipped her phone into her handbag and closed her computer to prepare for dinner with Aunt Pippi.

For the sake of Lina's sanity, the queen could wait.

CHAPTER 8

Ivo sat on the stairs of the Greenwich Village brownstone across the street from Lina's, watching and waiting. He'd taken a taxi to an adjacent block, then approached from the opposite direction he and Lina had taken last night, walking slowly in order to survey the neighborhood and make note of anyone lingering in doorways or holding a camera. Sounds carried from the next block—low chatter from outdoor seating at restaurants, the hum of cars, the occasional thunk of a delivery truck bouncing over manhole covers—but the area around him remained quiet. Only two pedestrians and a dog walker passed in the ten minutes he'd been here, and neither noticed him leaning against the stairs' iron railing, his attention riveted on Lina's building and the sidewalk that fronted it.

The tranquility gave him a sense of relief. For now, at least, she had her privacy.

Finally, Lina appeared at her window, her eyes searching the street until she spotted him. To his immense satisfaction, a smile bloomed on her face, then she waved for him to come over.

The door buzzed to admit him, then he sprinted the stairs. She opened the door as his foot hit the landing.

"You ran three flights. How are you not screaming in pain?"

"You're at the top." She looked amazing in a close-fitting lavender dress and dark brown heels. Her hair was up in a loose bun, as it had been the day he'd first laid eyes on her at Heathrow. This time, instead of smiling at a fussy child, she turned that radiance toward him.

"You brought flowers. And shaved."

"You answered my message asking you to look outside." A message he'd sent less than two minutes ago, once he'd ensured the coast was clear. He bent to give her a kiss, one intended to be quick but that instantly became heated. She tasted delicious, smelled delicious. He flicked a gaze toward the living room. "Is this a bad time?"

"Only a bad location." She eased him inside and closed the door. "Mrs. Metzger across the hall makes frequent use of her peephole."

"Mrs. Metzger needs to get a hobby."

"She's harmless. She's also incredibly wealthy. If the opportunity presented itself, she'd buy this condo and combine the units. I want to keep her on my good side, just in case."

That surprised him. "You plan to sell?"

"We haven't decided. I doubt we'd find a better buyer than Mrs. Metzger, though."

She located a vase in the kitchen, filled it with water, then unwrapped the flowers and trimmed the ends under running water. As she arranged the stems, he asked, "Dinner with your Aunt Pippi go well?"

"It did. Awkward at first. She was hurt to learn about my mother via the Internet, but she doesn't blame me or my brothers. She knows we were kept in the dark, too." She looked up once she'd finished with the flowers. "I suspect she's glad Jack never knew the truth. He loved my mother deeply."

"He loved you, too."

"Us, too." She regarded him with folded arms. "You could have called to ask how dinner went."

"True, but I also wanted to see if you'd finished your spreadsheets."

"I did. You could have called about that, too."

"I could have. But then I couldn't surprise you with this." He withdrew an envelope from the inside pocket of his jacket. "You deserve a treat after a hard week of work."

She approached to take it, but he jerked it away. "No, princess, not yet. Get a coat. We're going to see a show. Which one will remain a mystery until we arrive at the theater."

Lina started to say something, then quieted. He realized what he'd done and scowled. "Now I know why you told me to stop whenever I called you princess."

"I'm no one's princess."

"You're mine. Always will be. But I'll call you something else."

She gave him a grateful smile, then retrieved her coat from the closet. He didn't miss that her eyes lingered at his jawline before she bowed her head to fuss with her zipper.

"It's a bad scar, I know."

"It's better than last time I saw you."

"That's not saying much." At her frown, he asked, "What?"

"It's just...I had nightmares about your chin." She rolled her eyes and waved off her own comment as ridiculous. "When I arrived at the hospital, the doctors were focused on treating the biggest issues first. Your chin was at the bottom of their priority list. But to someone who isn't a doctor, your skin looked—" She puffed out a hard breath. "Let's just say that it was peeling. I could smell the burned flesh."

"I couldn't."

She grimaced. "I probably couldn't, either. I suspect my mind was playing tricks on me. But it looked painful."

"Lucky for me, it's not." The skin felt stiff at times, but there was no pain.

She aimed a look at the envelope. "What made you sure I'd agree to go?"

"First, I suspect you buried yourself in work all day and need the break. Second, since the tabloid types haven't found the condo, I thought you'd feel safe venturing out. It'll be good for you to have your mind on something other than work or family. Enjoy a Saturday night in the city." When she approached, he smiled and tucked a stray tendril of hair behind her ear. "Then, I'll walk you home and kiss you goodnight before I return to my hotel. You should settle in for a good night's sleep and a restful day tomorrow so you're fresh to conquer the world on Monday."

Her palms went to his chest. "What if I want you to come upstairs?"

"If you're especially tempting, which you always are, I'll kiss you a second time." He dipped his head, doing just that. He let his lips linger against hers, then pulled back. "But I'll stay at the hotel tonight and tomorrow. This is an important week for you. Make it count."

He'd been responsible for her career faltering once. He wouldn't be responsible for a second stumble, not after all she'd done to support him. He could be patient. If he got this week right, they'd be supporting each other's careers—and enjoying fantastic nights together —for many nights to come. Everything would be as it was before. Better, without the secrets between them.

"Sure you won't tell me which show?" she asked as they descended the stairs.

"Patience," he told her, "will be rewarded."

LINA'S FEET skipped along the sidewalk as she and Ivo left the theater. She even hummed a few bars of 'Cell Block Tango' before catching herself and glancing at him to see if he heard. He pretended he hadn't, keeping his eyes forward as he took her hand and slid it through the crook of his arm.

"I take it you didn't mind seeing it again?" As if he couldn't tell. Warmth flooded him at the knowledge he'd made her so happy. He'd had to force himself to stop stealing looks at her during the performance. Any signs of worry melted away with the bright music and snappy dialogue as she lost herself in the story. By intermission she'd become more radiant, more carefree. More *Lina*. The woman who loved to dream big, then find practical means to make her dreams happen.

"*Chicago* is my favorite. I love the music, the flirtaticusness, the dirty side of it…it's so much fun. The woman playing Roxie was phenomenal. The entire cast was phenomenal. I'm so glad you thought of it."

He squeezed her hand as they dodged traffic to cross to the south side of the street. "Me, too."

A busker stood off the sidewalk, occupying a gap between buildings, his fingers flying along the strings of an acoustic guitar for the music-minded crowd leaving the theaters. A couple walking behind them commented on the man's skill.

"He's playing Ottmar Liebert," Ivo said to Lina, recognizing the tune as they approached the guitarist. A few bars later, he added, "'August Moon.' Not a song most would choose. He's talented."

Lina paused, pulled a bill from her handbag, then dropped it into the open guitar case. The dark-haired man gave her a nod of thanks before she and Ivo rejoined the wave of theatergoers clogging the sidewalk.

"It always amazes me how generous you are."

"I appreciate the hard work that goes into sounding effortless." She glanced sideways at Ivo. "It always amazes me how well you know music and movies. How is it possible you've never seen *Chicago*?"

He slowed to guide her around a mass of people exiting a play. "The movie's been on my must-watch list for years. I'm sure I'll see it eventually. And I've never been to the theater."

"Never? Or never on Broadway?"

"Never." At her look of surprise, he added, "I saw outdoor theater in Rome when I was a kid, but not with a ticket or a seat. It was one of those summer tourist productions. I was working, but I caught bits and pieces."

"You've mentioned working when you were a kid before. I know you modeled, but what were you doing at a theater? Selling refreshments? Tickets?"

"I was too young to work at a ticket booth or refreshment stand." He'd also been too foreign and too dark-skinned at a time when immigrants were eyed with suspicion, despite the fact he knew nothing of life outside Rome.

They turned a corner to skirt the edge of Times Square as they made their way to the subway. A woman in her late teens or early twenties sat before an easel not far from the corner, drawing a caricature of a young boy perched on a stool. The boy's mother stood behind the artist, smiling at the image of her son. Ivo's childhood in Rome seemed far away most of the time, as if it had happened to someone else, but the sights and sounds of buskers and sidewalk artists exhibiting their skills brought back a wealth of memories.

To Lina, he explained, "I sold souvenirs from a blanket outside the amphitheater. Sometimes it was knockoff Roma or Lazio *fútbol* jerseys, if I had enough money to buy a box of them to resell. That was good money, but risky. The police will fine or chase off anyone selling fake goods and my mother would've killed me if I was arrested. She didn't want me selling the fakes. Holding that first profit from a box of jerseys, though...there wasn't a feeling like it. Like I was on top of the world. All for a few coins." He couldn't help but smile at the memory. Tough as those days were, they'd given him a sense of accomplishment, one that had driven him to pursue that feeling again and again. "Most days I sold postcards or plaster casts of landmarks like the Arch of Constantine or St. Peter's Basilica. Or candy bars and bottled water, depending on the crowd. A production that drew more children and teenagers meant I'd make more on candy. I learned a lot doing it."

She contemplated that. More than once, he'd seen Lina slip Euros to children working on the streets in Milan. She'd done it without judgment, without making a fuss, and despite the fact she was in the fashion industry, which had a lot to lose with unlicensed sales. It was one of the traits that made him sure of her innate goodness.

"You must have been young."

"It was the two summers before my first modeling job. Once I landed that, I quit working the amphitheater."

"You were only twelve when you started modeling." She stopped walking and frowned as they neared the subway steps. "You told me that when you were little, you lived with your mother and that your father was out of the picture. Where were they while you were out on the streets?"

He gave her a pointed look. "It's not time for an Ivo pity party. As you see, I'm doing fine."

"Of course you are. But you've never told me any of this."

"No reason to. It doesn't affect who I am now. Besides, there's out on the streets and there's out on the streets. I had a roof over my head in a decent part of town. I had clothing, food, and an education. My mother worked hard and took good care of me. Made sure I attended school and could speak both fluent English and Italian."

"Satisfy my curiosity, then. How did you end up selling souvenirs on the streets?"

He gestured toward the subway entrance and she fell into step beside him. "My mother was raised in a rural village in Nigeria. Life wasn't easy, but she made it through high school thanks to a UNICEF program."

"That's why you support UNICEF?"

He shrugged. He hadn't thought of it in that manner, as a tit for tat. He knew what good the organization did, he made donations, and he said yes when they made requests. "After she finished school, my mother traveled to Abuja twice a week to work at an arts and crafts stall that sold goods from her village. Handmade jewelry, carved wooden pieces, small furniture. She grew up speaking English and Yoruba—a local language—and picked up a little Italian and German from tourists."

"That's impressive for a teenager."

"She loved it. She once told me that she'd hoped to manage the stall someday, though I suspect her ultimate goal was to open and run her own stall. She has a good head for numbers."

"Life had other plans?"

He smiled at that. "My father worked in Abuja for an Italian import company. His job meant perusing the local markets for items that would sell in Europe at a higher price. They developed a professional relationship that turned personal, very much over her parents' objection. She found out she was pregnant at the same time he received a promotion that required him to return to Italy."

Lina's "uh-oh" was good-natured.

"I assume her first thought was more panicked, though she never said as much to me."

Lina pulled a subway pass from her bag and swiped them through the turnstile. Her attitude made it easy to continue the story. "Being a good Catholic, my father insisted they marry as soon as she told him. I was born in Abuja, but when I was six months old, he brought me and my mother to Rome. Their relationship didn't last. They came from such different backgrounds, I suspect the marriage was doomed from the start. She knew she'd be looked down upon if she returned to her village, so she stayed and built a life in Rome."

"Your father didn't support her after they divorced?"

"To my knowledge, they never divorced. Simply went their separate ways. I don't remember anything of the time he lived with us, though my mother assures me he once did. I try not to ask too many questions. I think it makes her uncomfortable to discuss it. He's part of her past, not her present." Ivo put a protective hand to Lina's back as they walked to the platform for the train that'd take them to Greenwich Village. "I haven't seen him in several years, though he sends me notes for my birthday and on Christmas. When I was growing up I saw him every so often. He'd take me to the zoo or to sporting events. He was always kind. Always asked how my mother was doing. Always tried to give me money. I never took any, though I'd occasionally find some in my pocket after I returned home. My mother" —he lifted his face toward the station's tiled ceiling— "was too proud to take his money."

He lowered his chin, then shook his head. "Actually, that's not true. It wasn't pride so much as her own moral code and upbringing. She insisted that while she'd felt pressured to marry, it was still her choice. She also told me it was her choice to separate when she realized their marriage wasn't, in her words, as a marriage should be. Therefore, it was her responsibility to work to earn a living rather than take what she considered a handout. I suspect that's why she's careful in her choices now."

"It must have been difficult for her, working in a foreign country when she had an infant."

A howl to their left caused them to turn before Ivo could respond.

A group of teenagers raced along the platform, laughing and screaming, oblivious to those around them. A girl near the front of the pack carried a hot pretzel in waxed paper, holding it aloft as if it were a prize to be won. Ivo and Lina stepped out of their path, then watched as a boy caught the girl around the waist, lifted her, then spun her in a circle so another boy could pluck the pretzel from her hand.

"She doesn't seem to mind being caught," Ivo observed.

Color suffused the girl's cheeks and she laughed as the boy who'd caught her released her. A beat later, she turned and gave him a playful swat.

"No, I suspect she's fine with losing the pretzel if it means she gets the guy."

Ivo pulled Lina closer to his side. He loved how they fit. That he had only to gaze at her to feel warm inside, no wild flirtation or chasing her for a pretzel required. Unable to resist, he lowered his head and to give her a quick kiss. She tightened her grasp on the arm of his jacket, sending a pulse of electricity straight from her fingers to his groin.

Dear God, he wanted to take her back to the condo and make love to her, despite his promise to give her breathing room tonight.

He angled his head to deepen the kiss and was rewarded with a low, sultry sigh that nearly undid him.

Some promises were more difficult to keep than others.

CHAPTER 9

Ivo ran his hand along Lina's back, melding her body to his. At the same time, a drawn out chorus of *woooo* erupted from the teenagers.

Lina tensed, but didn't pull away. With her lips close to his, she murmured, "You'd think they'd have seen it all, living in New York."

"They're fired up. We're simply an excuse to continue." He gave her a final, gentle kiss and let go. A wave of giggles burst from the teens. Ivo shot a look their direction, one intended to quiet them without being threatening. It worked.

Once the teens moved to the far end of the platform, Lina asked, "So how'd she do it? Taking care of you and working?"

It took him a second to pick up their earlier conversation. His mind was on Lina, rather than his upbringing.

"I spent the mornings with neighbors who'd emigrated from Cameroon while my mother worked at a bakery near our flat. Her day started around four in the morning, but she was home by two. When I was old enough to go to school, I did. Luckily, the modeling offer came along to keep me busy. A woman who ran advertising campaigns for an Italian clothing company took photos of me selling jerseys one night outside the amphitheater. I thought she worked for the police at first." The memory amused him. He'd been certain he was going to be arrested. "Turns out she had seen me there before and thought I had the look she wanted for a promotion. My mother met with her. Before long, I had an agent and a series of six ads booked for that clothing company."

"It must have been lucrative."

"The first batch didn't pay well. More than selling souvenirs, but not enough to change the way we lived. My mother was happy that I could book the work around school. And that I wasn't trying to sell counterfeit jerseys."

"It didn't take long, though."

"No, it didn't." Anyone with access to a computer knew his story from that point. He landed a public service campaign on the importance of vaccinating children, a job that put his face in every hospital and doctor's office in Italy. It enabled his mother to move from their leaky one-room flat into a two-bedroom across the street. More clothing ads and occasional runway work came after the government campaign, then he landed a series of commercials for a soda company. One spot was shot at a racing kart track. During breaks, he asked questions about the karts and one of the drivers gave him a demonstration. The moment Ivo obtained his driver's license, he returned to take lessons. He became obsessed with racing and showed a knack for it early. The first race he entered brought a third-place trophy. After graduation, he quit modeling and used a chunk of his savings to pursue the sport. Over the years, he worked his way through the echelons of racing, all the way to a prestigious F1 contract.

Once they found spots on the train, Lina said, "Your mother must be proud of your career."

"I like to think so." She hadn't been happy about his decision to leave behind a modeling career with pending contracts. Nor his decision to forgo a university education, which she viewed as the ticket to security.

Surprise flickered in her eyes. "You don't know?"

He raised one shoulder and let it fall. "It's not a topic we discuss."

"What do you talk about?"

"The usual parent-child topics, I suppose. Her health. Her job.

She's still at the bakery. The owner is semiretired, so she manages the place, though her Italian isn't the best." His hand went to Lina's waist as the train left the station with a jerk.

"You must discuss your personal life, at least occasionally. Your work. Your relationships." She explained, "When I saw your wreck and flew to San Rimini, I couldn't get access to your room without consent from your next of kin. The hospital called your mother. She granted permission without asking any questions."

"I told her several months before the accident that I was seeing someone. I thought she should know."

His gaze raked over her blond hair and full lips as the train slowed, sparking a flame of desire. It hadn't occurred to him before this week that she'd care whether he'd told his mother about them. But for some reason, it did. He could see it in her posture, in the way she shifted closer as they waited for the doors to open. He liked it.

On the other hand, while his mother had been a good parent, ensuring he had all he needed, she wasn't the type who spent her days dreaming of her son's wedding. Their conversations weren't what Lina had experienced with her own mother. Emotion, dreams…they weren't practical. His mother had needed to be brutally practical to survive. He needed to burst Lina's bubble on that front.

"I never gave her your name. She must've assumed that you were my 'someone' when the hospital called."

A divot appeared between her eyes, though it disappeared instantly. "I see."

"No, you don't." What mother wouldn't be curious about her son's life? "But I appreciate that you want to. Once she left Nigeria, I was her whole family. Everything my mother did, she did for me. The long hours at work, the tough discipline. Taking me to the park on her days off, even when she was exhausted, so I could kick a ball around with other kids. But she's more comfortable staying in the dark about my personal life unless there's something she needs to know. She's skeptical of relationships. Understandably so, given her experience. I do my best to keep her concerns minimized. If she doesn't ask, I assume she doesn't want the details."

He wasn't sure why he felt compelled to explain her to Lina. Maybe it was that when he walked beside her, it was as if they'd created an island of calm in the midst of Manhattan's lights and noise. He craved that calm as deeply as he craved fresh air and sunshine following a long day strapped into a simulator.

He'd never realized it, not until now, but he'd felt the same way when he and Lina spent time together before his accident. His time with her allowed him to relax, to take a break from the immense pressure of his everyday life: the focus required on race weekends, the intensity of his daily workouts, and the time he spent listening to engineers discuss the pros and cons of adjusting the steering or braking systems. Lina even provided a refuge from the scrutiny of the F1 press and ferocity of its fans. With her, he could be himself. They could talk movies and books. Art. Astronomy. News. Politics. Everything that didn't interest his racing friends. Their discussions helped him view the world in new ways.

Next time he saw his mother, he needed to tell her more, whether she wished to hear it or not. Lina deserved that.

It took until they were exiting the station near her condo for Ivo to realize how stiffly he held himself. He made an effort to relax, but not before Lina noticed. She looked sideways at him. "You have a difficult relationship with your mother."

He didn't respond. He didn't have to.

"You've never mentioned it. Why?"

"Maybe because you always seemed to have such a good relationship with yours."

Her lips rose in a crooked smile. "The operative words being 'seemed to.'"

"You did." He wrapped an arm around her shoulders, craving her closeness as they walked. "My mother loves me very much. While your mother and mine are different, you shouldn't doubt her love. She supported your education and career because she knew it would make you happy. She may have had a lot of other things going on in her life, things she kept hidden, but she loved you deeply."

Lina paused as they reached the stairs fronting her mother's condo.

"You told me your childhood doesn't affect the person you are now. I think the opposite is true. It's made you a caring, conscientious man. The kind who walks a woman home in the rain. Or who pays close enough attention to know what kind of flowers she'd like or what show would be the perfect choice to take her mind off work. Maybe you don't have the best relationship with your mother—I can only imagine the challenges she's faced—but I'm sure she appreciates the man you've become. I do."

Warmed by Lina's words, he turned to face her, keeping her in a loose embrace. Much as he wanted her to invite him inside, to continue the kiss they'd shared on the subway platform, he'd keep to his word. One easy kiss, maybe two, then he'd keep his word and return to his hotel.

"What's your plan for tomorrow? More spreadsheet excitement?"

She grinned at that. "I have some reading to do. Then I'll rehearse my sales pitch a dozen times more than necessary out of nervousness. After that, I'll go for a run to try to work that nervousness out of my system. What about you?"

"Tomorrow? Leaving you alone so you can work. The hotel has a decent fitness center, so I'll visit whenever I can catch it empty." Mostly, though, he'd catch up on technical reading. He'd fallen behind during his time in the hospital.

"What about Monday?"

"I have a workout scheduled with a physical therapist. I imagine I'll be sore afterward, so I may try to book a massage. I have a quick business meeting after that, then I plan to find a tea shop I've heard about on the Upper East Side. Thought I'd have a gift box sent to my mother. The family who cared for me when I was little still live in the neighborhood. She has them over from time to time and they enjoy trying tea and cookies from different places."

She brushed her hand along the side of his body, pausing at his waist. "You make an effort to stay close to her."

"It was hard on her to be estranged from her family. Neither of us wants our relationship to feel strained. We both make the effort."

Lina nodded in understanding. "Monday sounds like a busy day for you."

"Busy, but not stressful. At least not the part where I sample tea and cookies."

Lines formed around her mouth, though she quickly looked away in an attempt to hide her reaction.

"What's wrong?"

"It's nothing."

He framed her chin. "It's enough to distract you. And disturb you."

"I received a text yesterday." Though they were out of earshot of other pedestrians, her voice dropped before she said, "Queen Fabrizia asked Rocco for my contact information. She's in New York and asked me to meet her for tea tomorrow. I didn't respond—I told Rocco to warn her I wouldn't—which I think is for the best. Until you mentioned tea and cookies, I'd put it out of my mind."

"You should go."

"Go?" She jerked back. "Why would I do that?"

Ivo ticked off the reasons on his fingers. "She's married to your biological father. She went to the effort of arranging a private meeting. Her time is in demand, so she must believe this is important. What harm would there be in hearing her out?"

"What good would there be? The kindest reason I can conceive is that she wants me to reach out to Carlo. I'm not interested."

"Rocco seems to get along with the man."

"So?"

"Like it or not, they're your family. At least Carlo is, as are his other children. They're close to your age. Accomplished. Good reputations. I don't imagine the queen has any purpose in contacting you beyond making peace with all her husband's children." Having lost both her mother and Jack Cornaro, Lina could use more people in her corner. She deserved that.

"I'm happy with the family I have. I couldn't ask for better brothers."

"You're fortunate to have them."

How often had he wondered about his mother's family in Nigeria?

Whether he'd get along with them? Whether he had cousins who could be friends?

Once he'd become famous, it felt wrong to reach out to them. It wasn't something he'd do while his mother was alive, anyway. Not when they'd rejected her. But Lina hadn't been rejected. Judging from what he'd read about Rocco and the royal family, King Carlo wanted a relationship with his illegitimate children.

He pulled Lina closer, then gave her a slow, soft kiss, followed by a brief touch of his lips to her forehead before he stepped back. "Think about seeing Fabrizia. Listen to what she has to say. If you don't like what you hear, you can always leave." He gave her a wry smile. "If you don't, I suspect you'll hear from her again. She strikes me as a woman who doesn't accept no for an answer."

"Ivo...no."

He smiled. "Good night. Let me know how it goes in White Plains on Monday. If you have the energy to talk afterward, you know where to find me."

"You really aren't going to stay over?"

He let loose a full-on laugh. "Lina...no."

———

LINA PLACED a clean bowl on the shelf, closed the cupboard door, then wiped out the sink.

From the moment she'd crawled into bed last night, a lead weight rested in her stomach. Ivo did everything right yesterday. He gave her much-needed time alone, brought her flowers, treated her to the theater, then walked her home. After he turned to head for the subway, he paused at the corner to ensure she'd safely unlocked her front door and stepped inside before moving out of sight. He'd done as he promised, ensuring she'd have a good night's sleep so she could spend today preparing for the week ahead. But their goodbye left her unsettled.

Perfect weather had greeted her on a quick morning jog, flushing her lungs with fresh air and invigorating her joints and muscles. Afterward, she'd treated herself to a croissant and latte from a Greenwich Village bakery she'd come to love, then enjoyed a relaxing shower. A run-through of her Isola sales materials had gone beautifully and she'd checked and double-checked on her transportation to White Plains. Still, Lina couldn't find her focus.

A glance at the clock showed it was quarter to two.

Damned Fabrizia. Why did the queen feel the need to encroach on her life this week, of all weeks?

And why did Ivo think it was so important she give Fabrizia a chance? Lina doubted it was concern that Fabrizia would persist, coming after her like a dog pawing the garden for a hidden bone. If that were the case, Ivo would've encouraged Lina to answer the reporters' questions and be done with them, too. She and Ivo both knew that wouldn't work, and she found Fabrizia more dangerous than any tabloid reporter.

She closed the dishwasher door and clicked off the light over the sink.

At three minutes to two, she snagged a cardigan from her bedroom and strode out the door.

She'd go, but she would *not* get dressed up to see the woman.

LINA RECOGNIZED the barista who stood on a stool behind the counter and carefully tipped a bag of coffee beans into the hopper of a fancy espresso machine. Last time Lina visited the shop, the young woman's hair ended in hot pink tips. Today it was all blond, but the tiny silver bar that pierced her brow remained the same, as did her bright smile.

Lina didn't recognize the man who occupied the small table nearest the shop's back room. On first glance, he appeared ordinary enough— close-cropped hair, a zip-up sweatshirt, a disinterested look on his face as he lifted his chin at her entrance, then returned his attention to his phone—but a second look made Lina realize he was positioned to see the entire shop. His slouch also hid a muscular frame. A rather tall, muscular frame. She'd bet anything if he stood, he'd be several inches north of six feet.

He wasn't as disinterested as he feigned.

"I'll be with you in a sec," the barista said over the sound of the beans hitting the funnel. "We're out of the coffee cake that's listed on the board outside, but I have plenty of everything else."

"Thanks. I'm actually here to meet someone. Is the back room open?"

The barista stopped pouring. She glanced at the man before returning her attention to Lina. "You're scheduled at two?"

Before Lina could answer, the man stood and moved within arm's reach. "She is. I'll escort her."

The barista scrambled down from the stool. "I'll take my break, then. The door will be locked and the Closed sign posted until two-thirty. You want me to knock when I return?"

"Thank you."

"I am Umberto Niro," he told Lina, then gestured toward the rear of the shop. "Please follow me. Ms. Rossi is expecting you."

CHAPTER 10

THE WOMAN DIDN'T RISE from her seat when Lina entered the room. Instead, she lifted her chin to meet the gaze of the man who'd called himself Umberto.

"I'll return with your tea in a moment, Your Highness. My team has the alley." He shifted his focus to Lina. "Would you care for a latte? Skim milk and one sugar?"

"Thank you." How he'd known her usual order…no, she didn't want to know.

Once the door closed behind Lina, Queen Fabrizia finally rose. She stood in a single motion, as if on strings, without touching the long table in front of her. Despite her small stature, she held herself with a dignity that ensured she'd command any room.

"It's a pleasure to meet you, Lina."

Lina knew she should respond in kind, but the pleasure was all the queen's. "I'm surprised you're in New York." She refused to add "Your Highness" to the end of the statement. "When did you arrive?"

"This morning." The edges of her lips rose a fraction. Queen Fabrizia was a striking woman. In her sixties, lean and fit with soft blond hair, she possessed delicate features that made her appear at least a decade younger. Lina was startled by the queen's bright green eyes as she approached and extended her hand in greeting. She was known for them—magazines loved to highlight Fabrizia's brilliant gaze on their covers—but it hadn't occurred to Lina that the beauty of those green eyes would be dwarfed by the intelligence hidden in their depths.

That canny intelligence made Lina remember how dangerous Fabrizia could be. How her mother once described the queen as a shrewd survivalist camouflaged by designer labels.

Lina accepted the queen's handshake and was surprised when Fabrizia put her other hand over the top, holding Lina in place. "When I learned you were in New York for the week, it struck me as the perfect opportunity for a private meeting. I'd never be able to arrange time like this in Europe."

The queen's surprise visit to Rocco's villa proved otherwise, but Lina refrained from mentioning it.

The queen gestured toward the end of the table where she'd been seated. "Come. Sit beside me. We have a great deal to discuss."

"I'm not sure we do." The words were out before Lina could stop them.

"Yet here you are." She resumed her seat, then waited for Lina to join her. "You needn't fear me. I've no wish to take advantage. This is no publicity stunt, nor does Carlo need a kidney. I contacted you because I believe that forging a relationship could be mutually rewarding."

The queen looked toward the door as the knob turned and Umberto entered with a tray. He set it at the end of the table nearest the door, then carried a teacup to the queen and placed a large, steaming latte in front of Lina. He returned to the tray for a plate of cookies and the teapot, then poured for the queen. He finished by asking Fabrizia if she required anything else, dipping his head, then departing.

"He's a fair butler." A note of amusement brightened her tone. "However, he's my head of security and far more capable in that position. We won't be disturbed. Now...where were we?"

"Carlo doesn't need a kidney."

"No, thank goodness, though he was diagnosed with a thickening of the arteries several years ago and must take care. Information I trust you'll keep to yourself, but that's important for you to know as the condition may be genetic." The queen selected a cookie from the plate, then took a bite. "I missed lunch and plan to indulge. If you want one, take it now."

"Perhaps in a moment." Watching the queen eat a cookie with obvious delight felt surreal, as if Lina had walked onto a movie set. This one was complete with a guard at the door and—apparently—an entire security team in the alley.

"I've unsettled you."

"I imagine you have that effect on a lot of people."

"I find it useful most of the time. In this case, however, I want you to be comfortable" —she waved a hand— "which is why I chose this shop. I see why you frequent it when you're in town. Becky is lovely. Says she's from Oklahoma originally. Did you know she's attending graduate school at NYU when she's not working as a barista?"

Lina flexed her hands under the table. "If you want me to be comfortable, here's a tip: don't offer me a cookie immediately after telling me I might have a heart condition. And stop telling me how much you know about me. No one should know as much information as you do. Not my schedule, not where I'm staying, and certainly not my favorite café or drink order in a town where I don't even live."

Instead of responding, the queen finished her cookie, then raised her teacup. After breathing in its aroma, she took a cautious sip. Lina suspected the woman was leaving her to squirm on purpose. Finally, Fabrizia said, "That knowledge is all superficial. I don't know *you*. I assume you know a great deal of superficial information about me, as well. Some may be correct, some may not."

She itched to retort that she didn't care to know any information. Correct, incorrect, she didn't care. She didn't want this woman in her life.

She could kick herself for answering the queen's summons.

"You weren't going to come," the queen said, as if Lina had spoken the thought aloud. "What changed your mind?"

"What makes you say that?"

"You were late. I don't imagine a woman in your position is late to meetings, certainly not when it's only a two-minute walk from your flat." Her tone was pleasant, but the rim of the cup didn't hide her all-knowing expression.

"I decided it was in the best interest of my mental health to let you say your piece." Steam drifted from the surface of her latte, so Lina took a treat from the plate to give her drink another moment to cool. "This place also has good coffee and cookies."

"Your mother was not my biggest fan. The two of you were close, so I can only assume she shared her opinion with you. Nevertheless, I hope you can put that opinion aside and listen to what I have to say."

"I'm here, aren't I?"

The queen remained silent, tempting Lina to fill the void. She resisted.

At last, the queen shrugged. "I despised your mother for many years. She preyed on my husband before I knew him, when he was young and vulnerable to such machinations. To his credit, Carlo does not place all the blame on your mother. He likes to believe that, at seventeen, he had the judgment to understand his choices. The fact those choices included fornication with—"

"If you wish to denigrate my mother, you've chosen the wrong audience."

The queen's lips thinned. "My point is that Carlo does not entirely blame Teresa for what happened between them. It took me many years to embrace my husband's point of view on those events. It was, to use your phrase, in the best interest of my mental health to do so. He loves you, you know. And as I love him, I cannot help but support him."

"He doesn't know me. He's never met me. That's not love."

"If you knew Carlo" —her green eyes darkened, as if she fought back an emotion she'd confronted many times before— "you'd know that he is incapable of having a child without also having a deep, abiding love for that child. However, that love has come at a high price. For you, for Rocco, and for Enzo...year after year, he has sustained deep wounds to his heart, first in private and now in public, and he has done it without complaint. He did it because it was best for you. Not because it was best for him."

"By keeping my mother's secret."

"Yes." The queen set her teacup on its saucer without so much as a clink. "I knew about Rocco when I married Carlo. What I didn't realize was the extent to which your mother would use Rocco to keep control over him. When Teresa informed Carlo that she was pregnant with you and Enzo, she threatened to leave the country with you if he didn't divorce me. He confessed everything to me that same evening. He was certain it would cost him our marriage, but felt it was the moral thing to do."

The queen raised her hand in a silent request to finish her tale uninterrupted. "He finally recognized your mother for what she was. He didn't love her and had no intention of marrying her, even if I left him. Even knowing she'd carry through on her threat. It was the most difficult decision of his life, but he made that decision believing it would be best for *you*. He was certain she'd never expose his secret. To do so would risk public censure and perhaps even jail time…which would mean risking her ability to care for the three of you. He also knew she'd raise you well—give you a good education, a good home, and love—which she did. Her vengeance was aimed solely at him, and she hit him directly in the heart."

Fabrizia let out a long breath and stood, gesturing to indicate Lina should remain seated. Not that Lina was going to follow protocol and stand when the queen stood.

"I wanted to see you today not to dredge up the past, but to look toward the future. Your mother's passing must not have been easy for you. No child who loves her mother says goodbye easily. You had to endure fallout for actions that were not your responsibility, which is regrettable. However, I believe this could be a new beginning, both for you and for Carlo."

"You want me to get to know him." Lina raised her latte to her lips and took a long sip, hoping she projected calm rather than the uneasiness she felt at the idea.

"I do." A note of regret tinged the queen's features before she said, "You and I share no bonds of blood and I know I have no right to ask. However—right or wrong—since you were born, part of me has considered you my responsibility. I love Carlo dearly. Each of his children, therefore, has a place in my heart. In my orbit of care. I'd be happy to arrange a meeting. I can ensure it's kept private."

Lina set her latte on the table and smiled at the queen. "I understand the inclination" —though she didn't— "and I appreciate that you've gone to the effort to meet me, but I must decline."

"May I ask why?"

The question was one of Lina's pet peeves. It always made her want to respond, *you just did*. Instead, she said, "I don't care to debate my reasons with you."

"I'd still like to hear them."

As Ivo said, the queen wasn't the type who accepted no for an answer.

She raised her thumb. "First, I have a business to run. I don't have the time to go to Sarcaccia." Her index finger followed. "Second, as much as it has hurt to lose both my mother and father—and by my father, I mean Jack Cornaro—I don't need anyone to step into their shoes. I'm quite happy with my life."

The queen nodded before standing to pace the length of the table. She glided a well-manicured finger over the tea tray Umberto had left behind. "You should be proud of what you've accomplished. Isola may be small and fairly new to the market, but your products are high quality. You have an excellent reputation. Personally speaking, I appreciate that you are socially conscious in your sourcing of materials and manufacturing practices. I've fought for many years to decrease the worldwide child labor rate. It's been a cornerstone of my social programs, and it's not always easy."

An image of Ivo working the streets of Rome flashed through her mind. She exhaled it away. "Thank you."

"You have a backbone and a strong sense of self." The queen raised her gaze to Lina's. "I like that about you. It's clear you don't need a father to be happy. Nor does Carlo need to have you in his life as a daughter. He's found his way to happiness, as we all do." A small smile lifted her mouth. "What's fortunate for us, as human beings, is that we can always accept more love. More friends, more connections. Once you become famous—whether for your work, your marriage, or as an accident of your birth—it's hard to know when and whom to trust. There are those who will approach you, offering friendship and love, but who don't have your best interests at heart. Carlo and I will always have your best interests at heart. Carlo, particularly."

Fabrizia returned to her chair and retrieved a small pink handbag she'd left tucked to the side. Even without handling the piece, Lina could tell the leather and stitching were exquisite. Fabrizia could afford any handbag on the planet, of course, but Lina appreciated the queen's taste in this one.

"Much as I'd love to put you on a plane to Sarcaccia and force you to meet Carlo, I won't." The queen placed a crisp white business card beside Lina's latte. "This is my private line. You may call any time, day or night. No one else will answer. If you change your mind, the invitation stands."

She pocketed the card without looking at it. "Again, I appreciate the effort, but don't expect a call."

Two short knocks sounded at the door, then two more.

"That's Umberto, letting me know that it's two-thirty and that Becky has returned to the counter. We should allow her to reopen so the shop makes money, don't you think?"

Lina stood, then took a swig of her cooling latte before eyeing the queen. "Before you leave, I would like to ask one favor. Stop following me or doing whatever it is you do to keep track of me. I value my privacy and I don't like the feeling of being watched."

"It's for your safety."

"Knowing my latte order translates to my safety…how, exactly?"

The queen smiled at that. "I'll ask my security team to step back."

"Not step back, step away. Entirely."

Fabrizia didn't bother to hide her consternation. "Step away, then. But should you change your mind—"

"I won't."

There were two more knocks, then Umberto opened the door. "Your Highness?"

Fabrizia exuded her usual control as she looked toward her security chief. "Everything is ready?"

"The jet's refueled and cleared for takeoff. We can be on board in twenty minutes. We should arrive in Sarcaccia three hours ahead of your husband's flight from Dubai." Umberto eyed the table. "I'll ask Becky to clear the room."

"Thank her for its use." The queen turned to Lina as Umberto went to speak to the barista. "It was a pleasure meeting you. I do hope we'll speak again soon."

Unable to respond in kind, Lina merely nodded. As Fabrizia walked toward the door, Lina couldn't help but ask, "What brought you all the way to New York for such a short visit? You never said."

"What motivates humans to do anything?" The queen paused with her hand on the doorknob. Without looking back, she answered her own question, "Love, *farfallina mia*. Always love."

BALLOONS IN BLACK, silver, and Mediterranean blue emblazoned with the Isola logo floated over the lingerie section of Mirabeau's White Plains location. Two hours earlier, before the store opened, the manager gave Lina a quick tour, making sure to point out the signs at both the first and second floor mall entrances advertising the launch. Members of the sales staff greeted her with exuberance, gushing over the new lingerie and the displays. Their enthusiasm carried into the first hour of the event as customers detoured from other parts of the store to take a look.

Pride surged through Lina as she moved behind the display to return a bra to the rack. She'd already personally fitted four women for new bras. Each left with new lingerie and smiles on their faces. Better yet, each of the women had tried on multiple brands and selected the Isola bras as their favorite without Lina having to nudge.

"Excuse me, are you Lina Cornaro?"

Lina raised her head and smiled in greeting, though the fact the woman called her by name put Lina on guard. "Yes, I am. May I help you?"

"I was hoping to talk to you for a minute."

Lina forced herself to keep her smile in place. "Of course. I'm happy to answer any questions you have about Isola."

"Oh, I don't have any questions, I just…I wanted to tell you how much I love what you do." The woman was dressed for a professional office in a lightweight black blazer, ivory blouse, gray and black houndstooth skirt, and polished black heels. She tucked a strand of gray-streaked black hair behind her ear before gesturing to her ample bosom. "I'm wearing one of your bras. I was on vacation last year in Milan and went shopping in the boutiques. My husband wanted to treat me to some lingerie—something racy, you know?—and I tried to explain that racy and supportive don't mix, and that I can't wear bras that don't hold the girls in line. We stopped in your shop—over my objection, because I saw those bras on the mannequins and thought *no way*—and the woman running the store talked me into buying two bra and panty sets. One in nude, one in black lace. Let me tell you, they're now my favorites. I'm wearing the nude one under this blouse and it's so comfortable. And totally invisible!"

Relief washed through Lina. For a moment, she'd feared she'd been cornered by a reporter. "I never expected to meet someone in White Plains who'd visited the Milan boutique. I'm glad to hear my staff was helpful and that you're enjoying your purchase."

"That's why I'm here." The woman's face lit with happiness. "My name's Dottie, by the way. I'm playing hooky from work this morning so I can restock my lingerie drawer. I live here and commute to Midtown. When I saw you were doing events both here and in Manhattan…well, I wanted to be certain I had the earliest pick of the merchandise. I suspect certain sizes will go fast once word gets out."

"We do our best to keep all sizes in stock, but if yours is ever unavailable, let the sales associate know and it can be ordered free of charge." Lina reached into the slim pocket on the front of her skirt and withdrew a card. "If you show this at the register, the clerk will know it's from me. It will grant half off your highest-priced purchase today.

Isola generally doesn't discount, but this is my way of saying thank you for visiting the Milan shop and making a special trip here. It was a pleasure to meet you, Dottie."

The woman thanked Lina profusely, then excused herself to peruse the selection of bras on a nearby table. Lina noticed the store manager standing nearby and approached him once Dottie took her selections to the fitting room.

"Sales are robust," the manager said. "The staff reports the fastest morning start we've had in the section in at least two years."

"Your team is doing a wonderful job." If brisk sales continued, Mirabeau was sure to extend the contract.

"A great product makes our job easier," he replied. After looping through the section once more, he departed in the direction of his office. Buoyed by the positive feedback, Lina completed two more fittings before finding herself face-to-face with her first male customer, a man in his early- to mid-twenties. He sported khaki shorts and an untucked, short-sleeved button-down shirt in narrow purple and white stripes. A lightning bolt tattoo on his left bicep appeared freshly inked and his cropped facial hair seemed deliberate, rather than scruffy. Stylish glasses completed his look. Though men often seemed uncomfortable when shopping for lingerie, he looked perfectly at ease.

"May I help you?" she asked as he approached.

He responded with a broad smile. "I hope so. I'm from *DayBuzz*. I'm here to cover your event. Are you familiar with our site?"

"I'm afraid not, though I live out of the country, so I hope you'll forgive my ignorance." There were more fashion websites and blogs in recent years than she could follow. "I'll certainly check it out after today's event. What can I do for you?"

A customer approached on Lina's left, though she kept her focus on the man in front of her. Hopefully one of the sales associates could help while she was occupied.

"I have a few questions." He made a swooping gesture, encompassing the department. "Your company's American launch comes only a few months after your mother's history with King Carlo came to light in the European press. Do you think your notoriety overseas helped you get your foot in the door here in the States?"

"My—"

"Your notoriety." Swagger laced his words. "You know, the scandal attached to your name. Was that the key to launching your lingerie line with Mirabeau?"

CHAPTER 11

THE QUESTION KNOCKED HER BACK, but she refused to give the man the satisfaction of seeing it. She gestured toward the main display, where several customers spoke with members of Mirabeau's sales team. "The launch comes after several months of discussions between Isola and Mirabeau. Both companies prioritize quality, and we each spend a great deal of time and effort to getting to know our customers in order to provide them with the best possible products and service. Our two brands are a great fit for each other."

The customer on Lina's left stepped closer, even as the man frowned. "Don't customers question your honesty?"

Lina felt her smile grow tight. "I have a brilliant staff at Isola, from those who work in our Italian factory right through to the sales team. Our lingerie is crafted with fabrics sourced from producers where everyone receives fair pay, yet we offer tremendous value for the price. I think you'll find our customers agree."

She hated that her words sounded straight from a company script, but she would not give this man a quote he could twist. Nor would she deal with him any longer. "Now, if you'll—"

"One more—"

"You never gave me your name." Only questioned her honesty.

He jerked as if she'd slapped him. "I'm with *DayBuzz*."

"And I'm Lina Cornaro, founder and chief designer for Isola. I work with the mantra that while the high road might be the tougher one to travel, the view is superior. The hardworking people I employ share that philosophy." She paused a moment, letting her words sink in. "You do have a name, along with your position, do you not?"

"Adam. Adam Green."

"Adam, thank you. As I was about to say: if you'll excuse me, I have customers waiting. I'd be happy to speak with you after the event if you have questions that relate to Isola. I'm extremely proud of the company and the lingerie we create."

She graced him with a smile he didn't deserve, then turned toward the woman on her left. She realized her mistake a split second before the woman said, "Your mother raped a teenage boy. It never would've come to light if her victim hadn't become a monarch. What do you have to say for yourself?"

Lina felt her lower lip twitch at the word *raped*. Her mother's relationship with Carlo was wrong, but that was *not* what happened.

Then she realized the woman had filmed the entire *DayBuzz* exchange on her phone…and was continuing to film. She'd used the inflammatory language specifically to bait Lina.

Lina's muscles tensed as she fought to stop her reaction from becoming visible to those around her. No matter what, she had to appear professional, as if these people and this topic weren't making her cringe inside. She kept her voice low and directed so only the woman and Adam Green, whom she now realized were working together, could hear. "Your questions have nothing to do with me, with Isola, or with Mirabeau. They are completely inappropriate. If you'll leave me a card, I'd be happy to have my assistant send you all the information you could possibly want in order to write a piece about Isola."

"No one believes *you* raped a teenager, obviously." The woman's voice carried through the small lingerie section. "But you have to admit that your mother's predatory actions will have an effect on your sales. Especially when you're selling lingerie, an item long associated with sexuality. Don't your customers question your ethics?"

Now the woman was conflating lingerie and rape, which burned Lina to the core. Miraculously, she maintained her composure. In a low, level voice, she replied, "They do not. However, I question yours. First, your questions are out of line and based on inaccuracies. Second, professional journalists would introduce themselves and ask for an interview. Or schedule one—"

"This is an unusual circumstance, don't you think?"

The store manager appeared behind the woman. Lina wasn't sure whether to be relieved he'd arrived to assist or horrified that he'd heard the exchange. While she had nothing to hide—she certainly hadn't done anything wrong—it was the last thing she needed on launch day, which should be a celebratory affair.

"What's the issue here?"

Both Adam Green and the unnamed woman spun toward the manager. The woman smiled as if she'd won a million dollar prize. "We're from *DayBuzz*. Are you aware of Lina Cornaro's background? I'm sure you've heard about her mother, Teresa Cornaro, the tutor who seduced Sarcaccia's King Carlo when he was a teenager. Do you have anything to say about Mirabeau's relationship with Lina Cornaro and her lingerie brand? Any comments on her ethics?"

The manager's gaze went past the woman to gauge the reaction of the shoppers, all of whom had gone silent. Even the sales staff appeared stunned. If they'd known her background, they hadn't thought of it in salacious terms. Not until this moment.

Lina wanted to be ill.

The manager visibly gathered himself, straightening his spine and glaring at the two pseudo-reporters. "Mirabeau takes pride in our ethical practices, practices our customers not only value, but expect. We apply that same standard to all the companies with whom we do business. If you'll accompany me to the administrative offices, I'd be happy to provide you with the contact information for our head of public relations. She'll be able to address all your questions."

Lina could tell the woman wanted to argue, but the appearance of two security guards stopped her. She glanced at them, then looked to the manager. "Of course."

One of the sales team members jumped to fill the awkward silence, asking a patron, "Would you like me to put your selections in the dressing room while you continue shopping?"

"Ah…sure."

Lina watched as the manager escorted Adam Green and his accomplice toward his office, then turned to straighten one of the displays as the hum of conversation resumed. She tried to picture how many people were in the department when Adam approached her and determine what, exactly, they'd heard. While Lina knew she hadn't said anything to cast Isola in a negative light, the reporters' inflammatory questions might be enough to make shoppers think twice before making a purchase.

Then there was the Internet. Where would that woman post her video? And how might she edit it?

Once Lina finished arranging the display, she skirted the lingerie department to survey the foot traffic while keeping a low profile. There were plenty of shoppers, but the festive mood had dampened.

"May I have a moment?"

She turned to see the manager, who'd returned from his office. Forcing herself not to grimace, she kept her voice quiet and said, "I apologize for that. I hope I handled it appropriately."

"They were aggressive and completely out of line." He took a long look around the section, noting the quieter atmosphere. "I'm not sure how it'll affect the event, but I do need to report it when I meet with the other store managers to evaluate the launch."

"Of course." She felt she needed to say more, to explain that her mother had nothing to do with Isola, but the manager knew as well as Lina did that perception was everything. Right or wrong, if Mirabeau shoppers questioned a product—or the people behind it—they'd make a different choice.

She opted for a pleasant tone, rather than a defensive one. "Thank you for directing them to the public relations department. I don't expect another incident like that, but if anyone else has questions, I'll give them the same information."

He thanked her, but she noticed that he lingered in the nearby dress department to keep an eye on the event.

She answered a customer question about sizing and another on laundering, then saw Dottie walking into the section.

"Hello, Dottie. You're back!"

"Hello, Ms. Cornaro."

Lina paused. Dottie seemed different. More formal, perhaps even upset. Lina shot a pointed look at the Mirabeau bag in Dottie's hand and smiled. "I hope this means you found a few items that work for you?"

"I did. Or so I thought."

Lina knew what was coming before Dottie spoke. "I didn't realize that you're related to that Teresa Cornaro, let alone that you are her daughter. What she did is despicable. As much as I like Isola, I can't in good conscience wear it. I can't support someone who covered up…well, let's just say I'm returning my purchase and I wanted you to know why."

"If you've read the news accounts, then surely you're aware that I knew nothing of my mother's actions until after her death, and only days before the news became public. However, if you feel you must—"

"I do."

Lina fought to keep her voice steady. Somehow, this was harder than dealing with the *DayBuzz* people. "I'm sorry to hear about your decision, but I appreciate your honesty."

Dottie hesitated. For a moment, Lina thought she'd change her mind. Then the Dottie spun on her heel, marched to the register, and informed the sales associate of her desire to return the hundreds of dollars' worth of Isola she'd purchased that morning…and why.

Ivo skirted a woman pushing a baby carriage as he exited the tree-lined pathway he'd taken through Central Park. He jogged in place and adjusted the volume of his headphones as he waited for the crosswalk light. When the signal turned, he ran ahead of other pedestrians, heading south.

Despite a solid half-hour run through the park's most peaceful sections, his mind hadn't quieted. What he'd witnessed this morning in White Plains left him agitated.

He'd awakened early and met with both a physical therapist and massage therapist, then enjoyed a late breakfast at a diner near his hotel. He was en route to an appointment to discuss a potential advertising opportunity when a water line break in the building forced a last-minute postponement, leaving him idle.

He'd started to text Lina to let her know his plans fell through, then realized the launch event was about to start. She wouldn't see his message.

He'd taken the train to White Plains, then a taxi to the massive mall where Mirabeau served as an anchor store, arriving about an hour after opening. Keeping his head down so he wouldn't draw attention, he'd browsed the merchandise at one end of the men's department, where he had a partial view of the lingerie section on the other side of the escalator. Business appeared brisk, and no wonder: the store had gone all-out to advertise the event, with posters throughout the mall and signage at each store entrance. For nearly thirty minutes, he rarely caught sight of Lina. She'd appear near one of the balloon-adorned displays, chat with a customer, then disappear in the direction of the dressing room.

Happy to know the launch was going as Lina had hoped, Ivo left to walk a lap around the mall and stretch his legs. He returned to Mirabeau for a last look before his scheduled train back to Manhattan. As he approached the men's department, he noticed a man and woman observing the lingerie section from where he'd stood to watch Lina previously. Ivo hung back, keeping an eye on the pair. They soon split up, entering the lingerie section separately. The man spoke to Lina while the woman stood off to the side, recording the exchange on her phone.

Ivo moved closer. Before he could hear their words, his gut told him the pair didn't have Lina's best interests in mind. They were too sneaky, too self-assured. Nor had they approached any of the Mirabeau sales associates or the store manager when the opportunity presented itself. Instead they'd waited, then put themselves directly in Lina's path.

Once he heard the man's questions, Ivo had to force himself to stay out of Lina's line of sight. And to keep his fists firmly at his side.

The woman's questions were far worse. Twisted. Calculated. Based on false premises in order to provoke an angry reaction.

Lina handled the pair as well as could be hoped, but they were determined to grab the attention of the shoppers around them, raising their voices when Lina refused to be baited. If the manager hadn't appeared when he had, Ivo wasn't sure whether he'd have been able to stop himself from interrupting.

Spotting a relatively empty side street, Ivo turned a corner to cut toward Eighth Avenue. With the dinner hour waning, those who worked late had started to clear Midtown, but summer tourists clogged the Theater District and Times Square and he didn't want to dodge pedestrians. Given that his joints and muscles felt good, he figured he could go a little while longer and circle back to the hotel.

On a long inhale, he sprinted into the street to avoid running under scaffolding, then rejoined the sidewalk at the next intersection. He passed a group of women carrying shopping bags, one of which sported the pink logo of a famous lingerie shop. He shook out his hands, attempting to put his mind on his run, but found it impossible. He hadn't missed Lina's expression in the seconds before she'd turned to straighten a display and gather herself. When a new customer approached she'd been her usual professional self, but in that brief glimpse he'd seen the depths of Lina's heartbreak.

He wanted to fix it.

He reached another cross street and waited for a break in traffic to race across, ignoring the light. He jumped the curb, then picked up his pace as he chewed up block after block, heading away from the noise of Midtown.

Every instinct made him want to protect Lina, but he couldn't. Not without her express request. Isola was hers. She held herself responsible for its success and the path she chose to achieve that success was as much a part of her dream as the lingerie itself. Much as he knew his experience with the press would help, much as he knew a well-placed word or carefully timed distraction could turn a combative reporter into a docile one, he couldn't do it. Lina would have to come to him.

Except…

Damn. Good-natured shouting to his right made him realize where he was. He'd run all the way from Central Park to Greenwich Village. All the way to Lina's. Her mother's condo was only a few blocks from where he now stood, panting alongside the fence that surrounded a neighborhood playground and basketball court.

He turned his back to the fence and leaned into it, his weight causing the chain link to sag as he yanked the headphones from his ears and shut off his music. His lungs ached and his heartbeat thundered in his ears as he braced his palms on his thighs.

At least his back didn't hurt. In fact, it felt great.

"Hey, brother, you good?"

He raised a hand to the basketball player on the other side who'd stopped to check on him. "Hard workout. I'm fine. Thanks."

The man gave him a quick once-over and returned Ivo's wave before rejoining the game.

Ivo consciously slowed his breathing, then used the hem of his shirt to wipe his face as exhaustion hit him with the force of taking a car full-tilt through the Eau Rouge corner at Spa. He knew better than to run so far, so fast, before he was at one hundred percent, but he'd allowed himself to get distracted. No doubt he'd pay the price tomorrow. So long as it didn't delay his overall recovery, he'd consider it a lesson learned.

He glanced down at the sidewalk and mentally prepared to push off the fence for the long walk to the hotel. The seams between sidewalk sections wavered. He blinked to clear his vision, but darkness crept in at the periphery and he started to pitch sideways. Only grasping the chain link prevented him from falling.

Vertigo. He hadn't experienced it since the first week he'd left the hospital. Even then, it only occurred when he stood too quickly. Now he knew he'd overdone it.

He straightened, keeping one hand on the fence for balance, and focused on the sidewalk seams until his equilibrium returned and the lines remained still.

Once he was certain he wouldn't topple, he crossed the street to a convenience store, purchased a bottle of cold water, and took several refreshing sips before turning north, in the direction of his hotel. He slipped his headphones over his ears and put on meditative music to remind himself to keep to a slow pace so the dizziness would stay at bay. As he punched phone buttons, a text from Lina appeared on the screen.

White Plains done, back at the condo. Good sales numbers. You at your hotel? Day go well?

Not that he could judge Lina's tone from a text, but the note about sales numbers reassured him, as did the fact she'd contacted him so quickly after returning home.

Just finished a run. Walking from the Village toward the hotel to cool down.

Almost as soon as he hit send, the reply appeared: *You're in the Village now?*

When he answered in the affirmative, she typed back: *Maybe you need a bath to relax those muscles. Someone I trust gave me that advice recently. I happen to have a large claw-foot tub.*

He moved out of the flow of pedestrians to answer: *There in ten.*

It'd be easier to make the trek to the hotel after he took some time to cool off, he reasoned. If he wasn't steady after a shower, he could always call a cab.

She was waiting at the window and buzzed him into the stairwell before he could ring. As he rounded the second floor landing, the stair treads began to wobble. He slowed and held the railing for a moment to shake off the sensation before continuing his ascent.

Lina opened the door as he reached the top of the staircase. When she'd texted, he'd hoped she'd join him in the bath, but to his surprise, exhaustion and the itch of drying sweat made him grateful to see her fully dressed.

The smile he offered felt weak. "I reek and have nothing to change into. You may regret this."

"Enzo left clothes last time he visited. Second drawer. You're welcome to borrow what you need."

"Enzo's considerably taller than I am."

She guided him inside and closed the door, then gave him a welcoming kiss, ignoring the sweat and the smell. "I think you can manage. I assume you haven't had dinner?"

"Not yet."

"Let me handle it while you relax."

For once, he wouldn't argue or offer to pitch in. Food would be as helpful to his recovery as water and a washcloth.

He burned to ask about White Plains, but gave her a grateful smile and headed for the bath rather than let on that he'd taken the train to the event. When he emerged, having scrubbed his body and stretched his muscles, the tantalizing scent of jasmine rice and curry greeted him. Lina had changed from the knee-length skirt and blouse she'd worn to the Mirabeau event into a summery, navy blue skirt and light blue T-shirt. She stood on her tiptoes in the kitchen, her back to Ivo as she reached into the cabinet for plates.

"Find something of Enzo's?" she asked.

"I did."

She turned to set the plates in front of each barstool so they could eat at the counter. Ivo spread his arms so Lina could see the shorts and T-shirt he'd located. They weren't in a size he'd have chosen, but they were clean and the fit wasn't so poor as to draw attention.

Lina put her hands on her hips and gave him an open assessment. Flirtation laced her words. "Looks better on you than on him."

"Hope you don't look at him that way."

"Never." She gestured toward the drawer that held the napkins, urging him to lend a hand as she located the appropriate flatware. "I assume you haven't lost your love of chicken with green curry and vegetables. I ordered from a place Mrs. Metzger recommended. You can tell me what you think of their version."

Warmth spread through him. This—*this*—was what he'd craved in the days since he was hospitalized. Lina knew his likes and dislikes better than anyone. She knew exactly how to make him comfortable and ease his cares so he could give his entire focus to his job when he was away from her.

Better still, she did it despite the fact his career presented risks that frightened her.

Lina set flatware beside the plates. When he added the napkins, she brushed against him. "Next time, I'll cook instead of ordering. I found a recipe for chicken with hot pepper sauce that I think will be healthier than the restaurant version. It looked spectacular."

Ivo surveyed the counter to see what else was needed. Lina had filled a large glass with ice water for him, knowing he craved hydration in the hour or two after a workout. An unopened bottle of wine and a corkscrew sat nearby, just in case. She'd thought of everything.

"Assuming you have plans to be in Milan," she added. "For the next few months I'm sure you'll be occupied with training, meeting the Ferrari personnel, doing whatever you need to do to get behind the wheel again. It'll be a busy time."

She turned away to reach into a bag emblazoned with the logo of a Thai restaurant. It took him a moment to realize she didn't feel as carefree as she appeared. He walked behind her and wrapped his arms around her shoulders. Slowly, she set down the containers of food, then relaxed into him.

"You're not hungry?" Her voice was thready.

"Very hungry."

He pressed a kiss to the juncture where her neck and shoulder met, then whispered, "You're wondering whether I want this to continue after we leave New York. If we're back to the way things were before the accident."

Her hands came up to his forearms. "Not because I'm needy. You have to prioritize work. You should. You've been off a long time and it's a big part of who you are—"

"And Isola is a big part of who you are."

He spun her to face him. As always, he was struck by her beauty. He could stare into her honey eyes or kiss the smooth skin along her cheekbones for hours. Play with the loose strands of her dark blond hair. Breathe in the welcoming scent of her and savor the way she made him feel as if he were invincible. Familiarity didn't lessen his fascination. Nor did it take the edge off his desire.

He followed the line of her shoulders with his thumbs. "Our relationship works because we respect each other's goals, but after what happened in San Rimini, and after our talk in my hotel room, I don't think we can go back to the way things were."

Her lips tightened fractionally.

He waited a beat. "If I have anything to say about it, it will be better. Far, far better."

CHAPTER 12

Ivo THRILLED to the relief that flooded Lina's eyes in the brief moment before he brushed his lips across hers. No matter where they were—New York, Milan, or a hideaway hotel on the F1 circuit—she would be his center. His calm in the eye of the storm.

And he would be hers.

"I don't want to be a distraction." Unlike the emotion in her gaze, her voice remained matter-of-fact.

"I committed to chicken with hot pepper sauce, not a shared mailbox and six kids," he said, unable to keep from running his hands along her shoulders as he spoke. "But I've missed you. If I'm distracted, it's because I choose to be. There's a time to work and a time to recharge. I might not have as much recharging time as someone with a normal job, but what I do have, I want to spend with you. As long as you're interested in the same deal. When you're away from Isola, I want you to be with me. I want to be your respite. As long as we communicate, as long as we're honest with each other, we can figure out the rest."

Tentatively, her hands went to his waist. She studied him for several heartbeats before her fingers curled into the hem of his T-shirt. "I couldn't imagine anything better."

Her touch told him as much as her words. He drew her closer and sealed their promise with a kiss that began softly, then turned heated and passionate. When she rose onto her toes, he tightened his embrace and lifted her, sliding his tongue across her bottom lip. As she sighed in pleasure and shifted one leg to wrap around his, a wave of need surged through him.

It wasn't love. Not yet.

Perhaps never, his mind warned. If his accident taught him anything, it was that life couldn't be planned. But this was more than a fling, more than the series of hastily arranged nights they'd strung together over the past two years. Whatever road they traveled, for now they traveled it together.

He took her mouth once more, the kiss deep and greedy. Her urgency matched his as she opened to him and slipped her hands under his shirt. Her fingers dragged along his back, a promise of things to come when he had her naked and sprawled across the bed.

"Dear God, Lina."

At the exact same moment, she groaned, "You're killing me, Ivo."

His mouth went to her throat and he luxuriated in the taste of her skin for a drawn-out moment before moving lower to find his favorite spot, the delectable divot above her collarbone. When her hands dug into his skin, his control threatened to unfurl. Still, he couldn't let go. Not until she shivered in his arms and her bare leg rubbed against his, warning him that they were nearing the point where they'd have to stop…or not stop.

He gave her a lingering kiss, then touched his forehead to hers to recover. Smoothing a hand over her hair, he twisted a section around his finger before allowing it to fall. "Let's continue this after dinner. I want to hear about White Plains. And I want that green curry."

Her gaze hung on his lips. "More than you want me?"

"Never." He allowed himself one more kiss before tracing her lips with the pad of his thumb. "I'm saving my dessert for last."

After they filled their plates and settled in to eat, he moved his barstool close to hers, so they sat shoulder to shoulder. Much as he wanted to ditch the food and make love to her, he needed Lina to know he meant what he said about being her respite. That meant time and attention outside the bedroom as well as in it.

He glanced sideways as he placed his napkin on his lap. "So… White Plains?"

Telltale lines of tension formed at the sides of her mouth. "It started out well. The advertising was all in place, the merchandise was displayed exactly as I'd hoped, and the staff was brilliant. Lots of foot traffic, lots of sales in the first hour. Then I had a run-in with two people who called themselves reporters. That didn't go so well."

Wanting to hear Lina's take before giving his own opinion, he asked, "What happened?"

"They were working together, though I didn't realize it at first. Asked me leading questions about my mother and whether my customers had issues with my ethics. I handled the situation as well as I could have." She took a long drink of water, then shrugged. "I've played it over and over in my head, and I didn't give them any quotes they could use against me. Not easily. Even so, the entire encounter made me feel awful. They were loud and drew the attention of some of the customers before the manager escorted them out. And their questions were based on false premises. Salacious premises."

"Glad the manager was on top of it."

"Me, too, but I suspect it dampened his enthusiasm for Isola. It's human nature. Not long after the reporters left, a customer who'd been in earlier returned her purchases. Said she couldn't support the brand, given that I covered for my mother."

Ivo's heart sank for her. He'd missed that. "You didn't cover anything. You weren't responsible in any way."

"You know that and I know that, but…human nature. When people are horrified by what they see happening in the world, they want to place blame. Particularly when they see bad things happening to children and teens. My mother's not here to blame and I'm a convenient target." Lina took another bite of her dinner, then raised her water glass. "On the bright side, sales picked up again after the reporters left. I was scheduled to leave at four but stayed until five, just to help the staff with fittings. If Mirabeau looks at the numbers rather than the disruption, Isola looks like a win for their stores. I'm trying to focus on that."

His admiration for Lina kicked up another notch. "Did the reporters identify themselves or where they worked?"

"I didn't get the woman's name, but when I pressed him, the man introduced himself as Adam Green of *DayBuzz*. I've never heard of it. Haven't had time to look it up yet. Haven't wanted to." She rolled her eyes at her own procrastination. "I'll do it after dinner. I need to know what I'm facing."

They talked about his visit with the physical therapist, then he offered to wash the dishes while she discovered what she could about *DayBuzz*. While he scrubbed, he occasionally glanced at Lina, who'd settled into one of the living room chairs with her laptop computer. Whatever she read didn't appear to bother her.

Finally, he wiped off the counter and took the seat across from hers. "Find anything?"

"*DayBuzz Westchester*. Local news and views, according to the website. Only four people on the staff, including one Adam Green. The only woman is Maisie Linkwell. There isn't a photo of her, but in a section on hobbies, Maisie describes herself as a royal-watcher, which makes me certain that's who was at the store today. The articles on the home page are about local celebrities and events. Fundraisers at country clubs, art auctions, that type of thing. Looks like it's web only. And…oh, wow. They've only been in existence for three months."

"Westchester's…a town?"

"It's the county that includes White Plains." She clicked a few more times, searching the site as she spoke. "Westchester is well-to-do thanks to its proximity to New York City. People with high-paying white collar jobs and families live there and commute so they can have a house with a yard."

"That explains country clubs and art auctions." As well as the high-end stores he'd spotted throughout the mall.

"They haven't posted anything about Isola, at least not that I can find. I'll check again before I head to my morning event."

"The flagship store at Central Park, right?"

She nodded. "I'm there from opening through lunch, then I have an hour to get to the SoHo store. I'll stay there through the evening rush."

"Big day. Any concerns?"

"I'm always concerned. You know me well enough to know that."

The enticing smile she flashed made him want to pull her from the chair to finish what they'd started earlier, but he buried the idea as she set her computer on the side table and her expression turned serious. "What happened today was likely a one-off, a case of two opportunists trying to make a name for their publication by writing a piece salacious enough to get picked up by larger presses."

"You think that was their goal?"

She nodded. "They were unprofessional in their approach and I didn't give them much to work with. That makes them—and reporters like them—easier for me to ignore. From a professional perspective, at least, even if they upset me personally." He sensed the *but* that was to follow before she added, "But I doubt it'll be the same situation tomorrow. The more likely scenario is that I'll have to face the tabloid reporters who were outside Mirabeau last week. I'm far more concerned about their reporting. Their reach is significant."

He itched to ask her if she had a strategy for handling them, but she beat him to the punch. "You offered to attend my events to deflect attention from my mother."

Careful to keep his body position neutral, he said, "I still think it's a good idea. I might've been able to help today."

"Possibly. It also might've made it worse." She leaned forward and waited for him to meet her gaze. "I don't need a knight in shining armor. I don't want someone to swoop in to save me at the first sign of trouble. I'd much rather save myself. And I want the focus on my products rather than my personal life. Even if that's the dating side of my personal life, rather than my paternity."

He tucked his chin. "Are you asking me to attend your event tomorrow?"

"Assuming the offer is still open—"

"It is."

"I'm still debating whether it's the smartest course of action."

"Then this is where I make a confession." He ran both hands over his head and exhaled. "Today's business meeting fell through at the last minute. Your event was about to start, so I wasn't sure I'd be able to reach you. I made a judgment call and took the train to White Plains. I watched your event from the men's department."

"You were there?" Incredulity made her features go slack. "How did I not see you? How did the reporters not see you?"

"You were busy and your focus was on the customers. As to the reporters…over the years, I've learned to blend in when I need to. It doesn't always work, but it's easier here than in Europe. A lot of Americans couldn't name an F1 driver, let alone identify one." He shrugged. "I saw the two of them talking before they came to your section and realized they weren't behaving normally. I also saw how you handled them. I left fairly soon after they did—I didn't see the customer who returned her merchandise or how the afternoon went—but I didn't swoop in, as you call it, to save you when I thought you might be in trouble. I wanted to, but I didn't."

She blinked, but said nothing.

"After my morning therapy appointment, I had nothing else to do today," he explained. "Still, I wasn't sure I should go. Even after I bought my train ticket. Questioned myself the entire length of the ride. I didn't want to distract you or put your event at risk. If I'd spotted the reporters who recognized me outside Mirabeau, I'd have left immediately. I certainly wouldn't have spoken to them or run interference, not unless you'd told me that's what you wanted."

Lina was quiet for so long he became aware of his heartbeat thudding in his ears. He resisted the urge to ask if she was angry, waiting instead for her to speak. Finally, she looked at him and said, "Thank you."

He frowned, taken aback. "For what?"

"For respecting my wishes. For respecting *me*." She traced the arm of her chair with her fingertip. "When it comes to Isola, I want my decisions to be logical, but it's hard to be logical when my heart's involved."

Heat rose in his chest at the phrase *when my heart's involved*. "It's hard for anyone. Even hard-core race car drivers who feel the urge to punch people from *DayBuzz*."

She smiled at that, but only for a moment. "My mother meant the world to me. She taught me to sew. Urged me to study design. Encouraged me when I started Isola. I have a hard time setting aside my emotions where she's concerned. Part of me wants to push away the press to protect her. Another part of me wants to drag her from the grave and shake her, hard, then publicly disown her for good measure."

The heat dissipated as if he'd jumped into a locker room ice bath. He wanted to know Lina's emotions were involved because of him… and the recognition that he felt that way left him disconcerted. Their careers meant their hearts couldn't be involved, not too deeply. Not now. He'd even told her he was committing to trying a chicken recipe. Not a house and kids.

Lina shifted her position in the chair, meeting his gaze. "What she did is affecting my company. I've avoided the issue for weeks, but with the launch, it's impossible. I can't ignore it and succeed. And it's not only about me. My employees are as invested in Isola's success as I am. The seamstresses whose work hasn't been outsourced from Italy because I've hired them. The sales staff who know that when they have an opinion about what does and doesn't work in the store, I'll listen. Even the fabric suppliers in India who rely on me to give them a fair price so they can care for their families. How I handle this launch means a lot to them, which is why I can't let my heart rule my head."

"It's not easy to overrule your heart, even when it's necessary." He'd had to force himself to deal logically with his own mother over the years. It deprived him of sleep on more nights than he could count during his first years on the track, knowing that she disapproved of his choice to race. But his battle had never been public, as Lina's had become.

And then there'd been Lina herself. When they'd started dating, it hadn't been easy to visit her in Milan for a day or two, then take off again. Or to see her for a few short hours in their hotel room between practice rounds and qualifying races at a Grand Prix, only to know she'd be on a plane to Milan by the time his race ended. She'd made it easier with her relaxed attitude.

He had no idea how the few married men on the circuit did it. Mario Puglisi, another driver on Ferrari's F1 team, had a wife and two young children. It seemed every time Ivo turned around, Mario was on the phone or sending his wife a text to address issues at home. A leaky washing machine, a school form that needed his signature, plans for a visit from his in-laws. How Mario set aside the never-ending demands of a family to focus when it came time to climb in the car drew Ivo's admiration.

"When it comes time, you'll know what to do," Mario had assured him once, giving him a clap on the back and one of his deeply dimpled grins.

"That time is called retirement," Ivo had retorted. Every driver had an expiration date in the cockpit, usually in his early- to mid-thirties. Ivo could only name two who still raced at forty. That meant, realistically, he had two or three seasons remaining on the circuit, then he'd transition to another facet of his career. As far as Ivo was concerned, that was the time to consider making a formal commitment to another person. Not before.

Still, he and Lina could nudge closer to that line. Something more involved than a string of one-night stands, yet less than a house and a mortgage.

"No," Lina agreed, pulling him back to the present. "It's never easy. But in this case, the decision isn't only about my mother or my employees."

She crossed the narrow space between them to sit on the arm of his chair. The heat in his belly flared again as she took his hand.

"It's a gracious offer, but the thought of dragging you into the middle of this bothers me. Even if your idea works and keeps the media off the topic of my mother, having them ask about our relationship could be a distraction to both of us. And if it doesn't work, if the questions become too much or the coverage twists in ways we can't predict, it wouldn't only hurt me or Isola. It'd hurt you, too."

"If I thought that could happen, I wouldn't have offered to be there." He raised her hand to kiss her knuckles. "I've spent my adult life dealing with the media. Sports reporters can be harsh. Blunt. Over the years, I've learned to steer their questions as easily as I steer my car. Let me be your partner in this."

She sighed. "Having a partner in this would be lovely. Far better than a knight in shining armor, no matter how chivalrous. Still—"

"Still…what?"

He eased his lips from her knuckles to the delicate, pale skin at the inside of her wrist. Her pulse quickened beneath his mouth, sending a spike of lust through him. When she spoke, her voice was ragged. "A partnership goes both ways. If we're going to do this, it needs to benefit you, too."

"We're going to do this. I'm going to benefit." His other hand went to her knee. He took his time shifting her skirt to the side, then sliding his hand along her thigh, all while continuing to kiss her wrist. He was growing harder by the second.

He wanted her naked. Warm and willing and naked and wrapped around him.

"Ivo."

He didn't miss the hitch in her breathing. After giving her wrist a final, lingering kiss, he lifted her hand and placed it at the back of his neck. Despite the protest hanging on the tip of her tongue, her fingertips spread across his nape.

"Tomorrow, I attend your event. I stand straight, I smile. I no longer look like a man who tried to smash himself against a wall and burn himself alive. The fashion press mention my presence. The F1 press picks it up. My sponsors have their confidence restored. I benefit."

"You're certain?"

"Absolutely. But there's more. I get to watch you work. I benefit." He reached the lacy edge of her panties and spread his palm across her hip. He loved the feel of that particular curve under his hand. It held magic. Made him feel as if each caress was the first. His eyes locked with hers. "I see you holding the world's most sexy lingerie, I benefit. I hear your beautiful voice explaining its wonders—"

"You benefit?"

"I benefit. Truly a partnership." He pulled her from the arm of the chair into his lap, stifling a grunt of pain as his spine absorbed their combined weight.

"You're going to hurt yourself."

"If I do, you'll make it better." He slipped his fingers under the lace at her hip.

"Only if you agree to move to the bed" —she raised her thumb before he could comply— "let me do the work so you protect your back" —she raised a finger— "and we stop if you're in pain. We have a few more days in New York. There'll be plenty of time to—"

"Deal. As long as you never again refer to anything we do in bed as 'work.'" He slid his hand to the juncture of her legs. The wet heat made him ache with a need so primal, the muscles of his stomach seized.

She inhaled sharply and reached for him. "I can agree to that."

CHAPTER 13

LINA'S BODY still hummed the next morning, more than an hour into her Isola event.

The first time she and Ivo made love, back in her flat in Milan, he'd made her entire being sing with pleasure. He'd done it every time since. From the pressure as his hands glided along her ribcage, to the masculine sounds that emanated from deep in his throat as he caressed her breasts or took an aching nipple into his mouth, to the way he framed her face or grasped her hips when they were in the deepest throes of passion, every aspect of his lovemaking made her feel worshipped and adored.

Even when that lovemaking was less-than-vanilla, like last night, when kisses in the living room chair turned into frantic, no-holds-barred sex that left them breathless on the hardwood floor before he'd wrapped her legs around his hips and carried her to the bed.

As the first hint of sunlight streamed through the transom over the bedroom door, he'd flipped around to grab one of her feet, massaging the arch and kissing her ankle, and told her how much he'd missed awakening with her at his side. "You always kick off the sheet so your feet are free," he'd said as he caressed her sole and glanced at her over her knee. "When I open my eyes to the dawn and see your foot peeking out from under the sheets, I'm seduced all over again."

"By a foot?"

"By you."

She'd eased her foot from his hand and captured his lips in a kiss that turned primitive, needful. He'd stretched her arms high over her head, wended her fingers through the slats of the headboard, and forbidden her from letting go. He'd made love to her again, first with his mouth, then with his body. All the while, he'd kept his dark, expressive eyes locked on hers. Daring her to look away, to deny him. She hadn't. She'd been grateful for the near-solstice sunrise that'd awakened them.

More than his words, or even his touch, there was an earnestness to Ivo that made her feel wanted. Respected. Sexy. She loved the way she felt when his arms came around her and he cradled her torso to his so they could sleep. It was the same earnestness that made racing executives sit up and take notice when he climbed into his car or when he spoke strategy. Ivo did nothing by half measures. His intensity inspired confidence.

Assuming he'd recovered from both his run and this morning's intimacy, she couldn't wait to make love to him again tonight, to experience the same rush that came with being the object of his undivided attention.

Lina peeked through the display racks, trying to catch a glimpse of Ivo without being obvious. He'd returned to his hotel to change this morning, so they'd arrived separately. She'd spied him as he'd circulated through the crowd, but it wasn't easy. Unlike the White Plains location, which sprawled over two stories at the end of a massive mall complex, Mirabeau's flagship location near Central Park consisted of eight smaller floors, each with their own specialties. Intimates shared the sixth floor with women's fitness clothing and the swimwear department. Doric columns punctuated the space, hearkening to the building's original use as a bank before the turn of the twentieth century. A wide, curved staircase with an elaborate railing was located adjacent to a set of three elevators. Antique crystal chandeliers provided the floor's primary illumination, though renovations to the space incorporated discreet modern lighting.

Finally, she spotted Ivo leaning against a pillar not far from the elevators, shoulder to shoulder with a well-dressed man with salt and pepper hair who kept one eye on the lingerie section. The man crossed his arms as he spoke, giving Lina a glimpse of a wedding ring. His relaxed manner made Lina suspect he was killing time while waiting for his wife. Both the stranger and Ivo appeared in good spirits, so Lina returned her focus to the task at hand. A woman Lina estimated to be in her early twenties glanced at the price tag on one of the Isola bras, then quickly withdrew her hand from the display. Moving to one of the other racks, she flipped the tag on a different style and, seeing the same price, she moved further down the line.

Lina approached and asked if the woman would like assistance, but she shook her head. "Thanks, but I don't think so. This, um, this pushes a student budget."

Streaks of pink appeared on the woman's cheeks. Lina smiled in sympathy. "I know the feeling. I didn't so much as cross Mirabeau's threshold when I was in design school. You might be surprised at what you can find, though. If you need a bra for a special event, one that you don't expect to wear very often, I can give you some recommendations for pieces at a lower price point."

Lina spent the next twenty minutes helping the young woman, Kati, try a variety of bras at different price points. When one of the Isola pieces turned out to be her favorite, Lina handed Kati a business card identical to that she'd given Dottie the day before, granting the student a discount. The young woman's gratitude made Lina's morning. After Kati left, Lina helped another customer find high-cut briefs in her size, then a sales associate approached to let Lina know that a reporter from *Fashion Backstage* hoped for a few minutes of Lina's time and was waiting near the register.

"Of course." A combination of nerves and excitement fluttered through her as she made her way through the section. *Fashion Back-*

stage meant huge exposure in the industry. A positive mention in the monthly magazine or on the publication's website could be the push needed to finalize a contract with the Frankfurt department store. Though Tomasina had sent press releases and an event invitation to *Fashion Backstage* in the hope they'd cover the launch, she'd never heard a peep from the publication.

Lina approached the register, but only saw a sales associate and a customer she'd helped earlier.

"Winifred, was there someone here to speak with me?" she asked the associate.

"Oh, yes, over there." She angled a look in the direction of the elevators. "He was speaking to your friend earlier."

"Thanks." Salt and pepper hair man. What had he and Ivo discussed for so long?

"Ms. Cornaro, I hope you're looking for me? I'm Salvatore Marcusi, from *Fashion Backstage*."

Lina shook his hand and thanked him for coming to the event. He surprised her by saying, "No, thank you for taking the time for an interview. I promise not to keep you long. Your launch appears quite successful."

"Mirabeau and Isola are a great fit." She urged him toward the far side of the section, away from the congestion of the stairs and elevators. "It might be easier to speak here, where it's quieter. If there's anything you'd like to know about Isola or our products, I'm happy to help."

After gaining her permission to record their interview, Salvatore began with general questions about Lina, confirming information that had been contained in the press release, inquiring about her educational background, and then moving to her passion for design. When asked, she explained that her interest in lingerie came naturally, after she'd grown frustrated with bras that were uncomfortable and expensive for what they were.

"After I finished school, I was fortunate enough to land a position with an Italian design house that focused on sportswear. I thought the fact I could afford to spend more meant I'd finally find underwear that didn't creep or a bra that didn't itch or lose its support after a few months of wear. When I still couldn't find what I wanted, I decided to design it myself. I spent nearly a year sourcing materials that are both durable and comfortable, from producers who treat their employees well, then creating prototypes in my apartment. I experimented with different sewing techniques to increase longevity. The final result is what you see here."

"The final results are also provocative."

She smiled at that. "I'd call them beautiful. If they're provocative, that comes from our customers. My philosophy is that if a woman is comfortable, she's confident. If she's confident, she can be the very best version of herself. That's what I hope Isola does for those who wear it."

Salvatore asked for details on the ethical sourcing of fabrics, then followed with questions about her factory in Italy before surprising her with a question about London Fashion Week. "You weren't scheduled for a full show, but you did have a sizable reception planned and meetings with several buyers. What prompted you to cancel?"

"It was a personal matter," she told him. "Someone close to me was in an accident and I needed to be there. It was disappointing to have to cancel the reception, but fortunately I was able to reschedule meetings with the buyers once the crisis had passed." She finished by touting Isola's sales at the London boutique and noted that she hoped to see the brand carried by more shops throughout the United Kingdom.

Salvatore rolled right to the next question, about the possibility of appearing in upcoming shows. As he spoke, Lina felt the tightness in her chest ease. Not only was Salvatore Marcusi a professional, Ivo had prepped him, and he'd done a fantastic job of it.

Instinct made her want to look for Ivo, to meet his dark eyes and signal her gratitude, but she resisted. Later, when they were alone, she'd make sure he knew exactly how she felt.

Her heart tripped, thinking of how she'd thank him.

Last night, as she'd rested her head on Ivo's shoulder before they went to sleep, he'd stroked her hair and broached the topic of how they'd handle press questions.

"I'm perfectly comfortable talking fashion. It's like breathing." She'd run her index finger across his chest, circling one flat nipple as she contemplated how best to describe her discomfort. "But when it comes to the personal, it's like my head is being held underwater and if I so much as flinch while my air runs out, I'll be punished. My ribs feel like they're caving in on me and it's all I can do to remain calm. The F1 press is so much more aggressive than what I've faced. How have you handled it for so long? And so well?"

"The trick is to ignore the worst questions, the way you did in White Plains," he'd said as he continued to play with her hair. As to the rest, Ivo assured her that the press would be more likely to take what she said as truth and report it if he gave similar answers and they didn't sound rehearsed. "My team and I do it before every major press conference. We brainstorm possible questions, from previous race results to track conditions to any personal issues the press might raise—because the F1 press is convinced that drivers take their personal issues into races—to ensure we give consistent answers. We try to think one step ahead of them so we can provide information they'll want to publish, but that also serves our purposes."

He'd given Lina practice questions, starting out easy with questions reporters would ask about Isola itself. Then he'd hit her with questions about the fact she'd missed London Fashion Week.

When she'd tried to skirt the subject, he'd shaken his head. "If a reporter happens to talk to both of us, they should get enough information to discover you canceled in order to care for me. I won't say it outright. I'll give them just enough information that it can be pieced together from a quick Internet search if you say you had to care for a friend who'd been in an accident. A call to the hospital will confirm it. They'll feel they've scooped other publications and they'll run with it. That's a much better story than another one that focuses on your connection to the Barrali family."

At the mention of King Carlo, she'd propped herself on one elbow so he could see her face. "I haven't had the chance to tell you yet. At the last minute yesterday, I decided to go to the café."

"You met Queen Fabrizia?" At her nod, he'd asked, "How did it go? What did you think of her?"

"Surreal. She's prettier than her pictures. And smart."

Lina had been in awe, though she couldn't bring herself to tell Ivo that. It'd been hard enough to admit it to herself when the sensation hit her after she'd left the shop. Fabrizia carried herself with a self-possessed air that Lina suspected came at birth, rather than with the title she'd acquired at marriage.

To his credit, Ivo remained silent, waiting for Lina to continue.

"She wants me to meet King Carlo."

"And?"

"I didn't agree to anything. I mostly listened." Lina exhaled. "She gave me a card with her private cell phone number and said she'd be happy to arrange a meeting when I'm ready. She's bossy."

Ivo'd laughed aloud at that. "In addition to being a queen with a large staff, she's a mother of six. I imagine bossiness comes with the territory."

"I suspect she'd be bossy without the crown and children."

His fingers drifted along her arm. "Were you seen? Will any reporters ask questions about the fact you met with her?"

Lina shook her head, then described the security arrangements and Umberto, the queen's head of security. "He was ready to whisk her to her private plane and off to Sarcaccia the minute we finished. He didn't strike me as the type who'd let anyone see the queen if she didn't want to be seen."

"All right." Ivo's hand went to her shoulder and he'd guided her head to the pillow beside his. They'd practiced answers to questions about the Barralis as he ran his hand along her arm and her hip, silently coaxing her to relax. It didn't take long before she realized she could twist nearly any question back to Isola. He'd finished by asking if she could draw up a list of the fashion publications that had received press releases about the event, highlighting the most important. "With that information and a few minutes on the Internet in the morning, I might be able to identify reporters. It'll make it easier to feed them information."

She'd agreed to share what she could and had fallen asleep with a sense of relief, rather than fear.

Now, as she stood facing Salvatore Marcusi, she was grateful for Ivo all over again. The reporter's gaze went beyond Lina for a moment. "Care to confirm a relationship with Ivo Zanardi?"

Ivo had identified himself? Since it wasn't in their plan, she frowned and said, "There's no Isola employee by that name."

Salvatore laughed, the deep rumble drawing the attention of several female shoppers. "No, I imagine not. I won't harass you about his presence here. I suspect you're keeping that quiet." He waited for Lina to say something. When she didn't, he went on, "However, I'd be negligent if I didn't ask about the recent coverage of your family. You didn't attend King Carlo's press conference a few months ago, but without giving your name, he acknowledged publicly that he fathered three illegitimate children with your mother."

"Yes, he did."

He waited for her to expand on her statement, but she kept her expression placid and waited. Ivo had urged her to resist the temptation to fill silences after she'd answered a question.

Finally, the *Fashion Backstage* reporter asked, "What is your relationship with King Carlo today? Do you feel the spotlight on his personal life has drawn attention to Isola?"

"I've never met the king, so I can't comment on that. As to Isola" —she waved a hand in a manner she hoped appeared casual— "the company has experienced slow and steady growth from the beginning. What we're enjoying today is the result of relationships we've built with stores like Mirabeau and with our customers over a long period of time."

He smiled, then tried asking about the royal family from different angles. Each time, Lina followed Ivo's advice and simply repeated what she'd already said, ensuring the only quotes the reporter had were those that would cast Isola in the best possible light. When he finished, he thanked her for her time, then took his leave.

As soon as he was out of sight, Lina released a long breath. While his questions went from professional to deeply personal, the interview felt completely different than what she'd faced with *DayBuzz*, due to both the reporter's professionalism and her own preparation. Intense as it was, it left her optimistic.

It didn't take long before the store manager, a statuesque woman in her mid-fifties, swooped in to congratulate Lina on drawing *Fashion Backstage* to the event. "I usually get a heads-up when Salvatore Marcusi is in the building. He must've come in one of the side entrances, rather than the front." She glanced around to ensure no one could overhear, then said, "He usually calls before he visits, then stops at the fragrance counters and talks to the employees before he comes upstairs. He likes everyone to make a fuss. But today I didn't know he was here until one of the sales associates said he was standing near the elevators watching you. Did you see him before he approached you?"

"I believe he was talking to a customer."

The manager puffed out a breath in shock. "This is all so unlike him."

"My assistant sent a press release last week with details on the event. Perhaps her copy was particularly intriguing?"

"Perhaps." The manager's gaze breezed over the floor, taking in the busy lingerie section. "My associates say that sales are going well. Congratulations."

"You've hired excellent staff. Their enthusiasm is making a big difference."

The older woman studied Lina, then ran her hand along the edge of one of the displays, her expression one of approval. "I've been here a long time. I'll admit, sometimes these product launches run together in my mind, as do the people behind them. And I hate meetings where I'm forced to sit at a table and watch slideshows about products. However, your presentation last week was the most helpful and practical I've seen. And I loved my gift bag. Believe it or not, I'm wearing the bikini brief now. It's quite comfortable." A wide smile lifted her features. "This is a difficult business, but I have a good feeling about Isola."

The manager tapped the edge of the table, as if punctuating her thought, then spun on her black stilettos and strode away.

On impulse, Lina looked across the lingerie section toward the elevators. Ivo met her gaze, his expression conveying approval for her actions before he deliberately cast his eyes toward her legs, then up again. His ravenous look sent Lina's heart into overdrive.

Success. If this is what it felt like, she wanted more.

CHAPTER 14

THE SIDEWALK outside Mirabeau's side exit was free of reporters when Lina emerged. A taxi sat idle at the curb, the light on top indicating it was out of service. She slid into the back seat and thanked the driver for waiting. A block later, the taxi stopped and Ivo entered.

"Salvatore Marcusi. Of all people. You're amazing! How'd you know it was him? I had no idea what he looked like."

"Research pays off," he said, giving her a quick kiss once they were out of sight of Mirabeau. "I spotted him standing near the elevators, watching the customers in the lingerie section, and thought he might be one of the reporters from your list. I double-checked on my phone, and sure enough, his photo was on the *Fashion Backstage* website. I made an offhand comment that he was on the wrong floor, but that I appreciated having a little testosterone while I waited for someone."

Lina admired Ivo's quick thinking. "Did he realize that you recognized him?"

"No, and he never identified himself. But I could see it on his face the moment he recognized me." Ivo's mouth lifted in self-satisfaction. "Took him a few minutes, but he's a red-blooded Italian male, most of whom follow two sports, *fútbol* and F1. My guess is that he'll tell his friends I was there."

"By friends, you mean sports reporters?"

"If he knows any, he'll tell them." He eased closer to her as the taxi slowed at a congested intersection. "I mentioned that I was at Mirabeau as moral support for the Isola event. My exact words were, 'The company's founder is a good friend. She helped me when I was hospitalized recently. I told her I was happy to return the favor by watching her sell lingerie.' We had a good laugh over that."

Lina could imagine. Ivo mastered the art of putting those around him at ease.

"You're still all right with me referring to you as a good friend?"

She nodded. It hurt her heart and her ego—not that she'd ever admit it aloud—but they'd agreed last night that it was the safest description to use with the media for now, should they need to use one.

It wasn't long before Mirabeau's SoHo store came into view. Ivo squeezed her hand when they recognized several people on the sidewalk as reporters who'd been at Mirabeau the day she'd been accosted. Making a quiet entrance wasn't an option.

"Ignore questions from the reporters out here. What you said this morning will stand on its own. If anyone enters the store and interviews you during the event—"

"I'll stay on message and repeat what I said to *Fashion Backstage*."

"I'll feed them what information I can." In other words, he'd promote Isola as a caring workplace. He'd drop hints about their relationship without confirming anything. And, if the situation allowed him to do it subtly, he'd mention the UNICEF fundraiser. Good for her, good for him.

"Ivo?" She put a hand on his knee before the taxi rolled to a stop. "Thank you. This means a lot."

His broad smile sent a ripple of heat through her. "I owe you one. More than one. In fact, I believe I owe you thanks for including me in your adventure. I'm enjoying myself."

"Maybe thank me tonight?"

"Definitely tonight." His gaze turned hot, his eyes saying even more than he could have with words.

Before she could respond, the taxi stopped and Ivo shot a look at the store in a silent instruction to walk ahead of him while he paid the driver. "Go in like you own the place. I have your back."

Six hours later, Ivo sat with Lina's back to his chest as they relaxed under the bubbles in his hotel suite's massive tub. He pressed his lips to her temple and ran a sudsy washcloth along the outside of her arm, using subtle pressure to soothe her muscles. Admittedly, it provided him plenty of enjoyment.

He'd never understood the allure of sitting in a vat of hot water. Showers were more his speed. In, scrub, out, dry, done. But as Lina rolled her neck, then settled her head into the crook of his shoulder, he savored the slide of her leg along the inside of his. The haze hanging over the surface of the water. The lemon-vanilla scent of whatever concoction she'd poured under the faucet. The sweet sound of her exhale.

Pure, unadulterated bliss.

He drew the washcloth up her arm, kneading her muscles as he went, then switched to the opposite side before encouraging her to lean forward so he could massage either side of her spine.

"You're spoiling me."

"I told you I'd have your back."

"I had no idea this was what you meant."

"I've learned a few things in my physical therapy sessions." He moved his thumbs in small circles along her shoulder blades, easing the knots under her skin. "I did promise to make it worth your while to come here instead of heading to the condo."

Her voice held a smile as she pointed out, "The condo was closer."

"We'd never have fit in your mother's tub. Not like this."

She sighed with pleasure as he found the base of her spine with his knuckles. At his encouragement, she drew in her legs so her knees peeked out of the bubbles and offered a spot to rest her forehead.

He'd left the SoHo store a little over an hour ahead of her and ordered room service so it'd be ready when she'd arrived. As they ate, they'd each shared their thoughts on the day's events. The SoHo sales appeared to have outstripped those at the Central Park store this morning, though that store reported robust traffic throughout the afternoon, thanks to the balloons and signs that continued to draw shoppers to the lingerie department long after Lina departed.

Better yet, the early press coverage was largely in Isola's favor. After dinner, they'd scoured the Internet for feedback on the events. The first hit had been the most painful. The *DayBuzz Westchester* homepage featured a photograph of Lina taken from an angle and cropped so it centered on a lacy bra and panty set hanging just in front of her. Adam Green had been cut out of the photo. The caption referred to Lina as "the lingerie purveyor with a shameful past." The article beneath it was short, highlighting the history between Lina's mother and King Carlo, then stating that Lina was "bringing her wares to Westchester as a test market" and that it would be "interesting" to see the response of Mirabeau customers who rely on the store for quality, high-end merchandise.

Lina's jaw clenched so tight as she read the article, Ivo worried she'd chip a tooth. Finally, she'd muttered, "It could be worse," and returned to her search results. He knew it was the "shameful past" phrase that bothered her most, as if she'd done something immoral, either by virtue of her birth or career choice. Thankfully, the *DayBuzz Westchester* piece was forgotten when Lina discovered that a fashion blogger posted photos of the White Plains store's display and raved about the comfortable fit of Mirabeau's "latest, greatest discovery from Italy."

"I don't know if her reach is greater than what they have at *DayBuzz*, but one can hope."

He'd read along over Lina's shoulder. "She posted photos that are easily saved and shared. Give it time."

"I'll forward this to my assistant. She can promote it through our channels."

A short time later, as Ivo cleared the table, Lina drew in a sharp breath. "*Fashion Backstage* just posted about me on their home page."

"And?"

"I'm reading." When she met Ivo's gaze, her eyes glistened. "Ivo, it's fabulous. It's only two paragraphs, but he mentions my education and why I decided to start a lingerie business, then talks about Isola's quality. He says there will be more coverage in an upcoming print issue of the magazine."

The relief in Lina's voice made his throat constrict. How many weeks and months of stress had preceded that mention?

"I could hug Salvatore Marcusi."

"I'd rather you didn't. Particularly when I'm right here."

She'd laughed at that. It hadn't taken long before they'd ended up in the tub, enjoying the steam and each other's company. She turned her head to the side as he continued to massage her back.

"You haven't said much about the UNICEF show. How's it coming?"

"There's a rehearsal tomorrow afternoon. Should be straightforward. Unfortunately, the advertising meeting that was canceled before I went to White Plains has been rescheduled to tomorrow morning."

She sighed as he kneaded her deltoids. "You never told me what it was."

"Men's fragrance. They're interested in having me as the face of their newest product launch. I don't know the name of the new scent—it's apparently top secret—but my agent says they want the marketing to connote an aura of speed and danger."

"Therefore, they want a race car driver."

"They haven't smelled one fresh off the course, obviously."

A soft laugh escaped her before her arms slipped down her knees and into the water. "I won't see you tomorrow, then. I'm at Mirabeau's Park Slope store most of the afternoon and evening."

"I wish I could be there."

She sighed her smile. "I'll be fine."

"I know you will." He inhaled the moist air, thick with the scent of the hotel's bath products. "What about Thursday?"

"No store events, but I have a conference call with a Frankfurt department store first thing in the morning. After that, I have a meeting at Mirabeau to get their initial feedback on the store events."

"Oh?"

She knew what he was asking. "They won't decide whether to pursue a long-term contract for at least a month, more likely two or three months. I doubt the meeting even lasts an hour. It's only to review what worked and what didn't. If there's anything the sales team believes I need to tweak on the display or merchandise, they'll let me know then. After that, I'll return to the condo to get ready for the Cooper Hewitt reception. That's the mansion that houses the Smithsonian Design Museum," she clarified. "It'll end after midnight. Friday morning I do a virtual visit with the Syracuse store. Instead of a launch event like we had with the other locations, they've issued invitations to their best customers to come in for a private breakfast in their bistro with the store manager, followed by a video question and answer session with me and first access to the line before the store opens at ten a.m."

"That's innovative. It also makes for an intense week."

"Nature of a launch. Adrenaline helps. You've made it easier."

He skimmed his fingers along either side of her spine, then gave her neck a final massage before easing her torso to his. Their week in New York was flying. He'd always regretted the end of their trysts, but this felt different. He wouldn't just miss her while they were apart. The thought of being without her company made him ache *now*.

Lina's hands went to the outside of his thighs as she relaxed into him. "Well, you and this bathtub made it easier."

He flicked her under the water and was rewarded with a wiggle. If she knew what that did to him, she'd think twice. Much more pressure would bring a quick end to the bath.

A moment later, she asked, "How do you feel about walking a runway for UNICEF? The modeling you did was mostly print work, wasn't it?"

"Mostly. But this is an entirely different beast than when the goal is to sell merchandise to stores. Instead, the focus will be on helping those in need. I suspect I'm the only one who's modeled professionally—print or runway."

Her touch did wicked things to his legs. He slipped his arms around her waist, then closed his eyes and savored the play of her fingers over his skin.

"Has it sold out yet?"

"Not that I know of, but the organizers seem happy. Most of the money going to UNICEF will be on the back end, rather than through ticket sales. The Midtown and Park Slope stores will run video of the event for the next month and have special displays highlighting the show's clothing and accessories, then the designers will donate proceeds from the sale of those items."

She needed to move her hands higher. Maybe turn around and use her mouth.

Definitely turn around and use her mouth.

"Sales should be good, then." Lina shifted so her feet slid alongside his as she continued her exploration of his leg. "If it's all right with you, I'd like to come."

Oh, he'd like her to come, too. To see the arch of her neck as she built toward release, hear her gasp as she spasmed around him.

He smiled to himself. All in good time.

"You're not too busy?" he asked.

"I'm done after the Syracuse event. My flight home isn't until Saturday evening." Her fingers stilled. "On the other hand, I don't want to be a distraction."

"The naked woman in front of me says she doesn't want to be a distraction." Raw lust filled his voice. He didn't care. "What were you originally planning to do that night?"

She swirled her fingers along the surface of the cooling water. "Sleep if I was tired. If not, get tickets to whatever Broadway show looked good at the Times Square discount booth. But as it turns out, someone bought me tickets to a show earlier in the week. And I have so much energy after the Central Park and SoHo events, I can't imagine spending the rest of my time in New York sleeping."

"We've established that you have an intense schedule for the rest of the week. That'll burn off a lot of energy."

"And I was so sure you were about to say that there's a difference between time spent sleeping and time spent in bed." She twisted to face him. Simultaneously, her hand dipped below the water to make lazy circles around his knee. Her gaze turned wicked as her fingers moved to his quadriceps, then she dragged her knuckles underneath him, from the base of his shaft all the way to the tip, where she lingered. "Would you prefer that I skip your show?"

"Absolutely not. If you want to come, I'd love to have you there."

Doubt washed through him. Never a fan of doubt, he shoved it aside to analyze later, opting instead to cup her breasts and run his thumbs across her nipples, which had grown taut from both the cool air and desire.

Her fingers circled him.

"You can have me anywhere."

She'd barely uttered the words before he captured her mouth with his own.

URGENT.

It was the only word Lina could use to describe the way Ivo kissed her as she caressed him with one hand. Beneath the water, his legs pressed against hers, locking her in place. Above the water, where the air cooled her skin, his palms imprisoned her breasts while his mouth demanded heat. She opened to him, her body melting against the crush of his hands and the insistent sweep of his tongue.

She grasped him tighter. He grew thick and hard at her touch, making her ache for him.

He lifted his head, his dark eyes intense. "I love your hands on me."

"I love the way you kiss me." Blood pounded through her veins, driven by the dissipating heat of the bath and the fierceness of Ivo's tone. "I want you in bed. The sooner, the better."

"Stay."

He was out of the water and back with a large, white towel before she could tell him how much she admired the way droplets sluiced off the hard planes of his rear. She tucked the image into a corner of her mind as she stepped toward him and reached for the towel. Instead, he started to pat her dry, but before she could protest, he silenced her with another devastating kiss.

Surrender was her only option.

"I want to be inside you," he breathed into her hair as he dropped the towel and unwound the band she'd used to hold her waves out of the water. "I hurt I want it so much."

The carnal edge in his voice nearly buckled her knees. Ivo was always passionate, but this was something else. A single-mindedness that should scare her, but only made her want him more.

She bracketed his face in her hands, angling her mouth in a kiss that said, *yes, yes, yes.*

His response was instantaneous. He had her on the bed in seconds, his fingers threaded through her hair, his granite-hard body pinning hers against the luxurious softness of the sheets. Then his mouth claimed her once more, his tongue swirling against hers in a dance that sent a scorching wave from her scalp to her soles. Lina's all-encompassing desire for him bordered on pain. As her heart thundered in her ears and throat, she held him as close as she could. It wasn't close enough. He tortured the skin along her jaw before moving to her collarbone, and she dug her fingers into the powerful muscles of his backside and groaned his name.

She wanted him desperately. He was the only thought in her head.

His tongue swept lower and she lost her grip on his damp skin. When his dark head dipped between her legs, she jumped at the first touch of his warm mouth against her. Awash in sensation, she cried out his name as he delved inside her, ratcheting up the tension with each touch until she thought she'd lose consciousness with the pleasure of it.

She couldn't wait to return the favor. To see Ivo's throat cord with tension as she sucked him deep. To know she could bring him to the edge of ecstasy. To hear the eroticism in his growl as he said her name.

Ivo's broad palms stilled her hips, trapping her where he wanted her until a white-hot spasm sliced along her spine. Even then, he didn't release her, didn't stop the wondrous motion of his tongue and teeth. The friction, the heat, the pressure of what he did to her drove her head back until her vision blurred and her breath came in choked pants and another, even more powerful spasm shot through her body. Finally, he released her, moved over her, and pushed inside, filling Lina so completely she pressed her open mouth to his shoulder to muffle her cry at the perfection of it.

Always she'd loved this moment, when he first entered her and they fit together. But this time the connection was different. New. Potent. All-encompassing.

Ivo didn't move. Instead, he cradled her to him, as if stunned by the same powerful sensation. As if he needed the moment to savor it, to wonder at it. To breathe in and out against her hair, to allow her to taste the skin of his shoulder and feel each beat of their hearts as she wrapped her legs around his, locking them together.

Tears eked out the corners of her eyes as her muscles tightened around him.

Never before had she felt so close to someone, nor felt anyone so in tune with her. She and Ivo had always been drawn to each other. But being in New York, talking shop with Ivo and knowing he cared about her work and had insights to share, strengthened that impulse. He'd been the sounding board she'd never had at the office, where there was only so much she could say about her hopes and fears to those who worked for her. But Ivo didn't judge. He listened with respect and a steadfast belief in her dreams, a belief that helped her spread her wings and pursue her passion.

It bonded them as never before.

She dragged her cheek to his, inhaling the unique scent of him. He turned, capturing her gaze and holding it. A long beat, then two, passed. Then he began to move. Slowly, deliberately, never allowing his eyes to leave hers. No words passed between them as she arched her back and met his long, languid strokes. Deeper and deeper he plunged, their bodies rocking in unison, their gazes locked. A tremor went through him and he bit his lower lip. Still, his gaze didn't leave hers. He didn't quicken the pace.

It was the most intimate, substantive moment of her life.

"Ivo." The simple syllable shivered.

He exhaled. Then, forehead pressed to hers, he thrust harder, his hands grasping her hips, possessing her. He was on the edge. She wanted him to shatter for her. Yearned for it.

Her lips parted as she moved with him, mentally cataloging the subtle changes in Ivo as he neared his peak—the flex in his fingers, the set of his jaw, the fervor in his dark eyes—then her own climax shocked her, crashing through her in wave after wave, leaving the surface of her skin aflame. With a low, masculine cry, his body convulsed in an extended, forceful release. His eyes never left hers.

Everything outside the room disappeared, leaving only her and Ivo.

CHAPTER 15

"Mr. Zanardi? Is everything all right?"

Ivo released the edge of the curtain at Caleb's question. A summer intern with Mirabeau, Caleb had been thrilled to be assigned the task of organizing the lineup of celebrities backstage at the UNICEF fashion show. Ivo had happily posed for a photo with the young man, who'd promptly sent it to his girlfriend back home in Arizona.

Ivo could understand Caleb's excitement, as well as his desire to impress a woman. The woman Ivo hoped to impress occupied a seat three rows from stage, but well off to the side and away from those who'd nabbed the most coveted tickets. She didn't look like herself, either, with her hair captured by a silk scarf that obscured her blond waves. A pair of glasses she typically only wore at the computer rested low on her face as she surveyed the crowd.

They'd decided that until they had more time to talk about their relationship, it'd be easiest if she flew under the radar at tonight's event. In that, she'd succeeded. None of the smartly dressed people milling around the seating area paid her heed. She was learning what he had after years in the public eye: one could disappear into a crowd, but it took planning.

Now that the show was about to begin, Ivo realized he had a case of nerves. Much as he wanted to chalk it up to the fact he hadn't strolled down a runway in more than a decade, that wasn't it. Nor was it the anticipation pulsing through the backstage area. It was one hundred percent Lina...and not because he feared she'd be recognized.

The night he and Lina shared after her SoHo store event had been transformative. Forty-eight hours later, he still couldn't shake what happened between them. Through two sessions with his physical therapist, the meeting with the ad agency, and even the UNICEF rehearsal, Lina permeated his brain.

I love the way you kiss me.

That quiet statement went straight from her lips to his heart, rolling through his body with a physical force unlike anything he'd ever experienced. Unlike anything he thought himself capable of experiencing.

Before the hospital, he'd always looked forward to spending his breaks with her. After the hospital, he'd craved the opportunity to make things right, to better value their time together, to find a respite with her and offer her the same. But this was something else.

When they'd been forehead-to-forehead in bed, when he'd been buried deep inside of her, the sensation went beyond physical. It was a moment of all-encompassing emotion. The type of emotion to which he'd believed himself impervious.

He'd been raised by a mother who'd survived because she'd buried her feelings for her husband when she realized he'd married her out of a sense of duty, before their relationship had time to mature. Because she'd focused on work and maintaining a stable home, and on ensuring Ivo had the education and opportunity to do whatever he wanted, opportunity that'd been scarce for her in Nigeria. He'd succeeded because he'd followed her example, maintaining that same focus. He'd climbed to the top echelon of his sport so quickly because he'd shunned the nights out, the parties, the socializing, and the womanizing that went along with life on the circuit. And, unlike the men with wives and children, emotion hadn't distracted him. The way he and Lina had conducted their relationship allowed him to succeed.

But now...now the emotion was there. He couldn't deny it. He had only to think of the woman on the other side of the curtain to experience a pull so powerful it simultaneously hurt his chest and made him thrilled to be alive. It was utterly, completely transforming. That was the crux of the problem.

He grit his teeth and ran his hands along the front of his suit jacket. If he wanted to have Lina—truly have her, spending every night in her arms, making love to her and waking up to the warmth of her lying beside him in the sheets—he'd risk the one goal he'd worked hardest to achieve. The goal for which he'd pushed himself mentally and physically for so many years. Studying, working in the simulator, analyzing track conditions and memorizing the quirks of each curve, running up hills and sprinting stairs so his heart rate remained low in even the toughest, hottest racing conditions. The goal that didn't merely earn him an income, but supported an entire team.

No, he wasn't ready to be transformed. Not like that. Not after what he went through in San Rimini and the battle he'd waged—was still waging—to complete his comeback and accumulate the points necessary for that coveted World Drivers' Championship. The timing wasn't right.

If he gave it all up to stay with Lina in Milan, they could end up like his own parents. Rushing into marriage had precluded accomplishing the goals they'd each set for themselves, which in turn had doomed their relationship. His parents' relationship may have fizzled anyway, if not for the pregnancy, but they'd never had the chance to find out.

He and Lina did. But they needed to communicate. And they needed to take things slowly.

Walking in front of Lina, using the adrenaline rush of the stage to raise money for UNICEF…emotionally, he wanted to go all out to impress her, utilize every tool at his disposal to ensure she experienced the same life-altering feelings for him that he did for her. Logically, however, he knew he needed to dial it back. Perform his best for UNICEF, yes. But perform for Lina? No. The last thing he needed was for them to fall crazy in love with each other when they weren't ready.

He'd recognized it last night, during that moment in the bathtub when he'd felt a niggle of doubt about having Lina at tonight's show. He'd pushed the thought aside. He had to face it now.

He turned to the anxious intern. "Everything is perfectly all right, Caleb. Assessing the audience before the show begins." One audience member in particular.

"We sold out this afternoon. There's even a line outside in case of no-shows."

A note in the young man's voice caused Ivo to scrutinize him. "You sound surprised."

"There's a, um, rumor that you have a girlfriend here, Mr. Zanardi. I think that helped sell the last few tickets."

Ivo directed a look at a nearby stool, currently occupied by a New York Giants player who'd been added to the lineup that morning. While the All-Star tight end wouldn't walk the runway to model Mirabeau fashion, he'd agreed to appear at the end of the show to auction tickets for front-row seats to a Giants game that included a meet-and-greet opportunity with some of the players. "You don't think he helped?"

Caleb shrugged. "Maybe, but the sports media picked up their tickets days ago. I heard the last few went to gossip sites."

"If handled properly, they'll gossip about UNICEF. That's good for everyone."

The lights in the hall dropped as music thumped from the speakers. Caleb hustled to the opposite side of the stage, where the emcee for the night prepared to make her entrance. The popular morning show host would welcome everyone to the venue and mention some of the celebrity models before a video started on screens mounted on either side of the main stage. Intended to inspire, the video would give the audience insight into important work UNICEF accomplished around the world on a daily basis. The first person to walk the runway would be Amira, a nineteen year-old accounting student at NYU who'd been helped by UNICEF when her family was forced to flee their Kurdish village.

Ivo closed his eyes and let the music wash through him. Lina's presence called to him like a siren, but he could do this. He could focus his heart on his task tonight, rather than on the woman in seat 308.

If he was so distracted by Lina Cornaro's presence that he couldn't manage to get through a simple event like tonight's fundraiser without thinking of her—of what'd go through her mind when she saw him take off his suit jacket and work the runway, of how he'd taste champagne on her tongue when they kissed later tonight, of how she'd press her hot mouth to his shoulder to bury her moans when she reached orgasm—how could he possibly keep her from his mind as he raced through the streets of Monte Carlo or circled the track in San Rimini?

The morning host checked her teeth and lipstick in a backstage mirror, gave her husband's hand a quick squeeze, then squared her shoulders and smiled broadly as she strode onstage to thunderous applause. Her husband, a reporter who covered finance for a major cable news network, remained hidden behind the curtain, watching as his wife brought down the house simply by walking onstage.

While his wife was beautiful, a striking woman of Vietnamese heritage who'd turn heads no matter her career, the finance reporter wasn't staring at her legs or glossy black hair. Nor did he revel in the adoration being heaped upon her by the audience. His bright-eyed expression made it plain he loved his wife for how she made him feel, and that he was deeply grateful for the life they shared away from the cameras and accolades. Ivo imagined the man often looked at her with a similar expression while they weeded flowerbeds, wrestled toddlers into car seats, or pursued other day-to-day activities. They were partners. The kinship they shared was what made her squeeze his hand before she went in front of the audience and what kept him rooted to the spot now.

He resisted the urge to peek beyond the curtain. Lina wasn't needy, yet she made him feel needed. Not for his money or his fame, but for how he made her feel. And he liked it.

We could be partners.

Someday.

"I'm not sure I can do this with so many people staring at me. I swear, I can see their diamonds and Rolexes from here." Amira, the

NYU student, had come to stand beside him. "I thought I'd gotten used to living in New York, but this crowd is insane. Makes me feel like I'm the last person who should be here."

"You did a fantastic job during rehearsal. Once you start walking, you'll draw from their energy. If it helps, remind yourself that as privileged as they are, most of these people wouldn't be here if they didn't want to share their wealth. They understand their good fortune and want to contribute to UNICEF. If anything, they'll admire you for your resilience and for clearing hurdles they've never been forced to overcome."

During rehearsal, while waiting his turn to go onstage, he'd been seated beside Amira. Fragile as she appeared in her NYU tank top and jeans in what had to be a children's size, with lean fingers that flew over the pages of a study packet she'd brought with her for their downtime, he'd sensed a toughness in her that reminded him of his mother. And of Lina.

Sensing Amira needed further reassurance, he added, "It doesn't hurt that you're in a spectacular dress and you wear it well. Once the crowd sees it, they'll envision themselves in it and they'll plunk down their credit cards. Think of all the education that could provide to kids in refugee camps. Or the number of pop-up shelters that could finance."

Amira smoothed her hands over the front of the blue-green dress, which was exactly the type a woman could wear to a cocktail hour or wedding reception with confidence. He hadn't lied to make her feel better. She did look great in it.

"It's pretty comfortable, too," Amira said on a long sigh. "I suppose if it felt so tight I couldn't breathe, I'd pass out halfway down the runway. Wouldn't sell many dresses."

Caleb scooted past with a reminder that Amira was on in less than a minute.

"I may pass out from anxiety, though," she said, her voice so thready Ivo barely heard her.

"You promise not to pass out, and I'll promise not to pass out."

"You have a huge advantage, but I can accept that deal." She shook out her hands in an attempt to relax, then gave Ivo a shy smile. "Thanks for the pep talk. It's not my personality to do this."

"Focus on UNICEF, not the audience." He grinned, then angled his head toward the stage, where he could hear the video transition to Amira's segment. "Break a leg."

Then he'd try to take his own advice.

———

LINA SCOOTED her rear end to the back of the folding chair at the end of the row, taking care not to muss its white fabric cover or knock off the card affixed to the backrest designating it as seat 308. A few seats away from her, at a better vantage point to the stage, a man wore an ID tag that identified him as a reporter for a popular online gossip site. His eyes went everywhere, taking in chandeliers sparkling overhead, the chic baby blue and white color scheme of the room, and, most importantly, noting the models, CEOs, and New York society mavens making their way through the rows to find their seats. He paid her no attention.

Secure, she let her own gaze drift. The last forty-eight hours had been a blur, between hosting the reception at Cooper Hewitt and engaging in the virtual visit with Mirabeau's Syracuse location. An evening that demanded nothing of her but to sit and discreetly people watch was a welcome relief.

Air kisses were exchanged and several squeals of delight bounced through the room as new guests entered. A well-known fashion magazine editor strolled to the front row with an A-list actress at her side, chatting as casually as if their attendance was no big deal, though the other guests looked stunned to see the pair. Diplomats, UNICEF staff, and Mirabeau employees were scattered throughout the crowd. Several used their phones to take stealthy photos of the editor and the actress. Fashion photographers ready to capture the night's highlights crouched near the runway, which extended from a sizable stage. On either end of the stage, giant screens displayed the UNICEF logo and a montage of photographs taken at schools, first aid tents, and refugee camps throughout the world. Each featured a child, though the circumstances varied. In some, distress and chaos dominated the scene. Others showed scenes of comfort: a toddler receiving vaccines, a girl with her hand raised in a makeshift classroom, a little boy hugging a UNICEF volunteer.

Mirabeau had gone all-out for the event. Lina noted with her designer's eye that not only would the room show well on video in the coming weeks, the celebrities in attendance had flattering backgrounds for any photos they took of themselves during the evening. They'd also feel pampered during the entirety of their attendance, from the welcome glasses of champagne being passed near the entrance to the soft fabrics used to cover the seats. Both factors would make them more likely to share the event on their personal social media platforms and—hopefully—draw attention to UNICEF and boost sales of the featured fashions.

UNICEF was worthy of such a fuss. As was Ivo, she realized. He was as famous as any of the guests in attendance, the Hollywood actress included. She'd only spent time with him in relative privacy, away from the venues at his events, where he was the center of attention. On the world stage, Ivo was so much larger than life. His confidence and his talent, which had attracted Lina from the start, felt magnified in comparison to his quieter traits, such as his kindness.

They'd had a wonderful time in New York …once he'd dragged her to his hotel room and forced her to listen to his apology and face her own responsibility for their breakup. They'd connected on a deeper level than ever before. But suddenly, with the air of excitement thrumming through the room, worry spiraled through her, settling in the pit of her stomach.

Ivo's career—and everything that went with it—was much larger than hers would ever be, even if she were to reach the top of the fashion industry. While she had notoriety and the attention of the press, thanks to her mother, that would fade. Even if she were to accomplish every goal, sell her product into every store, and become known within the industry, it was the rare designer known outside of it.

The entire sports world knew Ivo Zanardi. Even when he stopped racing, he'd be a household name. He might model, focus on advertising opportunities, or join a racing team from the technical side. He might even cover races for broadcast. He'd never *not* be recognized, particularly in Europe. He'd always have new goals to achieve, new challenges on which to focus.

Was she kidding herself, believing she could throw herself into a relationship with him in the here and now, without needing to know what the future held for them?

The overhead lights flashed twice, then lowered, leaving only the stage illuminated. Music swelled, its thumping beat more in line with a street party than the mood suggested by the stylish decor. Guests slid into their seats, then applauded as the night's master of ceremonies took the stage. Throughout the room, cameras flashed as the vivacious morning show host smiled in welcome. After introducing herself and thanking Mirabeau for hosting the event, she gestured to the photos displayed alongside the stage.

"What you see on the screens is a small part of what UNICEF does. The organization makes a huge difference in the lives of children around the world. My parents were born in Vietnam, a country where UNICEF has operated for decades. They told me from the time I was born how vital UNICEF has been in ensuring that Vietnamese children have access to health care and education during times of great strife. Recently, when months of extreme weather in rural parts of the south rendered water supplies unsafe, it was UNICEF who moved in to help the local government focus on sanitation. They also provided critical nutritional supplements to children and families at risk of illness and malnutrition. When we see images like these on our television screens, or at fundraising events like this, it seems very far away. But the world is getting smaller and smaller. We're interconnected. What affects people—what affects children—in one country affects us all. When you support UNICEF with your donations, you're ensuring that these children will contribute to all of our futures."

She moved closer to the front of the stage, her sweeping gaze encompassing the entire audience, as if they were friends in her living room. "To kick off tonight's event—and the fashion show you're all here to see—I'd like you to meet Amira Barakat. Born in a Kurdish village in northern Iraq, she was forced to leave her home after her father and several of his male friends were killed by an armed group of anti-Kurdish extremists and threats were made against the rest of her family. Amira's mother fled twenty-three miles to reach the Turkish border with Amira, her younger brother Ibrahim, and their grandparents. At the time, Amira was only six years old."

The morning host glanced at the screen. A photo of a frightened child in somber gray clothes appeared. She stood between two tents identical in color to the sun-scorched hills of the desert behind her, staring directly into the camera. Too-large sneakers, one with a hole in the side, covered her feet. Her wide eyes conveyed the cold reality of a child who'd seen too much, one who had nothing left to lose and no hope for future days.

"That was Amira then. This is Amira today. I'll let her tell the rest of the story."

The morning host moved to the side as the curtain opened and a gorgeous young woman emerged in a dress the color of the Mediterranean just after sunrise. The spotlight narrowed on her, drawing applause from the crowd. She started down the runway, a nervous smile lifting her features. Lina watched her progress until she was distracted by movement at the narrow gap between the curtains and the wall at the edge of the stage, a view she was afforded only because her seat was off to the side, rather than in the prime positions occupied by the VIPs in attendance.

With his fingers holding the edge of the curtain, Ivo stood watching Amira from backstage. The sweet expression of pride and admiration on his face was unlike any Lina had seen before.

Unbidden, tears sprung to her eyes. She propped her chin in her hand with two fingers splayed across her mouth to keep her reaction from being obvious to those around her.

Ivo Zanardi was unlike any man she'd ever known and unlike any she'd ever meet again.

CHAPTER 16

Lina sucked in her lower lip. This wasn't the time or place to get teary.

However, even from this distance, Ivo's tenderness for Amira was obvious. Though he was too far in the shadows for her to read his exact emotions, Lina could see that his eyes had narrowed into the thin lines of a man whose heart was involved in the scene before him. Then there was the subtle nod of his head as Amira started her walk, and the tight bunching of the stage curtain in his long fingers.

All Ivo's energy seemed concentrated on willing the young woman forward. Lina felt the emotions coursing through Ivo as powerfully as if he were a parent standing at the back of an elementary school auditorium, silently sending a wave of protective warmth toward a child who'd rehearsed endless hours for the lead in a play, knowing that the moment of their audition had arrived and they had one chance to prove themselves.

A youthful voice came over the sound system, dragging Lina's attention away from Ivo as additional photos of a young Amira graced the screen. First, sitting at the side of a dusty road on an upside-down crate, holding a boy nearly as big as she. Then, wearing a clean, long-sleeved white blouse and sitting at a table in a tented classroom, her head bent over a calculator and pad of paper.

We arrived at a refugee camp in Turkey with what we wore, enough of my grandfather's medicine to last a week, my parents' wedding photo, and copies of our birth certificates. We left behind our chickens. The tomatoes we'd planted three weeks earlier. All of our clothes and jewelry. Our friends and neighbors. My school. My books.

Two miles from camp, my sandals broke. I walked the last part barefoot. A man at camp saw my dirty feet and gave me his son's shoes. He didn't tell me what happened to his son and I was too shaken to ask. He showed us an empty tent with two folded blankets in the middle and told us to use it. We never saw him again.

We didn't know where we would go or how we would survive. We curled up in the middle of the tent to stay warm and we slept.

The next morning, a man and a woman from UNICEF came to our tent. A translator asked my mother what we needed. She was too scared to ask for anything, but they told us where to get food and made sure my grandfather saw one of the camp's doctors. Two days after that, the UNICEF people came back. They told my mother that I could go to school right there in the camp, starting that day. They also had a safe place for Ibrahim to play. My mother didn't cry, but when she told the UNICEF people we could go with them, she turned away so we couldn't see her face.

Other families from my village came to the camp that winter. We hoped they would have good news, but we learned we couldn't go home. Our house had been burned and the well poisoned.

Amira reached the end of the runway and the monitors transitioned to a photo of her standing in the square near Istanbul's Hagia Sofia mosque with her brother. They each carried messenger bags and appeared dressed for school.

The spotlight around her widened. Lina noticed then that Amira wore a microphone on the bodice of her dress.

"UNICEF made it possible for me to believe in my future," she told the crowd. "I was given what all children need to survive and to thrive:

food, clothing, shelter, and access to medical care. More than that, I was given an education and the opportunity to live up to my potential, which is crucial even in the most dire of circumstances. I could have easily been married off to an older man, sent to work, or worse. Instead, I learned math. I learned English. I read literature important to my own heritage, as well as many Western classics. I was given all the tools I needed to pursue my dreams, to make the world a better place, and to ensure that if I chose to do so, I could help other children who find themselves in the same situation I was in on the day I walked into a refugee camp carrying broken sandals. That education was—to me—as important as the tent that protected me from the cold and the food that kept me alive."

Amira's smile broadened with confidence as a photo of her standing on a hillside above the blue waters of the Bosphorus Strait lit the video screen. "UNICEF eventually helped us find a home in Turkey where my mother could work, my grandparents could live in safety, and my brother and I could continue to attend school. I applied to NYU and received a scholarship that helps to fund my education. I'm studying accounting and hope to work for UNICEF or another organization that educates children in developing countries.

"One thing I've learned as an accounting student is that resources are not infinite. That's where you come in. UNICEF can only continue its work when caring individuals and corporations are forward-looking, too. When you invest your time and your money in ensuring that UNICEF can continue its work in the years to come, we all benefit. Tonight's fashion show not only gives you the chance to see and purchase the latest in designer fashion, it gives you the opportunity to help people like me and my brother, Ibrahim."

Amira looked over her shoulder to where the morning host stood on the right side of the stage. Amira did a slow spin, then made her way back along the runway as the host described Amira's dress and noted that the designer hoped to sell enough to support fifty children at UNICEF camps for five years. "It's an audacious goal," the host claimed, "but no more audacious than the goals these children set for themselves. Amira is a great example."

As Amira disappeared stage left, the host noted that all the fashions being modeled would be included on a special page of the Mirabeau website, launching simultaneously with their presentation at the night's show. They'd also appear at specific Mirabeau locations for a limited time, with all proceeds going to UNICEF.

"Before we see the rest of tonight's spectacular designs, how about a big hand for Amira for being bold enough to lead off tonight's show, and for the cadre of designers who are donating their time, their creative brilliance, and all proceeds from these fashions directly to UNICEF?"

Cheers ripped through the room with enough enthusiasm to shake the seats. Lina was carried along for the ride, clapping for both the designers—whose effort she truly understood—as well as for Amira.

Again, Lina spotted Ivo in the gap between the curtains, his smile broad as he clapped for Amira. Even at this distance, she sensed his heartfelt appreciation for the young woman and her accomplishments. He radiated the pride of a parent who knew his child had blown the doors off their audition and earned the lead in the play, whether they were awarded the role or not.

Lina's heart squeezed as powerfully as when Ivo had held her gaze while making love to her. She exhaled and pressed a hand to her chest, willing away the sensation.

He committed to chicken.

Ivo's compassion for those who struggled to make the most of their potential ran deep. But Lina couldn't let the tone of the event color her perspective where Ivo was concerned. Yes, he was a good man—a man with a caring heart, a man who saw the best in others and encouraged them to pursue their goals, a man who led by example—but her relationship with Ivo was laid out.

Given where they were a month ago, or even a week ago, it'd be better for her to stay focused on enjoying the here and now.

The host introduced the next models, married television chefs well known to the New York crowd. The emotional mood set by Amira's appearance ratcheted to one of celebration as the pair took the stage, with the music shifting to a dance beat and the video screens showing images of children eating in the dining tent at a UNICEF-sponsored camp, then learning the basics of nutrition and sanitation as they worked alongside staff to prepare food.

The audience was carried along with the tempo, internalizing the message that by celebrating UNICEF here tonight and by enjoying the fashion show and making purchases, they'd make a difference in the world. At one point, Lina even pulled her phone from her pocket and ordered a sheer floral blouse sported by one of the models. When she tapped in her information, she caught Ivo's name in a hushed conversation from the reporters' direction. She completed her transaction seconds before Ivo took the stage to a roar of applause.

At his appearance, Lina remained silent, hands in her lap, breath caught in her throat as the room thundered around her. Unlike the celebrities who'd gone before him or the young people like Amira who'd walked the runway to support the organization that'd given them a hand up when they needed it, Ivo moved like he owned the boards. He wasn't the tallest of the models, nor was he the best-looking in the traditional sense. Rather, Ivo had charisma that radiated throughout the room. No doubt it was what drew that executive who'd spotted him selling shirts outside a Roman amphitheater and the dozens of other advertisers who'd hired him after that.

A woman seated behind Lina gasped, the sound one of unmistakable lust. Another female voice muttered, "I know."

Down the row from Lina, one of the reporters uttered to a friend, "They're going to sell out of that suit."

The screen lit with an overhead view of Ivo's car making an incredible outside pass on the Suzuka Circuit's famous 130R turn, then zoomed in as Ivo overtook another racer near the finish line. The emcee's voice blended with the noise of the engines.

Formula One is characterized by adrenaline-pumping races in such diverse locations as the Old World streets of Europe and the high-speed tracks of Japan, Canada, and Abu Dhabi. The danger and excitement of the sport attracts fans by the millions. Then there are the F1 drivers, known for their focus and determination. Ivo Zanardi is one of the circuit's top draws. As many of his admirers know, Ivo is a gritty competitor. He also modeled professionally in his teens. He's proud to walk the runway for UNICEF tonight.

Ivo aimed a shameless smile at the front rows, eliciting a burst of applause and a few whoops. Oh, he knew how to work the crowd. The lessons he'd learned posing for the print ads carried into his runway appearance tonight. Lina had seen him flash that same smile at F1 press conferences, using it to his advantage when he wanted to move reporters from one topic to another.

The man occupying the chair in front of Lina's leaned toward his wife. Speaking over the music, he told the petite brunette, "He might've made it bigger as a model than a driver."

She placed a hand on his knee, then gave him an easy smile, one full of flirtation. "I can tell you which I'd rather pay to see."

"You're paying to see the man model right now."

"As I said." Her eyes flashed. "Then again, he does know how to rev an engine."

The man eyes went dark as he shifted to give her a quick kiss. Lina bowed her head to hide her smile. She'd have to tell Ivo about the exchange later.

What many of Ivo's fans don't know is that he has a personal connection to UNICEF.

Ivo paused at the end of the runway, turning to show off the dark suit he wore. The immaculate cut of the fabric skimmed his torso to perfection. Holding the crowd mesmerized with the heat of his gaze, he unbuttoned the jacket, then slipped it from his shoulders. One of his knees appeared to buckle as he hooked the jacket on his index finger and flipped it over his shoulder, adopting a classic pose with the jacket dangling down his back. No one else seemed to notice and Ivo's demeanor didn't change, making Lina wonder if she'd imagined it.

Behind Ivo, on the screen, a tattered photograph of a teenage girl in a traditional dress and matching headgear made of bright green and blue patterned fabric. She stood behind a counter constructed of wood slats, proudly displaying a leather belt in her outstretched hands.

Ivo's mother, Noomi, was born and raised in a rural village in Nigeria, during a time when raids by warring factions hungry for terri-

tory and power were common. UNICEF provided the children in her village and others in the surrounding area with a safe place to continue their education. This photo was taken the month following her high school graduation. She was proud to have a job in Abuja, working at a stall that sold goods handmade by artisans in her village.

Today Noomi manages a bakery in Rome. The skills she learned in high school—skills that allowed her to make a living independently—wouldn't have been possible without UNICEF intervention.

Another photo appeared on the screen. It showed Ivo at around eight or nine years old, his eyes crossed and his fingers in his ears as he displayed a gap-toothed smile for the camera. His mother stood behind him, her gaze locked on something behind the camera as she laughed. It faded from the screen, followed by a photo of Ivo in a suit at what appeared to be his high school graduation. His mother stood beside him in a yellow dress and headgear suitable for the occasion, her chin held high and shoulders squared with pride.

Those skills allowed her to raise Ivo and ensure that he, too, had an education. Since his first paycheck, Ivo has given back to UNICEF. He's a valued member of his Formula One team, but we're delighted to have him on our team, too.

The emcee appeared onstage to describe Ivo's suit and the designer behind the sleek creation. Ivo moved with his cues, spinning to demonstrate the cut of the slacks across his backside, the fit at the waist, and the ease with which a man would wear it.

Again, Lina could swear she saw Ivo bobble. This time, however, his face changed. He blinked twice, then turned toward the curtain at stage left, where Amira exited following her walk. The emcee was midway through her pitch for Mirabeau's tailoring services—complimentary with the purchase of the suit—when the jacket slipped from Ivo's hand.

He dropped to his knees, then pitched face-first to the runway.

Ivo blinked at the harsh, unfamiliar light directly over his head. It was surrounded by the gridded panels of a drop ceiling.

He blinked again, squeezing his eyes harder this time. Snippets of a baseball game came to his ears. A television announcer talked pitch count not far from the bed…but not *his* bed. The mattress wasn't as pliable and he lay on top of the sheet rather than beneath it. The whole place smelled wrong. Not his detergent. Not Lina's.

He was propped slightly, not prone.

Hospital.

He ground out a curse as the memory came to him. The vertigo that struck as the spotlight tracked his movements along the catwalk. Tapping into muscle memory so his body would move, turn, and display the clothes in the performance the crowd expected while his mind fought to stay alert and finish the job.

He'd managed the alert part. Finishing the job, not so much. Even as he'd gone to his knees, he heard the crowd gasp behind him. His stomach pitched and he almost got a hand down on the floor before his face hit. Almost.

Noise had surrounded him as he pushed to his knees. The hem of the heavy stage curtain bobbed in his vision as he insisted he was all right, had simply taken a misstep. He'd managed a smile and a wave for the crowd, attempting to play off the episode while Caleb arrived at his elbow.

"Stay close so I don't fall over but don't make it obvious."

Caleb had acknowledged the request with a look, then waved to the crowd and yelled, "He's good!" before waving backstage and asking for a towel to clean the floor, acting as if it were a basketball court in need of a sweat wipe in order to prevent players from slipping.

The college student directed Ivo to a chair as soon as they were safely behind the curtain. On the stage, the host cracked a joke about the slick flooring before making a smooth transition to the next models, women who worked at a camp in Ecuador.

In that moment, Ivo had been grateful they'd recruited an adept morning host, one whose professional career revolved around her ability to steer a broadcast when it went into a sudden skid.

"I'm calling an ambulance."

"No—"

"We can be discreet. There's a parking garage under the building. It can pull alongside the elevator."

"Private car. Less showy. I don't want anyone out there" —he'd waved in the general direction of the stage— "to know I've left the show." Especially the sports reporters. He'd recognized a couple who covered Formula One.

"I'll see what I can do. Mirabeau's insurance might require me to call an ambulance."

Another protest died on the tip of his tongue as he'd slipped on the chair, nearly ending up on the floor. Every time he'd moved his head, patches of black spread across his field of vision. "All right. Do what you have to. As long as I go under my own power. No stretcher. I'll meet them."

"Done."

The single word had conveyed understanding Ivo hadn't expected. He'd put a hand on Caleb's arm. "Find a way to get the woman in seat 308 to the hospital. But no reporters."

"Done."

Caleb had accomplished the first request, recruiting another intern to drive Ivo to the hospital in a borrowed Toyota. Ivo had hope the young man could pull off the second. He'd waited until he'd sat through a half hour in the emergency room, a discussion of his recent medical history with a nurse, then the annoyance of a CT scan before he dared ask if anyone had come for him.

"There's a woman in the ER waiting room. Said her name is—"

She'd looked at another nurse, who finished with, "Dina, I think."

Lina.

"Can she come here?"

"Is she family? We have a family-only policy—"

Ivo had given the nurse an of-course-she's-family look, but said only, "That would be wonderful. Thank you."

"I'll find her."

Ivo blinked at the overhead light once more, then ran a hand over his eyes to clear them of grit, but the fog remained in his brain, if not his vision.

He rolled his head, saw a curtain to his left. A low moan came from the other side. Still in the ER, then. He hadn't been moved into a room.

"I know you hate hospitals, but it's not so bad this time," Lina's voice floated to him.

He turned her direction, but a black mist clouded his eyes for several seconds before it receded enough for him to see Lina's full mouth curved into a smile. She sat on a metal folding chair wedged between the side of his bed and the wall.

Now he remembered. After the CT scan, the nurse who'd offered to find "Dina" guided him past a row of curtained-off bays and had him lie down in the farthest. She'd drawn the curtain, then promised the doctor would be back shortly. He must've drifted off after talking to the nurse.

"Definitely not."

He hesitated before asking, "How long have you been here?"

"Only a minute or two. One of the nurses came to the waiting room and had me follow her. Not sure I could find my way back there. It's like a rabbit warren in here."

"Do you need to find your way back there?"

"No." Her hand clasped his. Warm, reassuring. "The nurse said you had a CT scan."

It already seemed ages ago. "They're being cautious, given my medical history. I was lightheaded during the show."

"I know."

"I imagine everyone knows. So much for my grand plan for using this week to draw positive attention to Isola and to convince the world I'm perfectly healthy."

"Well, the first part succeeded. And you did a reasonable job of faking a fall."

"Reasonable. Not convincing."

"Not entirely. Not when it's on video for everyone to play on repeat."

"Thank you. That's the reassurance I needed."

Her laughter soothed the worry. "The crowd had the impression that your mishap wasn't serious. And before I left, one of the models tried to take off his jacket and spin the way you did and ended up tangled for a solid ten seconds. I imagine his performance helped you off the hook."

"Who was it?"

"Someone from an American sitcom. Not a show I've seen, but the audience all knew him."

Ivo had met the man backstage. "He's a comedian. It may have been intentional."

"Intentional or not, it means people are less likely to remember your bobble."

Bobble. That was one word for it. With any luck, the coverage wouldn't rise to a level that would cause his sponsors to doubt his comeback. Of course, it all depended on what doctors said after they analyzed his scan.

He flicked a look at the clock. "Did the nurse tell you when the doctor would be in?"

"The doctor is in now." A lanky brunette with impossibly large breasts and hair almost short enough to be described as a buzz cut strolled through the gap in the curtain with an open laptop computer cradled in one arm. "Just got the results of your scan."

She introduced herself to Lina as Dr. Rademacher, then focused on Ivo. "You don't remember meeting me when you arrived?"

He didn't, though now that she spoke, her voice sounded familiar. "You came in right after the nurse took my blood pressure," he fudged. "What's the update?"

She moved beside the bed and spun her computer so Ivo could see. First, she pointed out a spot he knew was the result of his crash, one she'd studied in records forwarded to her from San Rimini while he was getting his scan. "I'm glad you were coherent enough when you arrived to discuss your prior injuries or I'd have been rather alarmed by this."

He was glad he'd been that alert, too. The fact he couldn't remember the discussion, though…that wasn't good.

Was she aware? If so, her expression gave no clue. Her features were arranged into the same inscrutable look most doctors perfected early in their careers.

"I don't think your prior injuries are the issue, though they may be a contributing factor." One dark brow lifted. "Given what we discussed earlier, and what I'm seeing now, I'm inclined to believe what happened today was self-inflicted."

CHAPTER 17

"When I hear 'self-inflicted' I think gunshot wound," he told her.

Dr. Rademacher's smile was polite, as if she'd heard the line a hundred times before when she told a patient their issue was their own fault. "You're extremely fit, Mr. Zanardi. Low blood pressure. Low heart rate. Those are typically good things to have. However, I suspect a blood draw would show your blood sugar level as very low. When's the last time you ate? Or drank anything besides water?"

"Noon." A protein bar.

"Nearly twelve hours. That's a long time."

Longer than she thought, given that breakfast had been a double espresso. Not his typical daily diet, but he'd been tired after a long day yesterday and slept late. He'd gone for a run after awakening simply to boost his energy levels. He'd even kept it short. After the episode by the basketball court in Greenwich Village, he hadn't wanted to overtax himself, particularly when combined with the physical therapy sessions he'd completed this week.

On the other hand, he'd craved a run through Central Park before flying back to Europe and this morning was his only opportunity. He hadn't been hungry afterward. He'd forced himself to eat a protein bar, showered, then made several overdue work calls before heading to the venue for the Mirabeau show.

"I forgot. I did eat something backstage, just before the show." At Dr. Rademacher's questioning look, he admitted, "A few pretzels."

"You need more fuel than that." She set her laptop on a rolling table, then slid her hands into the pockets of her white coat. "I imagine, given the physical training you do, you're well aware of your caloric needs. Have you had an episode like this before?"

"Nothing like this, no."

The vertigo he'd experienced earlier that week hadn't been quite the same. Then again, he'd been able to stop and lean on a fence.

"Ever had a day where you've eaten so little in relation to the activity you've done?"

He shook his head. He hadn't eaten much the day of that run to Greenwich Village, but it had been more than today.

"The stage lights and adrenaline rush of the evening were likely contributing factors. Given that, I don't think there's anything concerning here, nothing long term, at least. Let's get you some food and hydration. If you're feeling better after that you'll be free to go. When are you scheduled to return home?"

"Tomorrow."

"As long as you feel back to normal, that shouldn't be a problem. I've already forwarded my report and tonight's scan to your regular physician. He says he'll be in touch once he's reviewed them and that he'll likely want to see you to ensure nothing is being overlooked."

Ivo would like to see him, too. He wanted to believe Dr. Rademacher, but instinct told him there could be more to it. He'd spent too much time in hospitals over the past year to believe himself invincible the way he had when he'd first started racing.

"You spoke to him? Italy is six hours ahead."

"When I called the hospital, they got him on the line. He happened to be working the early shift."

"I'll call Monday if I don't hear from him first."

"Good. In the meantime, my advice is to take it easy. No intense physical activity for the next few days. If you start to feel lightheaded, get to the nearest doctor. All right?"

The thought of being sidelined again, even temporarily, rankled, but he murmured in agreement and offered his thanks.

"She seemed competent," he told Lina once they were alone behind the curtain. "Of course, my opinion of the hospital on the whole depends on what they bring for food."

Suddenly, he was ravenous. The doctor was correct on that count. A few hundred calories wasn't enough fuel for him, not given his lean mass or his daily energy expenditure. Even thinking about food made his stomach twist with hunger.

When Lina didn't respond, he frowned. "You look worried."

"Of course I'm worried. You are, too." Her voice was modulated so the patients in the adjacent beds couldn't hear. "I'm always going to be worried about your health, but this is more than that."

When he waited for her to continue, her lips drew into a thin line. "You didn't tell the doctor, but you're concerned that what happened to you tonight is more serious than missing a meal. As worrying as health issues are to most people, your health is also the key to your career. Your dreams." Her eyes shone as she continued, "I know what it's like to worry that your dream could slip away due to forces beyond your control. I know how concerned you are."

"But you aren't going to lecture me about taking care of myself. Or tell me to reconsider my career plans." It was a statement of fact rather than an accusation.

"Never." The metal chair creaked as she recrossed her legs and braced her palms on the edge. "Look, Ivo, from the time I learned what you do for a living and understood how dangerous it is, I've worried. Flying through the streets, taking tight corners at high speed…it's crazy. But it's also your passion."

Her grip tightened on the chair. "I understand what it's like to want something that doesn't make sense to people around you. Dozens of people told me that leaving a steady job at a prominent design house— a job I was very fortunate to get in the first place—and investing all my savings into starting my own business was crazy. That the odds were against me. That the field was already too crowded, that I didn't have the skills or the business acumen or the connections it would take to succeed. And, if I did succeed, I'd likely have to hand over management to someone else."

"They were wrong." He shifted onto one hip so he could face her.

"They were wrong. Though if more contracts come through, there will come a point where I can't do it all."

"You'd give up management?"

"It'd be a leap of faith, trusting my company—my career and everything I've built—to someone else, but yes. Once the company gets to a certain point, I'll need to choose whether I want to design or manage if I want it to continue to grow. And I'd choose design." She sighed. "A sign of success, right? We all have to make these choices, to conquer our fear of the unknown. If we don't, we stagnate. So far be it from me to lecture you about your health or tell you to reconsider your career plans. No matter what the doctors say, positive or negative, you'll find a way to accomplish what you set out to do. If you decide to shift your goals, you'll find new and loftier ones. But you're literally in the driver's seat. It's your life. No one else's. You'll do what's right for you. I can't imagine doing anything but supporting you."

He extended a hand. How had he ever found such a miraculous woman? And in Heathrow, of all places? When she placed her hand in his, he squeezed. "Thank you."

"It's exactly what you'd do for me. What you've already done for me."

"I was an idiot to throw you out of my hospital room."

"I was an idiot for failing to trust you."

"You had your reasons." He raised her hand and leaned far enough to place a kiss on her knuckles. He expected the dizziness to kick in, but it didn't. When he met Lina's gaze, he saw nothing but tenderness. "She supported you when you wanted to start your own business."

Lina's eyes widened as she realized who he meant. "She and Papa both did. He passed away before the boutique opened, but my mother was there the day I signed the lease. She didn't cringe at the rent or what I paid the contractor to refurbish the space. She said I'd picked the perfect location and told me what she liked about the design plans. She even went around the place cleaning while I set up the initial window display."

He remembered. Lina had mentioned it one weekend when they'd been in Belgium, enjoying lunch at a lakeside bistro before she caught a flight to Milan. He'd noticed Lina watching a man washing windows on a nearby shop, a contemplative look on her face, and asked her about it. She'd described her mother's attempt to clean the windows at Isola using an overturned shipping crate in place of a proper stepladder.

It had sounded like the kind of thing his own mother would do. She'd never let a mess go uncleaned, even if the necessary materials were in short supply.

"Next time you're faced with a customer like Dottie or you're questioned by a *DayBuzz*-type reporter, hold on to that memory. It'll keep the bitterness at bay and remind you of what's important."

Her eyes went glossy, but no tears spilled. She angled her chin and considered him. "You're in a hospital bed, you haven't eaten all day, and I'm here for the express purpose of comforting you. Yet somehow, you're the one comforting me."

"Give it time. I'm sure you'll have the opportunity to repay the favor."

Such a statement should've been filled with flirtation, a teasing of what would happen when they found themselves alone in the darkest hours of the night. Instead, his words held a serious note. A promise of something larger, more substantive. It wasn't what he'd intended, but he didn't regret it, either.

Lina stilled, her lips parted slightly, as if she were planning to lean over the bed and kiss him. Footsteps echoed on the linoleum nearby, then turned in their direction.

"I will give you one piece of advice," Lina whispered as she withdrew her hand and straightened in the metal chair. "Whatever food they offer, eat it."

LINA GAVE the hired driver the address for the Park Hyatt, then settled against the soft leather of the back seat as they departed the hospital's pick up area. Ivo's hand found her thigh within seconds.

Calm washed over her at the familiar touch. Given that her heart hadn't stopped racing from the time she saw Ivo tumble on the runway until he'd spoken to her in the emergency room, his brain clear enough that he grasped the time difference from New York to Rome, it was much-needed reassurance.

Orange juice and a sandwich had steadied him. Fifteen minutes after he'd eaten, the nurse checked his vitals and declared him fit to leave. In Lina's nonprofessional assessment, he looked much better. Ivo had popped out of the emergency room bed with the same ease as he did upon waking in the morning, but Lina caught the flicker of doubt in his eyes before he kicked his legs over the side and planted them on the floor. He'd been uncertain.

She'd exited the hospital beside him, giving no indication she'd noticed.

As much as she'd told him she wouldn't stand in the way of his dreams, everything in her feared for him. Even if he wouldn't admit it to the doctor, Ivo believed tonight's runway stumble to be more than a case of low blood sugar. He wanted to race—*needed* to race for his own mental health—and he was willing to do anything to get back in the driver's seat.

That scared her, even if she understood his instinct. What if he blacked out behind the wheel?

As the hired SUV slowed for a red light, she reminded herself that such a scenario was highly unlikely. Ivo had several weeks of physical therapy, time in the simulator, and a required medical clearance before he got behind the wheel again. If tonight's episode was his new reality rather than a fluke, it'd be apparent to his entire team long before he slipped into his racing gear.

She stole a glance at Ivo. He was so controlled, so responsible. Even without the checks in place, he wouldn't climb into the cockpit if he wasn't fit to do so. But what would it do to his psyche to sit on the sidelines?

She placed her hand over Ivo's and threaded her fingers through his as his thumb stretched to caress the inside of her thigh. If she were honest, her deepest fear was for herself. For her heart. After losing both her parents in the space of a couple years, she couldn't lose Ivo, too.

Being told he couldn't race again—or facing facts and admitting it to himself before either his doctor or Scuderia Ferrari did it for him— would change him. And that would change them.

She tightened her hold on Ivo's hand. There'd been a world of promise in his gaze just before the nurse entered to offer him the sand-wich. She'd marveled at the fact that he'd comforted her despite being the one in the hospital bed, then he'd promised she could pay him back later without so much as a wink.

The seriousness in his tone had shaken her as badly as seeing him pass out. It was a look that told her he was thinking of the future, not merely fun and excitement in the here and now.

Much as her emotional side craved that, her logical side knew it wasn't wise. Banking on a long-term, committed relationship with Ivo could leave her with a heart broken even more badly, more painfully, than when she'd left that hospital in San Rimini with the words *get out and leave me alone* ringing in her ears.

"No one saw us leaving the hospital." Ivo's voice was so low, Lina barely heard his words. "Caleb earned his intern badge tonight."

"The man who found me at the show?"

Ivo nodded. "He's working at Mirabeau for the summer. He was backstage tonight, keeping the participants on schedule. He's the one who arranged my transportation to the hospital."

"He did a good job."

"Everyone backstage tonight did." His thumb moved up and down along her thigh. "What did you think of Amira, the first person to walk the runway?"

"Stunning." The word came instantly to mind at the mention of her name. "She had the audience's full attention when she walked onstage. Then, when she spoke..." Lina glanced at Ivo as she struggled to put her thoughts into words. "She's been through so much, yet her attitude remains optimistic. She has charisma, but it's understated. Not flashy.

She strikes me as the kind of person who will change the lives of a lot of people for the better."

Ivo made a low sound of agreement. "We spoke at the rehearsal and again backstage tonight. What you saw onstage wasn't a performance. Her ability to look forward inspires me. And you're right. I do think she'll change people's lives."

A taxi full of laughing twentysomethings pulled alongside them at a light. As if on instinct, Ivo angled his body toward Lina to keep them from seeing him through the window. "I hope it came across to the audience that UNICEF offers practical help to children in situations like Amira's."

"I left with that message. I imagine others did, too. And to see that Amira is building her future on helping others—"

"What an impact she'll have." His tone was low, respectful.

"Exactly." Lina angled her head and waited for him to meet her gaze. "You have an impact, too."

"Not like that." His jaw tightened. "Maybe when I retire."

She started to tell him that he had an impact now, but his phone buzzed. Frowning, he glanced at the screen as their car moved forward, pulling away from the taxi.

"Team doctor," he told her. "He wants to know when I'll return."

Lina gestured for Ivo to go ahead answer. While he did, a text appeared on Lina's phone. The name made her breath catch.

"You made the morning news in Europe. Well," she corrected herself, "in Sarcaccia. The woman I met at the coffee shop wishes you well."

Ivo glanced at the driver, who didn't appear to be listening, then looked at Lina. "That's kind of her."

"Perhaps." Or she saw the opportunity to insert herself into Lina's life and took it.

"Good for you, giving her the benefit of the doubt," he teased, reading her mind. "I still say you should consider her offer."

She was about to retort when Ivo's phone screen lit with a new message. "They want me to follow up with a neurologist in Rome."

He didn't sound as surprised as she'd expect. "That's rather inconvenient. Why not your regular doctor in Milan? Or one of the specialists who treated you in San Rimini?"

"He's worked with several teams over the years. Understands the sport, the nature of head injuries that can occur. Good man." Ivo typed back his response, then smiled at Lina. "I saw him for follow-up tests after I was released from the hospital, so he'll know if there have been any changes. I imagine this will turn out to be nothing."

The car nosed around a corner and the Park Hyatt came into view. Ivo pocketed his phone and resumed his caress of her knee. "So much for switching my flight home so I can join you on yours. On the other hand, this means I can deliver my mother's tea and cookies in person, which is probably for the best. If I made the news in Sarcaccia, I'll have made the news in Rome. She'll want to see for herself that I'm fine."

Lina eyed his hand as it moved higher on her thigh. "You're not *that* fine."

"Benefit of all the training I do. It improves my recovery time."

As Ivo rasped out the words, Lina caught the driver sneaking a look at them in his mirror. The older man cleared his throat. "The Park Hyatt is just ahead."

Ivo thanked him, but his attention never left Lina. The desire in his eyes was enough to tell her all the wicked things he wanted to do.

She placed her hand on top of his, slowing its progress even as desire rolled through her. She kept her voice to a whisper. "Recently, an impossibly attractive gentleman walked me to my condo, gave me a kiss goodnight, then left even when I wanted him to stay. Even when *he* wanted to stay. He did it because he knew it was what I needed that night."

"Did he?" Ivo's dark brow lifted. He waited. When he realized she wouldn't relent, he said, "He knew there would be other nights."

She squeezed his fingers. "When will you be in Milan again?"

"As soon as I can."

Her heart fluttered at the assurance, but reason kept her from kissing him goodbye quite yet. "Things will be different."

"Better."

"Between us, yes, thanks to you." He'd been bold that first day, dragging her to the hotel, and she'd always be grateful. Her gaze drifted to a group of people in formal wear standing outside the Park Hyatt, exchanging hugs before they climbed into the cars waiting to take them home from whatever event they'd attended. "But—"

"Now it's out there."

"Yes." Even if her relationship with Ivo escaped scrutiny tonight, their bubble of privacy wouldn't last. Particularly not in Europe, where Ivo was recognized nearly everywhere he went.

"We'll handle it. As long as we each know what we want, as long as we continue to communicate, nothing can go wrong." His thumb dragged along the back of her hand. "Let's promise each other that, shall we?"

She nodded, aware that if they'd been more open, they'd have avoided the blowup in San Rimini.

Ivo closed the gap between them and gave her a kiss that appeared perfectly acceptable should the driver look in his mirror, yet his touch on her thigh carried an intensity that pledged more in the days to come.

A half hour later, when she arrived at the condo and opened her laptop to check in for her flight to Milan, she prayed Ivo was right.

Then she prayed she could keep what she wanted in sync with what Ivo wanted.

CHAPTER 18

ASIDE FROM WAKING in Lina's bed or climbing atop a podium following a Grand Prix, Ivo's favorite activity had to be walking the streets of Rome in the early hours of a Sunday morning. Not a soul moved in the streets, but the air was alive with sound. Birds chirped, cathedral bells tolled, and—if one listened carefully—a low rush of water could be heard from a nearby fountain or sewer.

In Ivo's mind, the liquid melody always indicated the presence of a fountain. When he did think of the sewer, it was with a mind to Rome's ancient history and the millions who'd walked these streets in the centuries prior to his arrival.

Ivo glanced sideways at a bird fluffing its feathers in a nearby puddle, then turned his attention to wiggling his key in the lock of a graffitied, stucco-clad building on a narrow side street in Rome's historic district, cursing the owner as he did so. He'd sent the man money to replace the lock with a keypad, but it hadn't been done. Everything with the landlord was promised tomorrow. Had been for decades.

Ivo looked over his shoulder at the building across the street, which had the same owner. It was in even worse shape.

Shaking his head, he returned his attention to the lock.

The district was high rent, but in the days after Noomi Zanardi and her husband separated, she'd managed to find a one-room flat in one of the few affordable buildings in the neighborhood, sacrificing space and reliable fixtures in order to raise her young son close to Villa Borghese's expansive park and the adjacent city zoo. The area was also within walking distance of the bakery, allowing her to save on transportation, and offered access to a quality school. He couldn't fault his mother the location.

Ivo grumbled as he withdrew the key, then reinserted it.

It had been a battle to move her into this two-bedroom across the street from their original studio. Even then, she'd insisted on a place that skimmed the line of habitability, in Ivo's opinion. It wasn't that he cared what people would think of him when they saw that his mother lived in this building, rather than one of the dozens of updated places that surrounded it, because the neighbors knew he could certainly afford it. It was—he swore as he finally managed to open the door—that she deserved better. After a lifetime of hard work, he wanted her to live in comfort. He wanted her to have a caring landlord so she could see the difference. To know what life was like with well-insulated walls, burners that didn't require knob-jiggling, and a shower head free of rust.

Ivo took the stairs by twos, taking care not to smack the bag he carried into the wall as he climbed.

He wondered if his mother would ever move. He doubted it. Once she'd separated from her husband and established herself, she'd resisted change. She kept the same job, same neighborhood, and same friendships.

He sidestepped a missing square of tile and told himself the building was fine, given that the ceiling didn't leak and he'd never once spied a rat. It was safe. The residents were kind. And though the landlord was a stubborn old man, he kept the rent reasonable. With that in mind, Ivo resolved not to nag her about moving to a nicer place. If she was content, it should be good enough for him.

On the final flight, he spied the familiar ceramic umbrella stand and patterned yellow rug outside her door.

It'd been at least two years since he'd surprised his mother. Last time, she'd been giddy at his appearance. He'd planned it for one of her days off. They'd spent the afternoon chatting in her flat before enjoying a leisurely dinner at her favorite restaurant. She'd regaled him with stories about tourists and regulars who visited the bakery and talked endlessly about the young family who'd moved into the flat below hers. Given that it was her day off again—a day she often spent cleaning her flat or running errands—he hoped his impromptu visit would be welcome rather than an inconvenience.

The bag of tea and cookies he'd brought from New York might compensate if she wasn't as thrilled as he expected.

The low rumble of a male voice came from behind the door a split second before Ivo's knuckles connected with the wood. He stepped back to wait, wondering if the landlord had finally come to repair the broken vent in her entry hall or if one of the neighbors stopped by.

Then again, it was only eight in the morning. Decades of bakery shifts meant his mother rose before dawn, even when she wasn't working, but he'd never known her to have early guests. Nor was the landlord the type to drag himself here on a Sunday morning.

An unfamiliar face greeted Ivo when the door opened. A barrel-chested man Ivo guessed to be in his late fifties to early sixties looked at him in astonishment, though the reaction was quickly concealed by a stern nod. He was clean-shaven and smelled of toothpaste. The long-sleeved shirt, neat trousers, and leather loafers he wore made it appear he was heading to work or Sunday mass. Ivo would bet on the latter.

The man stepped out of the way so Ivo could see his mother. Her shock at his appearance wasn't as well-masked as the gentleman's.

"Ivo! I didn't know you were coming. I thought you were in New York."

"I flew in on the redeye. I have an appointment near the University of Rome this afternoon and decided to surprise you with tea and cookies. I can come back later if now is inconvenient."

The man slipped past Ivo with more grace than Ivo would've attributed to someone of his build. "No, no. I am now leaving. You visit your mother, yes?"

He cast an undecipherable look at Noomi and told her in Italian he'd see her soon, then disappeared down the stairs.

Ivo listened to the retreating footsteps and waited for the stairwell's entry door to slam shut before speaking again. "Truly, I can come later—"

His mother's stern look silenced him. He stepped into the entry area, placed his shoes beside hers on the wooden rack she kept to the side of the door, then followed her to the flat's compact kitchen. Nothing had changed in the months since he'd last visited, when he'd come for a week at her insistence following his discharge from the hospital in San Rimini. Even the fruit bowl she kept on the counter appeared the same, with precisely three apples and five bananas, her usual Saturday afternoon market purchase.

There was no sign of the mystery man's presence. No men's jackets on the coat tree or the back of the chair in the kitchen, no dishes indicating he'd eaten breakfast with her. Beyond the kitchen, the living space contained a sofa and two chairs, each sided by book-laden tables. A cozy crocheted afghan occupied its usual spot across the back of the sofa. The throw pillows on either end were the same as when he was a youth. The only things that ever changed were the book titles as his mother consumed story after story: thrillers, romances, mysteries, classics. She preferred reading to television, claiming that game shows were ridiculous and the news only made a person frustrated over situations beyond their control.

His gaze lingered on one of the spines. Rather than English, this title was in Italian. A favorite romance novel she'd read a half-dozen times before…in English.

A million questions went through Ivo's mind, each dismissed before he could voice them. Finally, he settled on a statement. "My appointment was booked at the last minute. I should have called first."

She extended a hand toward him, palm to the ceiling, in a silent request for the bag. "What kind of appointment is it?"

"Neurologist." He looped the handles of the paper bag over her outstretched fingers. "Nothing of concern. Ferrari always wants to double- and triple-check my health so I'm at peak performance when I drive."

"Everything is still on schedule to return next season?"

"Yes." After each meeting with Ferrari and his trainers, he'd called her to give her updates, both on his health and his plans.

She frowned. "Why on a Sunday?"

"Privacy, I assume. When I told Ferrari I could get here this morning, they said the neurologist would see me this afternoon."

She placed the bag sideways on the counter so she could look inside. Interest lit her gaze as she selected a box of tea and read the label.

"Does it meet with your approval?"

"I'll tell you once I've had a taste." She sniffed the box and gave him a rare smile. "Bergamot. I imagine I will enjoy it."

"That was my thought when I saw it. The shop came highly recommended."

Her smile dimmed. "You didn't spend too much?"

"It's tea."

"I would say you shouldn't have, but I won't." She set the box on the counter and placed her hands on her hips. "I don't mind a surprise visit every now and then, but what you should have done is call me from New York to tell me about your health. You passed out."

"It was a stumble. There was no—"

"Maria saw it on the Internet and asked me how you were doing. I pretended I knew all about it and told her it was of no concern." She gestured toward the door and the flat across the hall from hers, where Maria the Gossip lived, then reached into the bag to retrieve the cookies. "So is it of no concern?"

"If you'd let me finish?"

She harrumphed.

"I had a dizzy spell during the UNICEF show. I did *not* pass out. I went to the hospital afterward out of an abundance of caution. The doctor in New York thought it was a simple case of low blood sugar. I hadn't eaten all day, I went for a run, then I went on stage. Bright lights, no food, you get the idea. The appointment today is to be certain."

Her look of irritation prompted him to ask, "What?"

"You still should have called."

"It was less than forty-eight hours ago and I didn't think the situation warranted it." At her look of censure, he flashed a genuine expression of contrition. "In the future, if a similar situation arises, I will."

"Good."

She reached into the cabinet and withdrew a plate, one she'd owned as long as he could remember and continued to use despite its chipped edges. Long ago, he'd offered to buy her a new set. Nothing fancy, he told her, just newer. Predictably, she'd refused. As with everything in her life, his mother thrived on efficiency and hated waste. She'd use the plate until it broke in half. She'd even told him she had a few that were in better condition set aside for when the neighbors came to tea.

"It's too early for tea and cookies, but I'll leave this out so it's ready when we return," she said, placing the cookies beside the plate, then adding two napkins and her favorite teacups to the collection. "I need to visit the druggist. Would it draw attention if you walked with me?"

"No one seemed to notice when I arrived, but the streets are still empty. I'll find a hat in the front closet."

When they exited the building, his mother turned left, rather than right. He made a point of looking the other direction. "Did you change pharmacies?"

"The druggist doesn't open until ten. We'll circle the park and talk first."

They kept to small talk as they approached the park, discussing recent changes to the neighborhood. It wasn't long until they reached the expansive space and its packed gravel paths. They turned away from the Galleria Borghese, where tourists had already congregated to view the museum's art and architecture, and headed for the park's center. Locals meandered through the grass with their dogs and a souvenir vendor pulled a cart toward his usual shaded location along one of the park's central paths. Otherwise, the primary sounds were those of the birds.

Ivo savored the lush green scent of the park. It would be a lovely day. Hot later, but that was Rome in June.

"You wish to know who he is."

His teeth clenched. Ivo made a conscious effort to relax his jaw before replying, "He's your business. Not mine."

She moved closer, then slid her hand into the space between his elbow and his side. He bent his elbow, hoping she didn't notice his split second of hesitation. Noomi Zanardi had never been one to hold a man's arm while she walked, even Ivo's. "It is time for you to know. You have a partner in your life now. I want you to understand mine."

She couldn't have astonished him more if she'd body-slammed him against the nearest tree. He nodded, simultaneously wanting to know and not wanting to know.

"Your father and I never divorced."

"I didn't believe you had."

"I suggested it a few times, years ago, but he does not wish to make the effort. He believes it will violate his faith and that it is easier to continue as we are. He has a woman in his life—has had many women in his life—and as far as I know, he is happy."

"And that's not a violation of his faith?"

"That is between him and God." She shrugged. "I don't wish to fight him. It would be very expensive—"

"I have the money."

She shook her head. "It would also cause me a lot of stress. After all this time, and given who you are, it could become public. That would mean more stress. The way things are now, no one asks. No one cares." She cast a sideways look at Ivo. "I haven't spoken to your father in over ten years. There has been no need. He keeps in touch with you and that is enough for me."

The sound of bells cascaded from a nearby cathedral as Ivo absorbed that information. He'd ceased asking his parents about each other when he was in grade school. While he'd sent cards to his father over the years, and his father had done the same for him, their conversations never went deeper than that. And Ivo had other topics to discuss with his mother than a man who'd exited her life more than thirty years prior.

"Do you want a divorce?"

She sighed, but he let the question hang. Only the sound of their footfalls and the rustling of a nearby squirrel broke the silence. Finally, she told him, "What is important is what is in my heart. God knows my heart. He knows that your father and I have been divorced in our hearts for many, many years, even if we have not divorced in the eyes of the law and the church."

She slowed her pace as the path widened to circle a fountain. A young boy sat on the edge and stretched his fingers to the water as his father watched from a nearby bench. Ivo smiled at the boy, then guided his mother around the fountain in the opposite direction.

His mother's fingers flexed in the crook of his elbow. "I have been seeing Placido for three years now. We keep separate flats, but he stays with me most Saturday nights. We understand each other." Before Ivo could ask, she continued, "Placido is a widower. He and his wife were married for twenty-two years and raised three children. He is close to them, but doubts they would be comfortable seeing him with another woman. They do not ask and do not wish to know. To them, he is *Nonno*. A grandfather, a respectable man with a simple life. He wishes to keep it that way."

"You could have told me before."

"You did not wish to know."

He frowned at that. "Did you *want* to tell me?"

A mischievous smile lit her face, one he rarely saw. It was the same expression she'd get when he was a child, playing in the park with his friends, and she'd open her cooler to reveal not only water, but ice pops. Now that expression was reserved for gossipy moments during social times with her friends or when she knew she had him beat at cards.

"Yes, I did. However, I am the parent, so I will turn this on you, Ivo. Why haven't you told me about Lina Cornaro?"

CHAPTER 19

Ivo nearly choked. "You never asked me about Lina. Not for details, anyway. I mentioned I was seeing someone, but I assumed you, ah, didn't wish to know more."

She shook his arm. "You know better than that. I always want to know about what is happening in your life. You didn't tell me because you didn't want my opinion."

He started to argue, but stopped before a single word left his mouth. His mother was right.

"Every big decision you've made, you've asked my opinion," she continued. "When you started modeling, I told you what I thought of the people who hired you. You listened to me. I made sure you signed decent contracts. That you worked with honest people."

"And avoided some awful ones." His mother's instincts had been dead-on when it came to charlatans.

"Yes. But as you did more and more modeling, I allowed you to make some of those decisions, I wanted you to learn and grow, as a parent should. So when you told me you wanted quit modeling to race, I bit my tongue."

"I knew what you thought. Your face told me all I needed to know."

"I thought the risk was too great. You were making a good income, meeting important people." Emotion deepened her voice. "You're handsome, but you're also very likable and intelligent, Ivo. I knew that if you stayed with modeling, you'd have opportunities within that industry, opportunities other models do not have because they are not so smart or personable. Opportunities that would mean your security."

She lifted her chin to indicate a narrower path, one that twisted beneath a canopy of trees and carried them away from the more crowded areas of the park. As church services started in some places and concluded in others, more people would indulge in a Sunday stroll.

"It wasn't only your financial future that worried me, Ivo. Kart racing frightened me. That fear did not go away when you moved to faster and faster cars. It only got worse."

He'd known all of this, simply by knowing his mother. It'd grated on him for years, driving an unspoken wedge between them. "Why didn't you say any of that?"

"You didn't want to hear it and it wouldn't have changed your mind. In fact, you're never more determined than when you know I disagree with you."

He couldn't argue with her there. The times he was most aggressive on the track—and reckless—were those early days when her disapproval was palpable, even if she never gave voice to it.

"You believed I was too careful with money," she continued. "You saw what modeling did for your bank balance and had no concept of how quickly it could disappear. How difficult it might be to start over if you changed your mind about racing. You would have dismissed my opinions about it."

They rounded a corner. In a grassy area between trees, a young couple sat atop a blanket, watching as their toddler daughter pushed a tiny stroller nearby. A bedraggled doll occupied the seat. Ivo and Noomi nodded at the couple, who responded in kind.

His mother waited until they were out of earshot to say, "You've never been deterred from pursuing what you want. When difficulties are pointed out to you, you ignore them. Remember when you sold jerseys? I told you it was dangerous and that I didn't like it. You were sure you could outsmart the police, so you lied to me and did it anyway." She huffed, unhappy all these years later that he'd defied her and broken the law, even though it helped their bottom line in the days they were scraping by.

She tightened her grip on his elbow. "Your first driving instructor noticed it, too. He told me, 'Ivo is very good at seeing the obstacles in his path—'"

"But he remains focused on his goal," Ivo finished for her.

"Yes. He said it would make you a success, that determination. That absolute confidence in yourself and your abilities."

"I haven't done too badly."

"No, you haven't." She expelled a hard breath. "On the other hand, I have always been cautious. Practical. I worry about those obstacles, probably more than I should, especially where money is concerned, because I know what it is like to have none. My practicality has served me well. However, because I know this about myself, I am careful in giving you my opinion, even when you ask. When you took so long to admit to me that you had a girlfriend, I thought it was because you did not want to hear my thoughts. You believed I would be judgmental about relationships."

"You knew about Lina before I said anything?" They'd gone to great lengths to keep their relationship quiet, and those were the days before Lina's paternity became public.

"That she existed? Yes. Her identity? No." A knowing smile crossed her face. "Your off-season visits dropped in half, maybe less. Instead, you stayed in Milan. When you were racing, you didn't invite me to as many events, even when you knew I could get away from the bakery. It was months before you mentioned—in a very offhanded manner—that you were seeing someone. You told me nothing about her, not even her name, so I didn't push. When I received the call about your accident, the hospital in San Rimini told me a woman named Lina Cornaro was already there. I thought it best to stay here and gave my permission for her to have access to your room."

"That's why you didn't come to San Rimini until later?"

"I came when she left, yes."

He covered her hand where it rested inside his elbow, trapping her fingers before he scowled at her. "You said it was because you couldn't get away from work. That the owner was ill and couldn't step in to manage if you left."

"He was. But you have to know, Ivo, I would never leave you." Her voice hitched and she glanced away. When she spoke again, she was steadier. "Your doctors kept me updated. I knew about your surgeries, your medicines. I asked questions and I did research online to understand what the doctors told me. If Lina hadn't been there watching over you, I would have closed the bakery."

"You could have come. You didn't *need* to, but you could have." He hated to admit it—even knowing how she'd have reacted to the sight of him in lying burned and broken in a hospital bed—but her presence would have reassured him.

"Perhaps." His mother indicated a bench at the side of the path, under the shade of a giant oak. They headed toward it. "When I arrived, you did not mention Lina. I asked one of your doctors, but from the look on his face I knew something had happened, so I told him not to worry, I was sure you'd tell me when you were up to it. You didn't." She shrugged. "When Maria told me what happened at the UNICEF show in New York, she mentioned Lina Cornaro. She saw in the gossip paper that you were seen with her."

"We ended things in San Rimini," he admitted as he used his forearm to brush off the seat for his mother. "We're back together now."

"And still, you don't tell me anything. This has me wondering."

"I didn't think you wanted—"

She waved him off. "What you think I wanted is not the issue. You were afraid. You *are* afraid."

He started to protest, but she twisted on the bench and gave him a look so fierce he shut his mouth and sat back.

"Perhaps you feared my opinion because of my relationship with your father. You didn't want to hear me tell you that when a relationship doesn't work, it can crush your ambition." Her expression remained defiant as she put a hand to her chest. "Ivo, that was my experience, my fear. It should not be yours. You are my child. I want you to have all my strengths and none of my faults."

Her eyes closed for a moment, as if she needed to gather her thoughts. When she looked at him again, it was with a level gaze. "I almost told you about Placido when you first mentioned you were seeing someone. I wanted you to know that I would support you. That I understood. But I couldn't find the words. *I* was afraid of what you'd think of me. Then you were in the accident and it felt wrong to tell you. I am glad you saw him today. I should have told you earlier."

"He means a lot to you." He paused. "Do you love him?"

She hesitated before answering. "I have a great deal of affection for him. Perhaps it is love. We have known each other a long time. He's a good man, a kind man. He does not care that I am an immigrant or that I am still legally married to your father. There are many in Italy who look down on me for that. Nor is Placido interested in me because of you." She rolled her eyes in exasperation. "There have been many of those, too. I recognize them quickly. But Placido knew me long before you were famous."

Ivo didn't recall having met the man. At a questioning tilt of his head, she explained, "He works down the street from the bakery. He's the butcher."

"You're serious." Ivo tried unsuccessfully to stifle a grin. "The butcher and the baker?"

"Yes, yes, I know. But this is how I know who Placido is at heart. I've seen how he does business. I know he loved his wife and that their marriage was a good one. And I know he loves his children and grand-children."

"You're learning Italian for him. Better Italian, that is." He offered a half smile. "I noticed you're reading your favorite romance in Italian."

"Fiction is better than taking a class." Her lips thinned. "His English is not good."

Ivo had gathered that from the man's stuttering departure. "It speaks volumes that you want to learn more than the basics you've needed for the bakery."

"After so many years in Rome, my Italian is better than you think." She shifted, relaxing her shoulders against the bench. "I'm happy, Ivo. I want you to be happy. When you keep things from me, I fear it's because you know there are obstacles. And that you are trying to ignore them."

"Lina and I are taking things one day at a time. My career isn't conducive to relationships. She has a lot going on in her life, too. Her company is at a crucial point in its development."

"She is also in the news."

He resisted the urge to grimace. "It's affecting her business."

"I imagine." She scrutinized him. "I doubt that would stop you from becoming more serious, if that is what you want. Do you love her?"

His heart stilled.

He tore his gaze from his mother's as two women approached on bicycles. They rode slowly, chatting and laughing as they made their way toward the Villa Borghese. One smiled at Ivo and Noomi as they came closer. Then her smile slipped and her eyes widened. After they passed, the woman waved a hand at her friend and began speaking in low, urgent tones.

He'd been recognized. He doubted the women would do anything more than share excited conversation, but given the coverage of his stumble the day before, he didn't want to risk having his location broadcast. They needed to return to his mother's flat, just in case.

His mother stood once the bicyclists disappeared from view. "We can exit at the far gate, then circle around. Do you have time for lunch?"

"My appointment is at one," he said as he fell into step beside her. This time, she didn't take his elbow. "I can come back afterward for tea and cookies, then take you to dinner if you'd like?"

"Did you want to stay tonight?"

"I haven't planned anything after the appointment. I figured I'd see how you were doing, then either take a late train to Milan or stay overnight and go home tomorrow."

"Stay tonight, then. I'll make dinner for you." A beat passed before she added, "I could invite Placido."

"That's entirely up to you."

"I'll invite him, then."

A peaceful silence settled between them as they wound their way toward the gate on Via Pinciana. From there, they could zigzag through the streets and make their way to the flat via the druggist.

He knew his mother still wanted an answer to her question.

Do you love her?

Before the bicyclists had passed, his mind instinctively answered yes. He wondered if his mother had seen it in his expression, even though he hadn't given her a verbal answer. It wasn't an answer he was ready to give.

It wasn't one he had the right to give. Not now.

He waited until they'd picked up her prescription and were a block from the flat before saying, "Lina is good for me, Mother."

"I assumed as much or she would not be back in your life. Yet you are being cautious."

They approached a long line of parked cars, found two with a wide enough gap between bumpers to cut between, then crossed the street.

When he came alongside her again, he said, "We each have careers to consider. She's in the midst of an important deal and mine is in a precarious state. I need to concentrate on my return." The neurologist would tell him whether his brain was fit. Discipline would take care of the rest of his body. "My contract with Ferrari expires at the end of next season. I want to give them every reason to renew."

She took the step fronting her building, then stopped. Rather than pull her key from her pocket, she turned, cupped his cheeks in her hands and searched his eyes, the same way she had when he was a little boy and she wanted to determine whether he was lying to her. To his astonishment, it unnerved him even as an adult.

"Your health will be fine. I know this. The neurologist will say the same thing."

"You can tell this by staring at me? You're in the wrong profession."

"Shush. I know things." She lowered her hands, though her gaze didn't waver. "You feel you have to prove yourself and you will. Next season, you will race and you will win. Your career with Ferrari is not in jeopardy. You will continue to be a role model for young people. Not because you win and make money. Not because the color of your skin makes children who look like you believe their dreams can come true. It is because of your heart. Because you do not give up."

She said it as if his future was as predictable as tourists flocking to the Trevi Fountain on a summer night. Then her eyes narrowed and he sensed she had something far more important to say. "Your problem is that you keep your mind on racing because for you, it's second nature. It's easy to ascertain the answers. You adjust a diffuser plate or raise a front wing, you see the effect on aerodynamics. It's measurable. What's difficult is to consider what you want when you aren't on the track. What will make you as content with your life as I am content with mine? Those answers are not so easy."

Her eyes misted and she lowered her head to reach for her key. It was as emotional as he'd ever seen her. When she spoke again, her voice held a watery note.

"Whatever you want, Ivo, so long as you ignore your fear of the unknown in order to pursue the difficult thing, I know you will achieve it. You always have."

To Ivo's chagrin, when she slid the key into the lock, it turned easily. She braced the door open with one hand, then waved for him to enter.

He paused and smiled at her. "Thank you. It means a lot that you believe in me."

"My dear son, on and off the track, whether it is with this woman or another, you can have it all. But you must be brave enough to pursue it."

Lina concentrated on maintaining the same pace as other pedestrians as she covered the final two blocks to her Milan flat. Ivo texted to say he was waiting a discreet distance from her entryway, having walked from the central train station. Though he was likely looking forward to moving indoors, given the blazing late afternoon sun, she doubted it'd be good for the relationship if he spotted her sprinting through central Milan in high heels, proving how desperately she'd missed him in the short time they'd been apart.

A couple paused in front of her to debate purchasing more wine before friends arrived for a dinner party, forcing Lina to swerve to avoid them.

More wine is never the wrong answer. As soon as she thought of the retort, she dismissed it, taking a deep breath in order to settle her thrumming heartbeat.

Ivo had texted her from Rome on Sunday night to tell her the neurologist wished to run more tests, so he wouldn't be in Milan until Friday. The intensity of her disappointment had stunned her. Friday wasn't long to wait, especially with work to keep her busy, yet it felt like forever.

She'd also wondered what the neurologist had seen that required further testing. Ivo hadn't seemed concerned, so she'd stifled the urge to ask for details.

Lina had arrived at the office at the crack of dawn Monday morning, ahead of anyone else. When Tomasina appeared shortly afterward, Lina told her surprised assistant that pending work and jet lag had combined to get her there so early. It'd been a lie. Lina's restlessness stemmed from thinking about everything from Ivo's health to the time they'd spent together in New York, from the details of their conversations to the nuances of his lovemaking.

She'd stared at the ceiling of her bedroom and shivered at the mental image of Ivo bracing his hands on either side of her head, then slowly lowering his body to hers. Nothing in his actions signified a long-term injury. Yes, he'd protected his back, but with both his words and his actions, he'd demonstrated his physical strength as much as he'd demonstrated his intense desire for her. The stumble at the fashion show was the only evidence anything might be amiss. As she spent the week returning phone calls and reviewing contracts for materials orders, she grasped that thought as a lifeline.

This morning, her body had thrummed with excitement even before she stopped at her favorite bakery for an espresso and croissant. She'd barely settled at her desk when another text from Ivo appeared, letting her know he was on the train and that he'd meet her whenever she finished work.

It'd taken all her discipline not to leave work early.

In front of Lina, a crosswalk light ticked down the final seconds to safely cross. Rather than hustle to beat the timer, as was her habit, she stopped at the curb to wait, then adjusted her handbag strap where it dug into her shoulder. Leaving work early wouldn't have made Ivo's train arrive any faster.

Two weeks ago, she couldn't imagine feeling the way she did now. She'd walked into that prelaunch meeting with the Mirabeau managers focused on one thing: selling lingerie. Isola and its success had become the most important thing in her life. The *only* thing in her life. She'd clicked through her presentation, talking price points and fiber content, quality and durability, with the singular goal of convincing those managers that Isola would make money for their stores. She'd been running on all cylinders for weeks, her stress level at maximum.

Isola remained her priority, just as it was that afternoon, but Ivo's return to her life brought with it a serenity she'd missed. He'd removed much of the strain of her mother's notoriety, eased the intensity with which she'd focused on her career these past months, and, best of all, he'd mended the heartbreak she'd experienced in San Rimini.

She needed to remember that—to be grateful for all the positives their reconciliation had brought—and to live in the moment, rather than worry about their future.

Across the street, a young girl in a red and white dress stood holding her mother's hand, tapping her feet with impatience as she waited for the light to change. Lina's gaze snagged on the girl's red leather shoes. They weren't made for running, but Lina had no doubt the girl would take off if her mother didn't maintain a firm grip. As Lina left work, she'd spied a dozen or so well-dressed children heading into the theater across the street for a private party. No doubt this girl felt she would miss out if she didn't hurry.

Lina understood the urge.

Keep it casual, she reminded herself. Don't rush. Enjoy the banter, the incredible sex, and the fresh pot of coffee that always seemed to follow a night of incredible sex. Enjoy the now.

If she could do that, life would be good.

Cross traffic slowed. Beside her, waiting pedestrians shifted, anticipating the light change. A familiar, masculine scent with a hint of spice came to her, making her skin tingle with awareness before she could turn to locate its source.

"You could have made that light."

The rich, gravelly voice came close to her ear. Before Ivo's hand spread against the lower part of her back to guide her across the street, she wondered how he could make her burn with nothing more than a few innocent words spoken on a crowded street.

Perhaps because there was nothing innocent about Ivo Zanardi.

She glanced at him. Unable to keep the flirtation from her voice, she said, "I was being cautious."

"Caution is overrated."

Once they'd navigated their way through the other pedestrians and turned onto her street, she finally allowed herself to meld her body to his, unwilling to wait until they were alone to slide her arm under his and hold him close.

They were acting like young lovers in the first flush of romance, unable to keep from touching each other. She didn't care.

It wasn't until they were safely in her flat that she dropped her bag and turned to face him. He'd taken steps to keep from being recognized. He wore a loose white shirt and summer-weight gray slacks, typical for a local walking the streets of central Milan in June. Dark glasses obscured the upper part of his face and he'd shorn his already-short hair since they'd left New York. So long as no F1 aficionados looked too closely, he'd blend in with the crowd.

Assuming the crowd was extremely good-looking.

He set his bag next to hers before his hands went to her waist and he drew her to him for a long, sensual kiss. Being here, in her flat, felt even better than when he'd kissed her in New York. There was substance to it, a confirmation this was more than a fling.

When his lips moved to her neck, she whispered, "You came to find me?"

"You were taking too long to get home from work. Didn't want to loiter outside." He eased aside the collar of her blouse. His tongue found the divot between her shoulder and neck, sending a shock along her spine, then his mouth closed on the same spot, sucking, kissing, testing.

Her hands went to the sides of his head. She explored the texture of his cropped hair as his mouth moved lower. Closing her eyes, she murmured, "You could have waited until I told you I was home to come over. Or I could have come to your place."

Cool air hit her skin as his hand slid between them to free the top button of her blouse. "My place is a glorified hotel room."

"I'd never describe it that way."

"You're right. The hotel rooms where I stay are far superior, especially those with bathtubs. My place is a glorified closet."

She inhaled sharply as he slipped the blouse from her shoulders and began walking her backward, toward her bedroom. With her arms caught in the sleeves, she offered little resistance. Not that she wanted to. At the entrance, he stopped, backed her against the doorframe, and levered his hips against hers. One hand came up to cradle her breast before he dragged his lips along her temple.

He smelled incredible, felt incredible. Her hands went to his hips, her thumbs to the top of his slacks. The tangle of her blouse kept her from reaching around to cradle his rear, but as he moved against her, she discovered she didn't mind.

The man's hip bones were lovely. The outline of muscle above his waistband, evident through the fabric of his shirt, even more so.

She drew a ragged breath. "I'll concede that point. Glorified closet."

Since they met, she'd only visited his flat a handful of times. Given his aggressive travel schedule, the minuscule space served as nothing more than a convenient home base close to both an international airport and the race track at Monza. It was also within a two-hour drive of Ferrari's facilities, where he had access to both the team's private simulator and test track, as well as to the mechanics and engineers who kept his car running at peak efficiency. The first time she'd crossed the threshold, he'd apologized, noting that he had no reason to maintain a house or live in an upscale flat with amenities that went beyond the essentials. That as long as he had a bed, a place to cook, and a washer and dryer—his one must-have feature, given the amount of laundry he generated with his workouts—he was happy. He'd much rather spend his time at home reading technical articles or watching race video than cleaning.

Ivo's lips moved closer to her ear, where he seduced her with both his rough tone and his words. "I'm happy to undress you in a closet. Or a kitchen. Or a shower. We could try them all. Experiment."

Then his mouth met hers, hot, insistent, and filled with the promise of pleasure. She reveled in the sensation, returning his kiss with all the passion that built over their days apart.

When he leaned back to unzip his slacks, she seized the opportunity to shake off the blouse confining her wrists. Once free, she made quick work of his shirt buttons. The firm, tightly muscled planes of his chest never failed to impress her. He hissed in a breath as she spread her hands across the smooth skin.

How utterly perfect he was. "Experimenting is good."

"I plan to remind you of that. Frequently."

Slowly, she moved her hands from Ivo's chest to his shoulders, peeling away his shirt so she could trace the dips and curves of his torso. His dark gaze penetrated her, as if he could see clear to her soul, could read every thought, could understand the depth of her cravings.

"I take it your appointments went well? You're healthy?"

His mouth lifted in a mixture of devilry and self-satisfaction, as if he were a hunter who'd trapped his prey after a long, challenging pursuit. "I'm about to prove how healthy I am."

She pushed against his shoulders. "I'm serious."

"So am I." He moved to kiss her again, then surprised her by catching her bottom lip and drawing it between his teeth in a slow, erotic nip. His hands spanned her hips and he drew her flush against him.

"Truly?" she whispered.

He pressed into her, giving her full evidence of his arousal. "I'm fine. Cleared for all activity. Now…if I could wait until later to share the details? My mind is locked on a singular purpose."

Relief washed through her. Until this moment, she hadn't realized how worried she'd been. Enough to stop her from entering the bedroom until she heard directly from Ivo that he was going to be all right.

Wrapping her arms around his neck, she answered him with a kiss. He smiled against her mouth, then opened to her, encouraging her with a slide of his hands from her hips to her waist. Their kisses grew hungrier, more frantic. His breath came harder, until he nipped her lip once more and eased away, slowing their pace. She murmured in protest, but he ignored her, taking his time as he caressed the sides of her body, his eyes following suit.

At long last, his fingers moved with a tender caress along the underside of her bra. His thumb paused over the lacy center, then traced the seam along the top of one cup.

"This is a new one."

"That familiar with my lingerie drawer, are you?"

He pulled her close and his low laugh resonated through her before he dropped a kiss at her temple. "Different cut than any you've worn before. A prototype? Or someone else's design?"

"I only wear the best. It's a prototype."

"Mmm." He palmed her breast. "Perfection."

She smiled. Two could play at that game. Her hands skidded along his spine, then she slipped one hand into the front of his pants. As she wrapped her fingers around him, she was rewarded by a hiss of breath. "Were you planning to remove it?"

"Let's leave it for now. But everything else must go."

She circled tighter, lower, then drew her fingers up and over the tip of him. Hard. A pearl of moisture met her touch. She closed her eyes against the need coursing through her before sliding her hand down again. "You first."

He swore. It took seconds for his pants to go, then he had her in the bed, his powerful body trapping her. A muscle jumped in his jaw, then he took her hand and guided it down. "Do that again."

She did.

Afterward, as they lay atop the mussed sheets, Ivo ran his knuckles along her shoulder, then hooked a finger beneath the strap of her bra. "Were you interested in feedback on your prototype?"

"Always." She snuggled closer, tucking her head beneath his chin.

"Hmmm." He slipped it back and forth between his fingers. "I can't speak to its comfort, but it meets Isola's high standards of style."

"Might need more durability testing." She dragged her hand along his abdomen, then lower. "If you're up for it."

This time when she captured him with her hand, he laughed.

Then he complied.

CHAPTER 21

Ivo woke to the rev of a motorcycle engine. Rolling to his side, he encountered Lina's soft, warm body. As if he'd beckoned her, she shifted and flattened her palm above his hip bone.

If he hadn't already been rock hard, her gentle caress would've accomplished the same result.

"Come here," he murmured, easing her closer so he could curl his arm around her. "I must have drifted off."

She wrapped her top leg around him so her toes slipped along his shin. "Wasn't long. Gave me the chance to watch you sleep."

"Sounds exciting."

"You have no idea."

He nuzzled the top of her head. Lying entangled in Lina's bed felt natural. Pure. He loved the scent of her. Then there were the small details he'd forgotten in the months since he'd last been here, like the polished nickel alarm clock on her nightstand, which she used despite having an alarm on her phone. The modern lamp with its base of sea-colored glass, and the ivory doily underneath the lamp, which Lina once told him her mother crocheted. If he opened the drawer of her nightstand, he knew he'd find lip balm, a travel-size pack of tissue, and her favorite hand lotion alongside her spare reading glasses. She likely had a book or two in there, though the titles changed every time he stayed, just as his mother's stack of reading material varied from visit to visit.

He let out a long breath, then kissed her hair.

He hadn't intended to make love to her the minute he arrived. They'd planned dinner, maybe gelato and a sunset stroll through one of the local parks, if they could do so without attracting attention. But when she'd taken her first full look at him after he'd approached her at the crosswalk, her designer's eye for detail noting his clothing, the sunglasses, and his fresh haircut, he'd also studied her. He hadn't missed the attraction that flared in those beautiful, light brown eyes. By the time they reached the flat, her expression had transformed into something far more primitive.

It was as if she'd punched the gas pedal with both feet. He'd wanted her with an intensity that nearly leveled him.

This afternoon, while he'd attempted to read a report on changes to the track for next season's Australian Grand Prix, the rhythmic chug-chug-chug of the train carriage and familiar landscape outside the window made him wonder if the rush of desire and adrenaline he'd experienced in New York would fade once he and Lina returned to their everyday surroundings.

He could state with confidence that it hadn't.

Then again, it'd always been this way with Lina. He couldn't look at her without wanting to be with her. Watching movies, debating ideas, walking through Milan at twilight, making love. If anything, clearing the air in New York—first by apologizing for the mistakes they made leading up to San Rimini, then by delving into the complexities of their unique childhoods—had bonded them more powerfully.

They'd each allowed themselves to be vulnerable as never before. They'd come out the other side stronger.

Closing his eyes, he traced the bones of her wrist. So delicate, yet resilient.

"You were right, you know."

He shifted so he could see her face. "About?"

"You're perfectly healthy. I'm glad you felt the need to prove it before dinner."

"Is that your way of telling me you're hungry?"

Her hand flattened against his abs. "I can wait."

He started to make a salacious comment, but was interrupted by a low rumble from her stomach. Gently, he eased her hand to a safer location.

"Dinner first," he told her. "Or I might never eat."

Lina had stocked her kitchen in anticipation of his arrival, so after dressing and debating the odds they'd have privacy at any of the restaurants in the area, given that it was Friday night, they decided to stay put.

"I stopped at the market yesterday for vegetables and made a gazpacho," she told him as she rummaged through the refrigerator. "How do you feel about gazpacho with a grilled chicken salad?"

Whatever spices Lina used on her chicken had converted Ivo to her salads soon after they'd met. He gave her an enthusiastic yes and asked what he could do to help. Once they were settled with dinner and wine, he asked about Mirabeau.

"No word yet, but I didn't expect it. They need to monitor sales levels now that the excitement of the launch is over. There are certain targets Isola is expected to hit. Doing so won't guarantee the contract, but missing them will mean a no."

"That's a lot of pressure."

She shrugged. "At this point, there's not much I can do beyond monitoring the stock. Mostly, Mirabeau wants to see return shoppers, which is a strong indication of brand sustainability."

Ivo filled his spoon with gazpacho. The rich scent of tomato, red bell pepper, and garlic made his mouth water. "Is there a timeline for when you'll hear?"

"The contract I signed gives them three months from the launch date to make a decision. During that time, Isola will be exclusive to Mirabeau in the United States. After that, I can pitch the line to other stores." She grinned over the rim of her wineglass. "I don't have access to all of Mirabeau's sales figures yet, but they've already restocked the

White Plains and SoHo stores. That's a good sign. I'm hopeful that Mirabeau will agree to a long-term contract within the next month to six weeks. That will allow them to expand Isola to locations outside New York and to their website."

"Which means more sales for you."

She nodded. "And if they want Isola to remain exclusive, they'd have to negotiate for that in the contract." The excitement and optimism in her voice was accompanied by a flush in her cheeks. "It'd be a good deal more money, which I could reinvest in the business. It'll be interesting to see what happens."

She swirled her wine, then set the glass on the table. "On the other hand, I don't want to get ahead of myself. Anything could happen. Sales could tank. Their current lingerie lines could change terms to offer better margins. Or Mirabeau could get backlash over my connection to the Barrali family." She lifted one shoulder, then let it drop. "I sent thank-you gifts to all the Mirabeau managers and followed up with *Fashion Backstage* and a few smaller publications who approached me during events at the other stores, then told myself not to think about it."

"That's practical of you."

"I'm always practical. Luckily, I had plenty to do this week for the Milan boutique. There's also a Frankfurt department store that's interested in Isola, so that required attention."

After another spoonful of gazpacho, he reached across the table to catch her hand. "Not luckily. The Milan boutique and the chance at another department store exist because you planned ahead and created those opportunities."

He knew most people would tune out Lina's business discussion, but it fascinated him. It revealed her thought process, her tenacity. Her optimism. All the things he admired about her.

Lina folded her fingers through his. He loved the sight of their hands like this, her long, pale fingers interlaced with his dark ones.

She saw him looking and flashed a smile that made his mouth go dry. "This from the man who plans workouts weeks and months in advance so you can be in perfect form on race days. I have a lot to learn to keep up with you." She gave his fingers a quick squeeze, then released his hand before adding, "That being said, I'm grateful to hear that you're healthy. Despite what the doctor said in New York, I was worried. I had the feeling you were more concerned than you let on and that you were trying to hide it from me. When you needed to stay in Rome for more tests, I wasn't sure what to expect."

"The longer stay was a request from Ferrari as much as from the neurologist." He picked up his wine and took a solid drink, wondering how she would react to his news. "Esteban Vargas, the Spanish driver who moved into my slot for the season, is good, but he's young and rough around the edges. He came from another team and has struggled as part of Scuderia Ferrari."

He took a hearty drink, fortifying himself for what was next. "The neurologist ran a full battery of tests and compared the results to the baseline taken when I started with Ferrari and to the scans taken in San Rimini. He tested my ability to handle the g-forces of a cornering car, my reaction times, my lung capacity, even my vision and hearing. I have a slightly decreased VO2 max, but that's to be expected since I haven't been training as hard. It's still in the exceptional range."

A laugh bubbled from her, causing him to frown. "What?"

"You talk about your VO2 max being in the exceptional range in the same way those of us who aren't superhuman share our shoe size with a store clerk." Her smile stayed in place, but her voice turned serious. "I take it this means everything else was normal. Well, what's considered normal for you."

He smiled at that. "Completely normal and medically cleared. What happened in New York was a result of low blood sugar and nothing more." To be certain, he'd conducted his own experiment, skipping breakfast his last day in Rome and going for a long run. Sure enough, vertigo set in shortly afterward. "I've lived such a scheduled life since I started racing, I doubt I've ever gone that long without eating. Now I know to monitor my food intake more closely on days with tough workouts."

"You must be relieved."

That was one word for it. It'd taken extreme mental gymnastics not to contemplate the worst case scenario when he'd walked into the neurologist's office in Rome. He suspected Lina knew that, but he merely nodded.

"Ferrari must be thrilled."

The statement was innocuous on its face, but he recognized it for what it was: curiosity about the team's intentions. It was the perfect opening. "They—and I—assumed this season was out of the question, but now they want me in the simulator and on the track as soon as possible. They believe that the more time I spend out of the car, the longer it'll take to return to peak form."

"They want you racing? This season?"

"If all goes as they expect, I'll serve as a reserve driver starting next month. They believe my presence will help Esteban focus. I've met him a few times—he has a lot of potential and he's earnest—and I think they're right."

Her brows drew together. "Sounds like they want you to train the competition."

Typically, Ivo would have jumped to the same conclusion. With only a handful of drivers at the F1 level, the competition for slots was fierce, even within teams. "With Esteban, I don't think so. I'm not sure F1 is his strength. Every type and level of racing takes slightly different skills. I get the impression they're trying to decide whether his talents lend themselves to another type of vehicle. I suspect he's making that same analysis."

"More of a mentorship role, then."

He'd never thought of himself that way, but looking back on recent seasons, Ivo supposed he'd gradually filled that role for younger drivers. They'd become his friends and were confident that when they asked him for advice or expressed concerns it would go no further.

His stomach clenched, hating what he had to tell her. "The upshot is that I won't be able to spend much time here in Milan. In fact, they want me to fly to Montreal on Monday to meet with Esteban ahead of the Canadian Grand Prix next weekend."

Her gazpacho spoon hovered above the bowl. "What did you tell them?"

"I agreed. They've already booked my flight." He didn't have much choice, not while he was under contract. Not that he would have declined. Racing took intense mental focus, both in and out of the car. The atmosphere of a big event like the Canadian Grand Prix would put him in the right frame of mind to return as soon as possible.

On the other hand, there was Lina.

She tucked a wisp of hair behind her ear and the knot in his stomach tightened. Even if she wanted to come with him, to face the inevitable scrutiny that would occur if she appeared alongside him at a major event, she couldn't. She was needed at Isola.

It didn't change the fact he ached to have her beside him on the long flight to Montreal, and on every flight thereafter.

"On the bright side, it sounds like you'll be on the track well ahead of wet tire testing in San Rimini. You won't have to start at the same location where you had your accident."

"True." He understood why it worried Lina. Returning to racing at the track where you nearly lost your life made for great sports copy, the kind that brought fans to the course in droves. However, Ivo had years of training that conditioned him to believe such coincidences didn't matter. He'd race with the same mindset no matter where he first jumped into the cockpit. His true concern was bigger.

He swallowed hard and looked directly at Lina. "I don't want this to change things between the two of us. What happened in New York was—" He struggled for the right word, unwilling to use *transformative* or to admit that after a single week—well, two years and a single week—he was falling head over heels in love with her. The kind of love that was deep and abiding. The kind of love that—eventually— meant the six kids and a shared mailbox he'd joked about.

"What happened in New York," she repeated, her eyes flickering with desire, "was wonderful because you were brave enough to hunt me down and apologize, and to demand the same from me. You were brave enough to be open and let me know where you stand. We'll be fine as long as we communicate, right?"

Before he could respond, she dealt him a blow he wasn't expecting. "You have your career, and I have mine. I'm perfectly fine with keeping things relaxed. I'm not going anywhere. When you're in

Milan, we can go to the theater, watch movies, have dinner. I even promise" —she stabbed a piece of seasoned chicken with her fork and twirled it slowly— "that the next time you're in town, I'll have the ingredients to make chicken with hot pepper sauce. Sound good?"

As long as he clung to the words *I'm not going anywhere.* While he smiled on the outside, on the inside, shock reverberated through him as powerfully as if he'd driven straight into a wall.

He'd wanted her to be sad. To protest. When it was the *last* thing he should want.

What in the world was wrong with him?

She leaned forward and held her glass aloft. "To finishing the season in good health and in style."

He touched his glass to hers and added, "For us both."

He polished off his wine, but he'd lost his appetite.

CHAPTER 22

Sunday evening came all too soon.

Ivo used his forearm to wipe sweat from his brow as he and Lina entered her flat shortly after sunset. The heat of the afternoon had settled into the cobblestones and asphalt of the city streets, leaving them both in need of a cool drink and time off their feet.

"Water, juice, or wine?"

"Water," he told her. "With plenty of ice."

While she filled two glasses, he strode to the bathroom to rinse his face.

After a late breakfast at the glorious food hall of Rinascente, they'd decided to escape the city center and head to the Parco di Monza. There, they'd rented bicycles and taken their time exploring the massive walled park. They'd looped through its expansive lawns, made their way along the edge of the Lambro River, and dismounted to watch the flow of water from the vantage point of a park bridge. Laughter had filled the air as they wandered. Local families walked their dogs, children ran in the grass, and tourists crowded around guides who described the park's windmills or the history of the Villa Reale. Everywhere, people strolled with gelato in hand and lazy Sunday afternoon smiles on their faces.

When the heat threatened to overwhelm them, they'd headed to the park's wooded area and walked alongside their bikes, discussing everything from politics to Italian history to places they hoped to visit. Ivo mentioned that during his stay in Rome, he'd taken his mother on a tour of the Catacomb of Saint Priscilla.

"Hard to believe she's lived in Rome all these years and never visited any of the catacombs."

"Had you?"

"Never. It always seemed like a touristy thing to do." And costly, given that during his youth nearly all their money went to necessities like food, rent, and clothing. "I wish we'd done it sooner. There are dozens around the city, but Saint Priscilla is unique."

Lina had listened attentively and asked questions as Ivo described the priest who'd led them deep underground and through the quiet of the ancient tunnels to see the early Christian frescoes.

"It sounds like you enjoyed yourselves."

"Very much."

Lina had smiled. "It was a good visit with your mother."

"It's the longest we've been together since I moved out of the house. We talked a lot. I fixed things around her flat. I even met her partner."

"Partner?" Lina's eyes had widened at that.

"Shocked me, too." As Ivo had described meeting Placido, the value of his visit to Rome finally sank in. "I wouldn't have stayed if the neurologist hadn't requested it, but it was exactly what we needed."

Lina had shifted so she held the handlebars of her bike in one hand, then slipped her other arm around his waist. "Rocco, Enzo, and I are completely different, and we don't see each other as often as I'd like, but we mean the world to each other."

He'd moved closer to her as she spoke and draped an arm around her shoulders. She'd sighed with pleasure—a sound that sent his heart soaring—then angled her chin to look at him. "Sometimes I take my relationships with them for granted. You and your mother might not always see eye to eye, but she's your whole family. Having a good relationship with her is important."

He'd tightened his hold. Lina understood him. With a few simple words, she made everything seem right in the world.

He'd slowed as they reached the edge of the woods and the last of the shade. Few people were in sight, and none within hearing distance. "On the subject of family—"

"You're going to ask me about Queen Fabrizia."

"Not at all," he'd protested. "I was going to ask about King Carlo."

"Ah. That makes all the difference."

"It might." He'd stopped walking to look at her. "I've made assumptions about my mother. Perhaps you're making assumptions about him? Fabrizia met with you in New York because she cares about her husband. She's seen the relationship Carlo and Rocco are building. If it was going badly, she wouldn't put so much effort into encouraging you to do the same."

He'd expected Lina to argue. Instead, she'd contemplated his words before responding. "My situation is different. You know your mother. She raised you. I don't know King Carlo at all. I don't know what I would get from a relationship with him other than more public scrutiny." Her mouth had pinched. "I know it's not logical, but part of me feels like I'm betraying my father by even considering it. That bothers me, too."

He understood that. Jack Cornaro was the only father she'd ever known. "What does Rocco think?"

"He's only met Carlo in person twice, if you don't count when he was a toddler. The first time was completely out of the public eye. The second was at the press conference. They had dinner together afterward." Lina had taken a deep breath and scanned the woods around them, as if nature held all the answers. "Rocco won't tell me what to do, but he made a point of saying that meeting Carlo was worthwhile. He said the same to Enzo."

"Did it make him feel like he was betraying your father?"

"I didn't ask, but I doubt it. He met Carlo the first time because my mother's death meant our paternity would become public. He wanted to get Carlo's side of the story before the news broke so we'd know the truth and understand what we'd face."

"But the two of them made a connection."

She'd nodded. He knew Lina was considering it, but her reservations weighed on her.

Ivo had chosen his next words carefully. "No matter what you decide, I have your back. If Carlo is as sincere as Fabrizia claims, meeting him won't hurt you. Whether you want him in your life or not, he's family. It could be a valuable relationship down the line."

Lina had moved closer to him. Her gaze held a wash of feeling: fear of meeting Carlo, possible regret if she didn't. And, beyond those two emotions, gratitude. He'd bent and kissed her. It had been brief, but tender. A promise of support.

They'd exited the woods, then mounted their bikes to meander through the rest of the park. The sunshine worked its magic, elevating both of their moods as they sailed along an empty stretch of path. By the time they'd decided to return the bicycles and start for home, they were both exhausted, but light on their feet. A group of locals recognized Ivo at the bike return and he paused for photographs. Otherwise, it was a quiet trip home. Watching the sun set as they covered the final blocks to Lina's flat on foot seemed the perfect way to end their outing.

As Ivo exited the bathroom, Lina stood at the windows. She held her hair on top of her head with one hand and a half-full glass of ice water in the other as she surveyed the traffic and pedestrians on the city street. Even with sweat at the back of her neck and a stray tendril of hair clinging to her shoulder, she made his chest ache. He'd known her for more than two years, yet felt as floored by her beauty as if it were the first time he laid eyes on her.

Her arm dropped and her shoulders squared when she became aware of his presence.

"I left your drink on the counter. If you need to add more ice, go ahead," she said without turning around. "The first heat wave of the summer does me in every year. I've lived in Italy my entire life, but my inner thermostat wants to run on a northern setting."

He joined her, downed his water, then took both their glasses to the kitchen for refills, adding a hefty scoop of ice to each. He gave her a pointed once-over when he returned to the window. While at the park, they'd discussed going out for pizza at a hole-in-the-wall restaurant near her flat, one they'd enjoyed previously and with a location that meant they were unlikely to be spotted by tourists. "You're less pink than when we left the park. Will you be up for dinner soon?"

"I need to shower first." She gave him the same once-over he'd given her. "How about you?"

"I could eat."

"Good, because if you're not hungry, I'm going without you. I'm starved." She took a long drink before asking, "And how do you feel?"

"Perfectly fine." Eating before the bicycle ride had done the trick. Despite the long afternoon of exercise and the intense heat, he'd experienced no dizziness. "Normal."

"It's that exceptional VO2 max," she teased, patting his chest. The fabric of his shirt clung to his skin, but she didn't seem to notice. Instead, Lina strolled to the kitchen and set her glass in the sink. "Mind if I shower first?"

"Is that a hint that I should shower, too?"

"Did you need a hint?"

He laughed at that. "Go ahead. I'll shower when you're finished. I'll check in for my flight while you're in there." He pulled his phone from his pocket only to realize the battery had died after their expedition to the park. "Never mind. I'll charge this while we're at dinner."

"Use my laptop if you want." She aimed a glance at the dining table, where her computer rested. "The password is already in, so you should be able to get online."

Before she disappeared, Lina asked, "How long will you be in Canada?"

"The Grand Prix itself is Sunday. My return flight is Monday. Ferrari has me scheduled for the simulator next week, then there are team meetings to get me up to speed. So to speak."

She grinned at his phrasing. "It'll feel good to return to your usual schedule."

As he plugged in his phone, she told him to help himself to anything he wanted to drink while she showered. He frowned as he listened to the sounds of her dresser drawers opening and closing, then to the stream of water as she started the spray. All typical sounds, but something felt amiss.

Then he pegged it. Lina's voice. When she'd asked about Canada, it'd been too perky. Too *bright*. It was the voice she used when practicing her sales presentations, not when speaking to him about their plans.

He dropped into the chair and opened her laptop. Now that he thought about it, she had used that voice with him earlier this weekend. It'd been when he'd told her his clean bill of health meant he'd return to Ferrari much sooner than he'd planned, and she'd given him that speech about their relaxed relationship. That she'd have the chicken with hot pepper sauce for him next time he came to visit.

He sat back and swiped a palm over his face.

She wanted him far more than she cared to admit. Oh, she'd admit to lust. Admit to wanting to spend time with him—with the "when we're both free" caveat—but she wanted more than that.

That she didn't feel she could admit it was his own fault. Just before she'd adopted that sales voice, he'd been flailing for the right word for what had happened between them in New York, too cowardly to tell her what it really meant to him. What *she* meant to him. She'd jumped to the most logical conclusion, given that when they'd stood in her mother's condo, he'd been the one who'd mentioned committing to recipe testing.

Much as logic had told him they should keep their relationship loose at the time he'd spoken those words, it wasn't what he wanted, either.

He huffed. They'd promised to communicate. They each needed to get over their fears and do better on that front.

He tapped in the necessary information to obtain his boarding pass, waiting to see the confirmation before he closed the laptop. The sound of Lina singing in the shower floated to his ears, making him smile, then laugh to himself as she went off-key.

Their single-minded pursuit of their careers was what made them successful, but it also meant they'd tried to rationalize their relationship into a neat, functional box. One that accounted for schedules, but not for feelings.

Ivo folded his hands on top of his head. What he had with Lina went deeper than feelings. Yes, making love to her, holding her gaze, knowing they were safe in each other's arms, felt wonderful. Enough to make any man fall hard. But this went deeper. It went further than a single moment or a single week.

Lina drove him to action. He wanted to be better at everything he did simply by watching her example. He suspected—he hoped—he did the same for her. He also caught himself thinking about what he could do for her, not to earn points or because he expected anything from her in return, but because it felt right. Like a true partnership, one that elevated each of them.

Like the morning show host and her financial guru husband from the UNICEF show.

Bottom line: He loved Lina. And damned if she didn't love him.

It was in the thoughtful questions she asked about his mother while they strolled in the park. In the way she automatically reached out to hold his bike when he'd stopped at the beginning of their ride to tie his shoe. In the fact she listened to his opinions about connecting with King Carlo and truly considered his thoughts, despite the entire idea going against her instincts.

It wasn't the behavior of a woman in a catch-you-when-you're-free fling. It wasn't casual for her. It wasn't casual before San Rimini, either.

They'd each been too scared to discuss it. He'd been too stupid to *see* it.

Closing his eyes, he blew out a long breath. *Why in the hell are you so scared?*

Perhaps his mother had nailed it. He was afraid of the unknown.

What was it Lina had said in the hospital, when she'd mentioned that she might have to give up management of her company?

We all have to make these choices, to conquer our fear of the unknown. If we don't, we stagnate.

He gritted his teeth. He may have had a fuzzy brain that night, but that statement stayed with him. He'd thought Lina brave to consider that she might have to give up day-to-day control of her company, a company she'd built, in order to build an even greater enterprise, though that greater enterprise could fail under someone else's direction.

It was a huge risk. It resonated.

Lina stopped singing. Water splashed against the glass door, a sound he'd come to associate with the last steps of her shower, when she rinsed her hair and smoothed her hands over the top of her head to eliminate the excess water.

Before he could second guess himself, he opened her laptop once more. He scrolled through her contacts, then punched a number in his own phone.

The only way to overcome a fear was to face it head on, whether that meant posing for photos, working a crowd of autograph-seekers, or climbing into a car and cornering at speeds that rattled a man's teeth.

Why would this be any different?

"Pronto?"

"Buona sera. Sono Ivo Zanardi." There was a second of hesitation on the other end, the type of lull that preceded a hang-up. Quickly, he added, *"Potrei parlare con Tomasina?"*

"Ivo Zanardi? Yes, yes, this is Tomasina diMassio. What may I do for you?"

He was about to ask how she knew he preferred English when she explained, "My father and his friends are lifelong *Tifosi*. They go to one or two races a year and drive to Maranello to watch you at the test track sometimes. There is a spot on a nearby roadway where they set up chairs and make an afternoon of it."

He grinned. "I know the place. Your father is a smart man. Has he attended any events this season?"

"Not yet," she said, but mentioned two in the fall he planned to attend.

"That's fantastic. Fans are the lifeblood of the team." He kept the affability in his voice as he told her, "I'm sure you're wondering why

I've called. I'd like to do something for Lina Cornaro. However, I need your help to accomplish it, if you're willing."

"Of course!" There was the sound of an engine being cut. "Forgive me, I am parking at my parents' house. Sunday dinner is mandatory."

"I can call later—"

"No!" A nervous laugh came over the line. "That is, it is not necessary. I am early. I…I know you have been seeing Lina, even though she has kept it very quiet. I will do whatever I can, as long as it does not make trouble with her at work. My job is my priority."

"I understand completely." He dropped his voice as Lina turned off the shower. "I don't know if Lina has any travel scheduled outside Europe, but next time she does, could you call me at this number and let me know beforehand?"

"Oh, I don't know—"

"I understand why you'd be concerned about revealing her travel arrangements. I'd be concerned if you didn't value her privacy." He straightened, bracing himself for the risk he needed to take. "I'll explain why I want to know. If you decide it's a violation of Lina's trust in you, I won't press further. I only ask that you keep it to yourself."

He could sense her inner struggle, even over the phone. "Go ahead."

He gave Tomasina the details, hoping he could convince her before Lina exited the bathroom and caught him on the phone. He finished by saying, "I know it's a lot to ask, but if you could do this for me, I'd be happy to get some autographed Scuderia Ferrari merchandise to you for your father. Actually," he added, "I'm happy to give it to you anyway, given what a fan your father has been."

"You are bribing me!"

"If that's what it takes."

She laughed in response, but he was completely serious. "It would mean a lot to me, Tomasina."

He heard a sigh, a rustle, then the opening of a car door. "All right. I will call you. But if I am fired for this, you will have to find me a new job. No matter what my father might claim, even a front-row seat on the finish line of the Monaco Grand Prix isn't worth losing my spot at Isola or my friendship with Lina."

Down the short hallway, Lina emerged from the bathroom in a thin robe, her hair wrapped in a towel. She saw him on the phone and gestured that the bathroom was all his whenever he was ready. He held up his index finger to let her know he'd be a minute, but gave her an up-and-down flirtatious look. She rolled her eyes in response and mouthed, "food first."

He faked a stab through the heart before Lina disappeared into her bedroom.

To Tomasina, he said, "Done," and in case Lina was listening, added, "The flight information is appreciated."

If he pulled this off, Tomasina would love the front row seat he'd offer in thanks. If not, well, it was the risk one took when steering off-track.

CHAPTER 23

L INA FELT RATHER than heard her phone ring in the side pocket of her handbag, which rested against her hip as she waited in line at her favorite Milanese bakery. Unwilling to answer it in the crowded space, she slipped her hand into the pocket and clicked the phone to silent as the person two in front of her reached the counter.

Most days, she basked in the atmosphere of Café San Giorgio. Despite the early morning heat—typical for the first full week of August in Milan—a hum of chatter filled the air, with the energetic conversation of the patrons in perpetual contrast to the brusque tone of Marcello, the owner, as he called for more rye bread, demanded another tray of croissants for the display case, or fussed over the espresso machine. The rich scent of coffee beans and buttery goodness of fresh pastry tantalized those at the counter into purchasing more than they intended. The affectionate smile of Magdalena, an older relative of Marcello's who waved off his grousing and shooed the stray cats from the entrance, made the place feel like home.

Today, however, Lina had awakened with a bizarre sense of dread hanging over her. Her morning shower hadn't washed it away. Brushing her teeth worsened the feeling, making her stomach pitch. Unable to explain it, she double-checked her calendar to ensure she wasn't forgetting anything. With everything as it should be, she'd chalked it up to a bad night's sleep. Perhaps she'd had a nightmare, one she'd forgotten upon awakening, that left her subconscious, and therefore her stomach, unsettled.

Then again, she'd experienced the same apprehension yesterday afternoon while reviewing sales reports from the London store. And during a lunch meeting the day before that. It was as if she'd forgotten something vitally important and would reap the consequences if she didn't figure it out soon.

Once she'd left her flat, fresh air had helped alleviate the sensation. But a few minutes ago, when she'd entered the Café San Giorgio and paused to talk to a police officer who frequented the bakery on a schedule similar to hers, it returned more powerfully than before.

Lina inhaled deeply, letting the carbohydrate- and coffee-laden atmosphere work its magic as she moved forward another spot in the line. She was running out of strategies to shake the sour feeling.

Before leaving work last night, she'd reviewed her punch list with Tomasina to ensure she was on top of everything. The discussion should have left her in high spirits. Though it hadn't been publicly announced, the Mirabeau offer came through a week ago. The initial terms included everything Lina had hoped to see. Isola would become a permanent part of the lingerie collection in the five stores that held launch events and would expand to Mirabeau's remaining locations over the next year. In addition, Mirabeau wanted to commission a bra and panty set that would be exclusive to its website.

Better still, Mirabeau was anxious to seal the deal, meaning a swift timeline for finalizing the details.

In the weeks since Isola's New York launch, the joys of Lina's personal life rivaled those of her professional life.

First, Ivo had returned from his Canadian trip on an adrenaline rush. It hadn't taken long for Esteban Vargas to realize that Ivo had his best interests at heart, and the younger driver had relaxed in a way he hadn't allowed himself to do since joining Scuderia Ferrari. The pair talked through the course at the Canadian Grand Prix and though the Spaniard missed the podium, he'd shown a major improvement over his previous outing. To Ivo, it felt like a victory. He was certain Esteban would capitalize on the knowledge for his next race.

The experience made Ivo all the more anxious to jump in the cockpit himself. Spending time with his team brought back the noise and rush of the cars, the intensity of a race weekend, and the strategizing required to win. Racing made Ivo more…Ivo.

He and Lina spent a wonderful few days together and shared a celebratory dinner before he left for simulator work and a meeting with Ferrari. A photo taken outside the restaurant appeared in a sports report, which was then picked up by several Italian and Sarcaccian papers, but the accompanying paragraph identified Lina only as the owner of Isola and "recently revealed illegitimate daughter" of King Carlo, without mentioning her mother or using inflammatory language.

Two weeks later, Esteban made a podium. When Ivo escaped to Milan for a short stay, they'd celebrated in private. He also revealed that he'd quietly taken two days of runs on the test track at Maranello and that both were successful.

It's all good, Lina reminded herself as she moved forward in the bakery line. No need to feel off-kilter.

Marcello himself came to the register when she approached the counter. She wished him a good morning, then ordered an espresso for herself and pastries for the office.

"*Bella, bella.*" He used tongs to arrange the freshly baked goods in a takeaway box, eyeing her as he did so. "What am I to do about you now?"

"What's bothering you, Marcello?"

"I read the papers." He said it in a tone only she and the other cashier could hear. "I want you to be happy. He makes you happy?"

"You know better than to ask me that." She gave Marcello the same dismissive gesture she'd seen Magdalena deliver hundreds of times. It wasn't as effective as when Magdalena did it.

"And you know what I think you need. A man who treats you like the princess you are. You should listen to Marcello." He whipped a long segment of string from a wall dispenser and huffed as he tied it around the box.

"The world would spin perfectly on its axis if only you ruled the planet and everyone on it, is that what you're trying to say?" At least once a month for the past few years, Marcello had asked her when she planned to marry, have babies, and bring them to his bakery. He'd also made the man-who-treats-you-like-the-princess-you-are comment, which made it easier for her to categorize as an offhanded figure of speech, rather than a reference to her paternity.

"Exactly." He placed the box on the counter and took her payment before gesturing for the barista to hustle with the espresso. In a low voice, he added, "He has a good reputation. His neighbors say that he is kind, but I do not know how they judge this as he is rarely home."

"Asked around, did you?" At his look of annoyance, she grinned. The man was as inquisitive as Queen Fabrizia, but he had her best interests at heart. "I'll see you tomorrow, Marcello. You keep my secrets and I won't tell anyone that your grumpiness is all an act."

"You don't share your secrets," he grumbled as he set her espresso on the counter.

"Then you're safe, aren't you?"

She chatted with Magdalena, then left the shop and turned toward Isola, cutting through a narrow cobblestoned alley to emerge onto a wide street that led toward her boutique. As she sidestepped pedestrians headed the opposite direction, another wash of dread rolled over her. She paused, flummoxed as to the cause. It wasn't like her to worry without reason. She had to have forgotten something important at work. It was the only explanation she could conceive.

On an exhale, she set the pastry box on an empty bus stop bench, finished her espresso, then fished in her handbag for her phone. Maybe the call she'd received in the bakery line would explain it. Her fingers connected with the phone at the same time a garbage truck rumbled past. The dank scent left in its wake roiled her stomach.

Biting back the nausea, she dropped to the bench and took several long, deep breaths. She hadn't felt this overwhelmingly ill since she had the flu two years ago, and the flu hadn't been accompanied by an impending sense of doom.

She could not afford to get sick. Not now, with the new Mirabeau contract. Not with her trip to India next week to meet with one of her fabric suppliers. And definitely not with Ivo planning to come to Milan again this week. Every minute her brain wasn't actively occupied with Isola—and admittedly, at times when it *should* be occupied with Isola —it was firmly on Ivo. Despite his ramped-up schedule with F1, she and Ivo had spent three hedonistic weekends together in the weeks since they'd reunited in New York. After being photographed at the restaurant, they'd kept a low profile. They'd taken walks through the city parks at off-hours, spent lazy afternoons reading, and then made love late into the night. On his last visit, she'd even prepared the chicken with hot pepper sauce she'd promised him in New York. It'd turned out awful, but they'd laughed until they cried as they foraged for the ingredients to make sandwiches instead.

"That didn't work the way I'd hoped," she'd told Ivo as he'd sliced tomatoes for their sandwiches and she'd scraped the chicken from their plates. "I hate to waste this, but it's inedible. I have no idea what I did wrong."

"Maybe nothing. Not all recipes are good." He'd shot a brilliant smile her way, one that made her sigh inside. "Good thing I'm flexible."

"Good thing I didn't hold you to your chicken commitment. You'd have been poisoned."

"I doubt that. I might've even liked it after a few more bites."

"You'd have kept eating if I didn't take it away from you?" How he'd managed to keep a straight face during the bites he'd consumed before she tried hers, she couldn't fathom.

"We'll never know, will we?"

She'd opened the best bottle of wine she'd had in the apartment. It had been the perfect accompaniment to the sandwiches.

Another garbage truck approached. This time, Lina turned her face from the road and held her breath. Once the truck turned the corner, she looked at her phone, then punched in the familiar number.

"*Buon giorno*, Tomasina. I'm two blocks away. You called but didn't leave a message?"

"It wasn't news I wished to leave on voice mail." There was a moment's pause before she explained, "Frankfurt is making an offer. They called about thirty minutes ago. Their legal team is working on a draft agreement and will send it this afternoon for our comments. Lina, it's a big order. After analyzing your report on the Mirabeau launch, they believe they can do better."

A mix of relief and elation coursed through her. She'd known the Frankfurt store would be a great partner for Isola. It was gratifying to know they agreed.

"They want a meeting at the end of next week to discuss a formal launch," Tomasina continued. "I asked if we could move it back since it's the day you're scheduled to leave for India, but their CEO is traveling to a conference then and will be on vacation the following week. I told them I'd discuss scheduling with you and call back."

"Let me double check the calendar when I get there, but I should be able to postpone India a day or two. I could fly from Frankfurt instead of Milan."

"Want me to call the supplier and see if he's flexible?"

"Yes, thank you." She pushed to stand and was nearly felled by nausea. This time, there wasn't a garbage truck in sight. Anxious to end the call, she said, "I'll see you in a few minutes. I have croissants from Café San Giorgio, so we'll celebrate."

"That sounds delicious." Tomasina's voice dropped. "Before you arrive, there's something else you should know. King Carlo just wrapped a news conference and was asked about Isola."

Curiosity pushed aside her queasiness. "A reporter asked a ruling monarch about lingerie?"

"We've had three calls for comment. I told everyone to let any others go to voice mail. I assume you will wish to handle any response."

She hated to ask. "What was said at the news conference?"

"The king was asked what he thought of your career. The question was apparently presented in a disparaging manner. According to the transcript I found, his exact response was, 'My wife is the design aficionado in our family, but she recently mentioned that Isola was profiled in *Fashion Backstage*, which gave the company a glowing review. My understanding is that it's a quality product and that Lina Cornaro's reputation in the industry is unassailable. Design is a difficult business, so my thoughts on her career boil down to this: it appears she's conducting it well.' He then chose a reporter in the front row and said, 'You mentioned earlier that you had questions about the summit in the Balkans. I want to be certain those are addressed.' That changed the topic. I'm trying to find video so you can see the exchange yourself."

She thanked Tomasina and said she'd look into it once she addressed the Frankfurt and India arrangements, then disconnected the call and turned to pick up the bakery box. Her stomach pitched. Within seconds, she was leaning over a public trash barrel at the end of the bench, vomiting the espresso and what little remained of last night's dinner.

Pedestrians covered their faces and gave her a wide berth. Several aimed looks of disgust in her direction. She didn't blame them. She was disgusted herself. She rummaged through her bag for facial tissue, thankful she'd worn her hair up this morning and had put on sunglasses as she left the bakery.

Embarrassment flamed her cheeks. On the other hand, now that she'd been sick, she felt marginally better.

Grabbing the box by its string, she strode from the bus stop. She'd brush her teeth again at work. Dive into the Frankfurt deal. Reschedule India. Figure out a statement—if one was needed—about King Carlo. Though she'd hoped coverage on that front would vanish, she'd gradually come to accept that it would always exist. The intensity, however, would ebb and flow depending on the activities of the royal family at any given time. How she presented herself and Isola to the world over the coming months and years would factor, but with much less impact. With any luck, she'd see the video and decide no comment was necessary on her side.

Rocco had done well navigating the press where the Barralis were concerned. Though her company had a bigger public presence than her older brother's did, Rocco's calm interactions with the media had proven a good test case. He often responded to inquiries with a simple, "No comment." It usually worked.

Thinking of Rocco reminded her that she owed him a phone call. He and Justine planned to visit Milan later this month while Justine, a professional skier, took a short break from her off-season training regimen.

A woman with a stroller approached. Lina couldn't see the infant, but tiny feet in striped knit socks kicked the air as the woman passed. Lina grinned inwardly, wondering if the socks would stay put or if the mother would be compelled to scrounge the stroller for them later.

Someday, after Justine retired, it would be wonderful if she and Rocco made her an aunt. Shopping for baby clothes in Milan would be—

Lina stopped cold as pieces of a puzzle snapped into place. The impact caused her lungs to seize as if she'd stood behind the garbage truck with the breeze blowing into her face.

No. No, no, no. This wasn't a puzzle she wished to assemble.

She blew out a long breath, horrified.

A pregnancy would ruin everything.

CHAPTER 24

AWARE of the people around her, Lina resumed walking toward her office. A cold sweat prickled her face and moved downward, causing a single hard shiver to wrack her body.

She'd noticed a couple weeks ago that her pill count was off when she stopped to refill her prescription, but she'd dismissed it, assuming she'd made a mistake. Her whole life, she'd thrived on schedules and routine. She didn't miss her pill.

Now she wasn't so sure.

Her gaze went to the green cross on the *farmacia* sign across the street. The metal grate on the door was half-raised. Behind it, a light flickered to life. Tempting as it was to wait for the pharmacy to open, she decided to return later, when there were fewer pedestrians and she wasn't carrying a bakery box. She'd wait for a quiet moment to make her purchase, tuck it in her handbag, then go home to take the test.

God willing, she was making something out of nothing.

By the time she reached the office, she was physically calmer. The sweat dried and she'd resumed normal breathing. She smiled as she greeted everyone and announced that there were pastries in the kitchenette. Travel to India was rearranged, her meeting with Frankfurt was scheduled, and she took a call from her attorney about the Mirabeau contract before she finally had a moment to herself.

She tried not to think about a possible pregnancy. She and Ivo had always been careful. Much as she wanted children of her own, it would be a disaster to have an infant now.

Babies didn't sleep. Even the most mellow needed nighttime feedings. Then there were the bodily functions and the crying.

She could deal with a lack of sleep—depending on how crushed she was at work—and she'd always been masterful at organizing chaos. A mess, even a diapered mess, was within her capabilities. As a teen, she'd babysat for several of her neighbors and never lost her head, even when the twin girls next door locked her in a closet, then accidentally dropped the key down an air duct and panicked.

But crying…no. Lina loved the silence of the early morning hours. She treasured the time she spent reading before bed and preferred movies that leaned heavier on the dialogue and lighter on the action. To be at her best at work, she needed time alone with her thoughts, time where she wasn't responsible for anything or anyone besides herself.

Then there were toddlers. They were as likely to lick the window at Café San Giorgio as they were to enjoy one of Marcello's pastries.

And Ivo—she pounded the computer keys harder than necessary as she opened her email—she couldn't imagine Ivo's reaction. He was on the cusp of his comeback, filled with fire and hope and high expectations. Plus his contract was up for renewal at the end of next season. He had everything riding on his performance over the coming months.

How in the world would she tell him? A hard lump formed in her throat. He'd be gracious, she had no doubt. Supportive, encouraging, everything a responsible and caring man should be.

It'd wreck him.

Tears sprung to her eyes. She blotted them with the tips of her fingers and shoved the thought aside. She couldn't think about it, not here.

She'd hit send on the last of her pressing messages when Tomasina knocked at the door.

Lina waved her in. "What do you have?"

Tomasina glanced at the hallway before approaching Lina's desk. Her voice barely audible, she said, "I found video of the press conference. I emailed the link to you. Two more calls have come in since you arrived. I let them go to voice mail."

"In that case, we'll need to respond sooner rather than later, even if it's to say 'no comment.'" She offered her assistant a look of gratitude. "Pastries don't quite make up for this."

"If any could, they'd come from Marcello." Tomasina waved a hand. "*Tranquillo.* King Carlo handled the questions well. If you do not mind me saying—?"

"If you can't be honest with me, no one can."

Tomasina offered a weak grin. "I imagine this is not easy. There are those, especially those with strong religious beliefs, who focus on the scandalous. But most people these days don't care about such liaisons. Look at France. They had no trouble electing a president who dated and married his teacher. Their opinion was" —she spread her hands— "so what?"

"In my mother's case, it wasn't the age difference alone," she reminded Tomasina. "In many countries, Carlo would be considered an adult at seventeen. It's that my mother was in a position of authority and used that relationship to manipulate a future monarch. A *ruling* monarch. That's a violation of Sarcaccian law. Then she and the king conspired to hide that relationship for decades."

"And most people say, 'so what?' They care more that Sarcaccia has a stable economy and a good standard of living." Tomasina shrugged. "He is loved by his countrymen and by his wife. If King Carlo says good things about Isola and our business model, it can only be good publicity."

Lina crossed her arms as she considered Tomasina's perspective. The incident at the White Plains store popped into her head. The accusations of the reporters, who'd wanted to bait her. The fact Dottie returned her purchases. The agony of waiting to see what news would come out of it. But, as Tomasina said, maybe most people didn't care. Aside from *DayBuzz*, no outlets had run negative stories about the company. "I hope you're right. Whether you are or not, I'll adopt that attitude. Thank you."

"*Prego*. All will be well, I'm certain." Tomasina asked planning questions about India, then left to handle the final details.

Before loading the video, Lina picked up her phone to check for messages. What she saw in her texts made her shake her head. Speak of the devil.

At a press conference this morning, an unexpected question arose concerning your company. My husband complimented your work and moved on. If anything was said that is incongruent with your wishes, please let me know and I shall pass it along. He wants to take the course that is best for you.- QF

Lina closed the message, then answered two others, letting the queen's words marinate in the back of her brain. Then she watched the clip of the press conference. King Carlo appeared comfortable at the podium, addressing each of the reporters by name and handling their inquiries as if they were guests in his living room. When a reporter deviated from questions on the economy to inquire about Isola, the monarch remained professional, yet relaxed. His demeanor remained the same as he switched to the topic of the Balkan summit.

She watched the clip a second time, studying the reporters' faces as best she could given the camera angle. Then a third time, with her focus on the king's expression.

She reread the queen's message. A full minute elapsed before she typed her response.

I appreciate the notice and the offer. Several weeks ago, you made an offer to me. When schedules permit, I would be pleased to accept.

She clicked send before she could talk herself out of it. She'd considered it ever since she and Ivo had taken their bike ride through Parco di Monza and he'd encouraged her to weigh the pros and cons of meeting the king. With the king's deft handling of the reporter, the pros outweighed the cons.

And Tomasina was right. If Lina treated the entire situation with an attitude of "so what?" perhaps that mentality would become reality.

Lina's phone screen illuminated, sending her heart to her throat as powerfully as if she'd hit the accelerator on Ivo's race car.

It would be our honor. Expect a phone call shortly from my assistant, Daniela, who shall make arrangements. She has my confidence. - QF

IVO BRACED his hands against the shower wall and rotated his head from left to right, then back again, allowing the warm spray to run off his scalp and down his face and back. He took easy breaths, in for a count of five, out for a count of five. Slowing his pulse. Relaxing his body. After every third exhale, he turned the dial down one notch until, at long last, cool water pummeled the top of his head, returning his temperature to a comfortable level.

It was a recovery ritual he'd followed hundreds, perhaps thousands of times. Gratifying as it was to clock a respectable time on the test track today, this felt even better. While engineers made adjustments to compensate for the effect of August heat on his car—addressing fuel consumption, tire wear, and engine efficiency—he was responsible for the effect on his body. Every minute he'd spent training in the heat had paid off today. A less experienced driver would've struggled.

He'd become the most experienced driver on the team by taking recovery seriously.

Ivo flexed his fingers, then stretched his arms over his head before reaching for the soap. He'd been cautious on a few of the turns today, ensuring he had the feel of the car. He could've gone faster. Tomorrow, he would.

This weekend, he damned well planned to make the podium.

He smacked his palm against the wet tile, confirming the promise to himself, then shut off the water.

Mario Puglisi, who'd moved into the top spot on Ferrari's F1 team following Ivo's accident, tripped over his daughter's scooter late last night. The doctors suspected he'd sprained his ankle. Though the first scan was inconclusive and they were forced to wait for the swelling to subside before performing a second, they didn't believe it to be a serious injury. Regardless of his prognosis, Mario's inflamed foot refused to fit his gear, leaving Esteban and Ivo to race in the Belgian Grand Prix. It wasn't what Ivo wanted, given that Mario had been Ivo's teammate for the past four seasons and was as close to a brother as Ivo had. But the opportunity was here and Ivo planned to make the most of it.

Unfortunately, moving from reserve driver to active status meant Ivo didn't have time to make the two-hour trip each way to Milan. He'd hoped to go tomorrow, spend a night—possibly two—then rejoin the team this weekend. Now that wouldn't be possible. Lina would understand, but that didn't lessen his disappointment. He craved the intimacy of the time they spent together. The easy rapport, the laughter, and especially the moments they lay curled against each other in bed, skin on skin, their hearts at rest.

More and more, he'd come to understand how Lina enriched his life. She viewed him as a person, not a driver or a celebrity. She forced him to evaluate his own assumptions about the world and about himself, challenging him in ways no one else dared. At the same time, she brought him peace. The moments spent with her in silence, whether riding bikes through a tree-lined park or walking hand-in-hand over a bridge at sunset, were the most glorious of his life.

Once dressed, he made his way to Ferrari's cafeteria for a dinner with factory employees, then retired to the room he used when staying overnight in Maranello. It was later than he'd planned to call, but he knew Lina would be awake. Probably reviewing spreadsheets. Or, if her lawyers had their way, the final contract from Mirabeau would have hit her desk this afternoon and she was reading it at this very moment.

He stretched out on the bed as he waited for her to pick up. Never in his life had the stars aligned more perfectly. His career was—literally—back on track and Lina's was firing on all cylinders.

Now that she'd landed Mirabeau, she might have to return to New York. If Tomasina would come through for him—

"Hello? Ivo?"

Lina's voice sent a buzz through his veins. He tucked a hand behind his head and adjusted the pillow. "No one says my name like you do," —*Princess* almost slipped from his lips, but he caught himself in time— "*Tesoro*. So provocative."

"All I did was answer the phone," she replied, then added in a sensuous tone, "Ivo."

"Mmm. Even better." His smile went so wide he felt it in his cheeks. "I'm sorry to call so late, but I have news."

"What happened?"

He recounted his day behind the wheel, then gave her the update on Mario and the Belgian Grand Prix.

"That's wonderful. Not for Mario, but for you. You're ready."

Her confidence bolstered his own. He wished he were in her flat, able to see the expression on her face.

"On the downside, it means staying in Maranello to prepare so I can head to Belgium on Wednesday," he told her. Lina knew the routine at these races. He'd do the pit walk and meet with fans on Thursday. Friday would be practice, then qualifying took place on Saturday and the race itself Sunday. "I won't be in Milan for another week. I know work is crazy for you now, but if you want to come, I could try to get a hotel room away from the frenzy."

"Much as I'd love to see you, it's your first race back. Focus on your career. Win." An odd note crept into her voice, but before he could analyze it, she told him, "I have news of my own. Frankfurt finally came through this afternoon. The official offer arrived a few minutes before I left work."

He gave the room a fist pump. "Took them long enough. How's it look?"

"Good. Fantastic." She shared the details of the proposal, her relief at finally making progress with the German department store evident. "Unfortunately, that means I won't be here when you're done in Belgium, either. To meet with the CEO before he goes on his summer holiday, I need to go to Frankfurt early next week. I'm flying straight from there to India."

"In that case, I'll make sure I'm in Milan when you return. Two weeks is my limit."

She murmured in agreement, then said, "There's something else. I've decided to go to Sarcaccia. Now that you're going to Belgium, I'll try to arrange it for this weekend."

He sat up at the unexpected pronouncement. "For work?"

"No."

He'd thought hearing that Mario tripped on a scooter would be the most shocking news of the day. "You decided to accept the invitation?"

"Yes. They offered to make arrangements. The flight takes around an hour, so I can be there and back in a day." She sighed. "I'm trying hard not to have second thoughts."

"Second thoughts are natural. But if you're asking my opinion…?"

"I know your opinion. I said yes because you're right. I need to take the risk." A mix of fear and grit edged her speech as she explained that the king was asked about Isola at a press conference this morning. The way he handled it made her believe a meeting was more likely than not to go well.

He smiled. "Would it be patronizing to tell you I'm proud of you? I know this isn't easy."

"Only if it's patronizing of me to say the same to you. You've worked hard to stand on the podium again and when you do, a lot of people will benefit. I'm thrilled you'll be on the circuit again. It's where you belong. "

The same odd note he'd heard earlier entered her voice as she mentioned his career. Particularly when she said, "It's where you belong." He frowned. It wasn't so much an odd note as an off note. Something was amiss. Something big.

"Lina? Did you have other news?"

"Frankfurt and Sarcaccia aren't enough?"

He changed position on the bed. "There's more. I can tell."

"Ivo—and that wasn't meant to be provocative—I have a lot going on here. It's just—" A feeble laugh slipped from her, one he was certain she didn't intend him to hear. "It's one of those things where I'd rather wait until we're together. You said you're heading to Belgium on Wednesday. Will you stay there the night after the race?"

The off note he'd heard before disappeared. In fact, her question sounded downright perky. *Bright.*

Experience in the simulator prepared him to absorb unexpected stops, turns, and even flips, honing his ability to keep his focus when his stomach dropped. His stomach never dropped quite like this.

"Lina." His voice was soft and filled with concern, even to his own hearing. "Tell me."

"Ivo, it's all right—"

"Tell me."

"We promised to communicate. Sometimes, though, it's hard. Especially when you're far away."

A long moment of silence followed. He closed his eyes. Waited. *Knew.*

"I'm pregnant."

CHAPTER 25

IVO BRACED one hand on the bed as he absorbed her news. He'd known what she was going to say a split second before the words came across the line, but that didn't lessen their impact.

What he didn't expect was for her to add, "I'm sorry."

"Don't apologize." He fisted the sheets at the edge of the bed. "Don't. Apologize. It takes two."

"I didn't mean—"

"Turn on the video." They needed to have this conversation face to face, even if they couldn't do it in person.

"It's all right, we can—"

"Turn on the video." He didn't mean to snap, so he softened his tone to add, "I want to see you."

"I'll move to the computer. Hold on."

He clicked the appropriate buttons on his phone and waited for Lina's image to appear. She was wearing the silk blouse she'd purchased at the UNICEF show, a blush pink with tiny flowers that made her face seem lit from within. Tasteful gold studs shone in her ears and her hair was styled for work. Seated at the table in her flat, she had a half-full water glass resting near her hand. Beautiful as she was, exhaustion was apparent in the lines at the edges of her eyes and her less-than-perfect posture.

"Better?"

"Always better when I can see you," he assured her. "Let's start over. You're pregnant. When did you find out?"

"Two hours ago." She stretched for something beyond his line of sight, then straightened to display a pink and white stick. "I haven't been to a doctor, but these rarely give false positives. I'm so sorry."

He shook his head. "Lina."

She waved a hand, dismissing her own apology. "I've felt strange the past few days. I had the overwhelming sensation something was wrong, as if I'd bungled a meeting or missed a work appointment. Then today I felt nauseous, and I'm never nauseous. I couldn't keep down an espresso from Marcello, if you can imagine that. I picked up a test on the way home from work."

He started to ask if she still felt sick, but she continued, "I know this will change things between us, but I don't want it to. At least not right away." A muscle jumped in her cheek. "I love what we have. I think you do, too. Seeing each other when our schedules permit, without having to deal with sharing finances or closet space…it suits both of our personalities. It suits our careers. It gives us the romance of seeing new places when you travel for races and keeps us from being distracted when we need to focus on work." She blew out a shaky breath in an attempt to gather herself. "Before either of us jump to make any changes to what we have, we should each take time to think about what we want. Separate from a pregnancy."

He inhaled on a count of three, then exhaled for three, an abbreviated version of his recovery routine. She'd rehearsed that speech in her head, even if she hadn't intended to deliver it tonight. He didn't need to rehearse a response.

"I know what I want."

With every fiber of his being. He knew it with a certainty he'd never experienced in his life, even more than when he'd seen the finish line of the Monaco Grand Prix and his hands moved ahead of his brain to turn the steering wheel enough to box out his nearest competitor and secure the win. More than when he'd first spied a kart and craved taking it around the track.

Even more than when he'd wanted to kiss Lina the very first time, that night they'd watched the stars in a park in Milan.

The want didn't scare him. A year or two ago, it would have. Maybe even a month ago. Now it felt as if it were the natural order of things. As if every choice in his life had driven him to exactly this point.

"How can you know when you haven't had any time to think about this? Aren't you even going to ask how I got pregnant?"

"Oh, believe me, I know how."

She scowled. "I mean how I got pregnant despite being on birth control."

"Accidents happen despite every precaution." He raised his chin to display the puckered skin of his burn scar. "I carry the proof. You can't plan for them. All you can do is adapt." He offered a smile intended to reassure her. "It's no different than when the reporters showed up in New York. You do your best. And you own what you do."

She shook her head, then smiled. "You're a good man, Ivo Zanardi."

"I'm a man who knows what I want. Lina, I want you."

"No, you don't. Not like that." Her fingers went to the screen and passion filled her voice. "You want to stand on a podium before this season is over. You want a World Drivers' Championship next season. You came so close three years ago. And again last season, when you had the Pole Trophy. You and I both know you can do it. You want it so much you plan your workouts months in advance and set audacious goals. Ivo, that dedication and heart is what makes you who you are. I would never, ever take that from you, any more than you would take Isola from me."

"You're not taking anything from me." He scrubbed his jaw, wishing he could be with her in person. "This shouldn't be a burden for you to bear."

She picked up the water glass then set it down again. It was one of those tics he would have missed if he hadn't insisted she turn on the video, and it told him all he needed to know about her mindset.

In the time between suspecting she was pregnant and answering the phone, she'd formulated a plan. Lina always had a plan. And, in this case, her plan didn't include him.

When he'd watched Lina from behind the curtain at the fashion show, it had occurred to him that she shared traits with his mother. This was one of them. She'd raise a child on her own, not wanting to rely on anyone else. Not wanting to burden anyone else. Wanting to control her own future.

But that wasn't at all what he wanted. He ground his palm into the bed.

He'd done it to himself, saying they didn't need a commitment. But damn it, he wanted one. He wanted to make one. Not because he felt a need to do better than his own parents had when faced with an unexpected pregnancy. Not to prove that he understood Lina wasn't her mother, using a pregnancy to manipulate. If that thought hadn't gone through her head yet, he knew her well enough to know it would. Though the situation wasn't the same as Teresa's, it'd occur to Lina that others would view her pregnancy—by a man with celebrity and fortune—through a certain lens, given the recent press.

He needed her to know that none of that mattered. He wanted Lina. Period.

Before he could find the words to explain what was going through his head, she said, "I'm not thinking in terms of a burden. My point is that we need to think about what we want. I know you. You're honest, you're steady under pressure, and you're dedicated. You also make snap decisions because it's what you're trained to do behind the wheel. It helps you win races and keeps you alive. But in this situation, that combination of traits may lead you to make a bad decision."

"You have never been a bad decision."

"That's good to know." Her smile made him want to reach through the screen. "Let's take this pregnancy news one day at a time. No rush, no making this more complicated than it needs to be. Can you do that? Can you put your mental energy toward Belgium?"

He wouldn't make any promises he couldn't keep. He matched her smile with one of his own, one he hoped would give her reassurance. "One day at a time."

The worry lines on her forehead eased. "Thank you. I really wish I could have told you in person. At the same time, I'm glad not to have to wait until I'm back from India."

"I'd rather know now. No matter what, we're in this together." Heartfelt emotion tightened his throat. "I'd hoped to tell you something in person, too, but I'll do it now so we're even."

She gave an exaggerated eye roll. "I can't imagine what else—"

"Lina, I love you. Whatever the future brings, know that."

Once more, she touched her fingers to the screen. He saw her swallow, fighting back moisture that sprang to her eyes. "I love you, too, Ivo."

His heart couldn't have expanded more. "Expect a terrific reunion after India."

That triggered a burst of laughter, though it didn't hide the passion in her gaze. "I can't wait."

THE MINUTE Ivo emerged from the crew meeting following his practice run, he dialed the number that had appeared on his phone screen an hour earlier. Tomasina hadn't left a message. He thought he'd come out of his skin as he waited to make the call.

By the fourth ring, he wondered if she'd already left for the day. He'd received a text from Lina almost simultaneously saying she was booked for "all travel" and would leave tomorrow. That, he knew, meant the daylong trip to Sarcaccia, a trip Tomasina knew nothing about.

But if Tomasina had finalized the Frankfurt and India legs and decided to share—

"*Pronto?*"

"It's Ivo. I saw you called."

"Ah, Tiziana! Thank you for returning my call about the airport transportation for Lina Cornaro. I was about to leave the office, so I am glad to hear from you."

He hesitated, uncertain for a moment, then asked, "Lina's within earshot?"

"Yes, yes. One moment and I will pull the travel details." He heard the tapping of a keyboard. "She will arrive in Milan next Sunday night just after seven p.m. She is coming from Mumbai via London Heathrow. I'll email the itinerary so you can track her flights in case of delays. You will have a sign with your company logo at pickup?"

"Thank you. I'll ensure she has a ride home from the airport that night." He provided his email address so Tomasina could send the information, then told her, "When you have a private moment, call your father. Have him call this number and identify himself." He recited the phone number, then explained, "I've set aside four tickets to the Paddock Club at the Italian Grand Prix next month in his name. He'll have great views of the track and garage, along with passes to walk around the pit area. I hope to meet him while he's there. You, too, if you accompany him."

He heard her sharp intake of breath over the phone, but her tone remained businesslike for Lina's sake. "That is…above and beyond. Thank you."

"No, thank you. This means more to me than you know."

If he pulled off this maneuver, it'd be the win of his life.

LINA GLANCED AT HER PHONE, ensuring she'd set the screen so updates from the qualifying day of the Belgian Grand Prix would appear, then sent a mental wish to Ivo in hopes he'd have a successful run. The press coverage for his return to Formula One had to be intense, yet he'd assured her beforehand that he'd remain focused on the race, not the bevy of cameras, while he chatted with fans and signed autographs on Thursday and ran through his practice routine yesterday.

Late last night, Ivo had called her from his hotel to let her know he'd done exactly what he'd predicted. He'd enjoyed a good practice run after feeding off support from his fans. He'd also offered encouragement for her trip to Sarcaccia today. Fortified, they'd each relaxed in their own beds, talking cars and lingerie, coworkers and pop culture. An upcoming movie by a favorite director dominated the conversation and they made plans to catch a showing in Milan.

Since she'd told him about the pregnancy, neither of them had mentioned it, aside from Ivo asking one seemingly blasé question about her health. She'd given a similarly blasé answer.

It was just as well. *One day at a time*.

Knowing Ivo loved her strengthened her mettle. Hearing it for the first time while they each traveled might not be the magical scene most women craved, but it was perfect. For *her*. She didn't want a man—even if that man was Ivo—changing his life's plan and swooping to her rescue out of a sense of obligation. She wanted their relationship based on their interactions, not on their circumstance.

Above all, she didn't want to be her mother.

Oh, she knew she wasn't. Ivo knew she wasn't. But the thought was difficult to push from her mind, particularly this morning, as she walked a street only a few blocks from the palace where her mother once tutored and seduced a crown prince. When she was compelled to leave home at a ridiculous hour and wear oversized sunglasses to lessen the chances she'd be recognized on a street in central Cateri, Sarcaccia's capital.

Lina stopped walking as she reached the intersection. The etched lettering on the glass door across the street identified number 45 Via Gallura as Angeletti Gelato. Lina frowned, then double checked her email, making certain the address Daniela sent matched that of the building.

Well, she was in the right spot. A gelateria probably shouldn't have surprised her, given the New York meeting with Maria Rossi occurred in the back of a coffee shop.

Pocketing her phone, Lina cut across the center of the street. Most shops on the island didn't open until ten on Saturdays, so at nine in the morning, traffic was light. The only pedestrians she'd spotted were tourists taking photos of Sarcaccia's famous cathedral or waiting to board one of the green and yellow tour busses that made the circuit of Cateri's medieval district. When the crack-of-dawn puddle jumper Daniela booked for Lina touched down an hour ago, even the airport had been quiet.

She had to give the royal family credit. They knew their island and its rhythm.

The gelateria appeared dark, but as Lina pushed her sunglasses on top of her head and approached the door, a blonde wearing a gray cotton dress and black Converse approached on the sidewalk. Between her laid-back outfit and swingy braid, she looked like a local out on an errand. Lina's gut told her otherwise.

"Let me guess, you're headed here?" the blonde said in American-accented English. "It happens to be open for two people right now. You and me. Come on."

The woman knocked twice, then opened the door without waiting and led Lina into the shop. A woman with thick black hair rose from where she'd been fixing a chair and crossed the shop, a smile of welcome on her face.

"Good morning, April," she said to the blonde, then focused on Lina and extended her hand. "And you must be Lina Cornaro. I'm Sara Angeletti."

"And as Sara said, I'm April," the blonde told her, offering Lina a firm handshake now that they were off the street. "It's a pleasure to meet you. I'm here to pick up the gelato my husband ordered and deliver it to the palace. I'll deliver you at the same time."

"April's married to Ryan Fournier, the palace's head chef," Sara explained. "The man discovered my gelato and made the wise decision to order it from time to time for special events." She glanced at April. "Did you park in the alley?"

"As requested."

Lina marveled at the shop's interior. While the decor took its cues from the historical building, with period-appropriate wood-framed mirrors dotting the walls and an elegant glass-fronted counter where customers selected and purchased their gelato, updates made the shop family-friendly. Two umbrella stands, one sized for adults and one for children, stood near the entry. Garbage cans tucked into the corners were modified so children wouldn't have to stretch to deposit their trash. In the center of the space, there were plenty of easy-to-clean tables topped with green and yellow tile, each with chairs that could be arranged to accommodate groups. Small yellow, green, and white Sarcaccian flags peeked from planters of greenery, offering another dash of color while giving a nod to the nearby palace and its occupants.

Best of all, the place smelled delicious. Like a warm embrace of vanilla, chocolate, and berries. Lina's eyes went to the menu, which was posted on a blackboard behind the counter and included selections for those with modified diets without sacrificing the flavors gelato fiends most adored. At one end of the counter, near the cash register, stood a glass display case designed to hold bakery treats.

"This is as perfect a gelateria as I've seen and I live in central Milan."

Sara's smile broadened. "Thank you. I'd offer you the grand tour, but you're expected at the palace. Follow me."

Lina couldn't help but trail her hand near the bakery case as they circled the counter. "Who did your design?"

"You're looking at her." Sara grinned, then pushed through a swinging door to a pristine kitchen. "The gelato recipes are all mine, too."

Lina knew in a five-second glance around the kitchen that Sara was a woman after her own heart. Not a single item was out of place. The stainless steel counters were so clean, they looked as if they were never used, though their patina proved otherwise. Mixing equipment was covered, utensils stored on racks ordered by size, and the massive freezer doors at the back of the room were completely free of fingerprints.

"I'm in awe."

"There have been a few misses with flavors over the years, but on the whole, we've done well." She opened the emergency exit door at the rear of the kitchen, looked outside to ensure the alley was clear, then used her toe to slide a wooden doorstop into place before crossing the kitchen to the freezer doors. A few seconds later, she emerged with a box and handed it to April. "There's a packing list and a receipt on top, and an extra carton of your favorite *pistacchio* tucked on the side. That's gratis for you and Ryan."

April beamed in sheer delight. "I'll get the order to my husband, the *pistacchio* to my fridge, and Lina to palace security. Thank you. This has been a huge help."

Sara's mouth quirked at the mention of palace security. She surveyed the alley once more, then indicated that it was all clear. April exited, tipping her head to indicate that Lina should follow.

Lina stopped to tell Sara it'd been nice to meet her, but Sara spoke first. "One piece of advice before you go to the palace. You're likely to be escorted by a man named Umberto Niro. He can be an ass. Don't let him intimidate you."

On that surprising note, Sara told her to enjoy herself, then kicked out the doorstop and waved Lina into the alley before the door slammed shut.

CHAPTER 26

Fifteen minutes later, Lina and April arrived at the palace. The drive should have taken five, by Lina's estimation, but April had taken a meandering route through central Cateri, chatting about various landmarks, describing her favorite restaurants, and mentioning a bar that offered a stunning view of the Mediterranean if Lina stayed on the island long enough to enjoy happy hour.

She wouldn't, but Lina appreciated April's ability to keep her nerves settled with easy conversation. She learned that April was originally from New York. Her work restoring buildings had caught Queen Fabrizia's attention when the monarch visited Manhattan years earlier and marveled at a project April had completed. "She made me an offer I couldn't refuse," April explained, "and now I handle repairs and restoration at the palace. It's a dream job."

"Sounds like it. Even more, I take it, once you met the chef?"

"Oh, I knew him in New York. *Left* him in New York, or so I thought." April's mischievous tone made it clear there was a story behind their relationship. "And here we are."

They turned into a fenced area, where an armed guard raised a bar and waved them past his station. Instead of proceeding straight ahead, toward the palace's main building, April turned onto a ramp that descended below ground, where they stopped at a metal gate. April rolled down her window, held a card against a panel, then the gate lifted, admitting them to a parking garage unlike any Lina had ever seen. Fancy carriages, the type seen in royal parades, were situated just inside the gate. Beyond those, several nondescript sedans lined one side of the garage, each parked nose out. On the opposite side were several cars with much higher price tags—a Mercedes, an antique she thought might be a Bentley, and several BMWs, though a few plain sedans and a red Jeep stuffed with fishing gear were interspersed with them. At the end of those, along a wall, stood a Cadillac limousine with tinted glass windows. A Sarcaccian flag and a flag bearing the crest of the royal family rose above the headlights.

A daunting man stood at the end of the line of sedans, his gaze tracking their movement. He gestured for April to back into the widest spot, one that provided a direct line to the exit. It was obviously the VIP position, at least among the staff vehicles.

April grumbled as she turned the sedan, then put it in reverse. "That's Umberto Niro, the head of security. Needless to say, this is his car. He'll take you the rest of the way. Don't let him intimidate you."

Lina glanced at April as April put the car in park and cut the engine. "Sara gave me a similar warning."

"She did? Huh."

Lina didn't get a chance to ask April what that meant before Umberto rounded the car and opened her door. "Welcome to Sarcaccia. I'll escort you from here."

He waited for April, who took her time removing the box of gelato from the back seat, then instructed her to go ahead. April gave Lina a, "nice to meet you," then crossed the garage to an elevator. Though the drive from the gelato shop to the palace had taken longer than necessary, Lina wished she'd had more time with the American. April had a mix of charm and practicality to her that made Lina suspect they could be friends.

Umberto watched April go, then shifted his focus to Lina. "Before we enter, I must ask whether there are weapons in your handbag."

Lina blinked. "No."

"It's standard procedure to ask. I must also request that you take no photographs for the duration of your visit, unless granted permission by a family member or at their request."

"Wouldn't dream of it."

"Thank you. Follow me, please."

This was feeling less like a visit and more like a test. She followed him to an elevator which opened to a service hallway on the ground floor. After several twists and turns he punched a code into a panel beside a door, then gestured for her to precede him. They emerged into a hallway with marble flooring and gigantic chandeliers, one long and wide enough to accommodate hundreds of people. She fell into step beside him and tried to concentrate on keeping her pulse at a normal tempo. When she'd first seen Umberto in Manhattan, wearing a hooded sweatshirt and acting as if he were any other coffee shop patron, Lina sensed that the Barrali family's chief of security wasn't what he seemed. His posture reminded her of a snake lazing on a sunny rock. Relaxed, yet able to strike with deadly force in an instant.

"Big place," Lina said as they turned the corner into yet another long marble hallway. It was an obvious, awkward comment, yet Umberto only angled his head.

"There are faster routes to the palace garden, but His Highness instructed that I avoid the public spaces."

The public spaces part she understood. "I didn't realize he wished to meet in the garden. I've heard it's beautiful."

Her eyes went from the oil paintings on her left to the expansive windows on her right, which overlooked a large fountain. Sprays of water went skyward, then fell to a blue pool in a mesmerizing rhythm. Around the fountain, low boxwood hedges surrounded a variety of roses in bloom. Two men in suits sat on a bench alongside a woman in a black pencil skirt and white blouse. One of the men took notes as she spoke. Beyond them, gravel paths disappeared into the greenery.

"Isn't the garden, ah, rather public?" Not only did palace employees and guests frequent the space, large swaths were visible from the rear of the palace. The gelateria seemed a more appropriate spot than behind the palace.

His expression didn't change. "Not where we're going."

Did he intend to sound ominous?

Umberto opened a cleverly hidden door between two of the oil paintings, then guided her down a flight of stairs under the watchful eye of overhead cameras and through an exterior door. He led her along a narrow path bordered by plantings that blocked it from view of those inside the palace. On and on they went, until they reached a chest-high wrought iron fence in front of large evergreens she assumed marked the rear of the property. They turned, following a path that ran perpendicular to the fence and evergreens. Beyond the evergreens, she could hear the low hum of traffic.

"Is that Via Floriana on the other side?" She'd approached Angeletti Gelato that way from the airport. The sight of the government security signs along a high fence on one side of the street captured her attention.

"It is." After a few minutes, he stopped and reached over the fence, releasing a latch on a hidden gate. Until he did so, she hadn't noticed the gap in the evergreens. "Through here."

She glanced at him, but he merely gestured for her to precede him. She ducked, went through the gap, and was stunned by the sight on the other side.

Umberto emerged beside her. "This is the family's private garden. Few know of its existence. King Carlo thought it would provide a secure meeting place without the formality of the residence."

"It's amazing." Given the thick greenery and the secret latch in the fence, it was perfectly disguised from those outside. And though it was situated at the rear of the palace grounds, bordering the shopping streets, the tall evergreens kept the noise of the city at bay.

It was easily accessible, yet secluded. And wildly romantic.

"Yes, it is." Umberto's mouth lifted into a grin that transformed his entire being. "I'm rarely here, as it's for the family only. It's my favorite location on the grounds."

Before Lina could process the fact Umberto actually smiled, the guard's gaze went to the center of the garden and his intense demeanor snapped back into place. "I believe Princess Sophia is here with King Carlo."

"Princess Sophia?" She didn't mean to blurt it out, but surprise got the better of her. "I didn't realize she'd be joining us."

"The king's schedule is blocked for a meeting with his daughter. If he returns to the palace from the garden with her by his side, no one will ask questions."

"I see."

Her gaze followed Umberto's, but she didn't see anything. A few beats later, movement on the other side of the fountain caught her attention, then the king came into full view.

Beside her, Umberto gave a slight bow. "I shall wait outside the garden."

The king's voice sounded just as it did on television when he replied, "Thank you, Umberto."

The monarch approached with a cautious, yet pleasant smile on his face. Lina knew she should move to greet him, but her feet weighed as much as boulders. He strode toward her and offered his hand. "It feels odd to say this, but it's a pleasure to meet you, Lina."

She took his hand. Shook it. Saw the bright gleam in his eyes as she released her grip. "Your Majesty." She paused. "Or is it Highness? I admit, I—"

"Please, King Carlo."

"King Carlo."

Though he wore a suit, one in a lightweight fabric appropriate for the summer weather, Lina would have recognized this man as powerful and important even if he'd walked past her barefoot in a swimsuit and T-shirt on the beach. He stood ramrod straight, his neck lengthened and head high. It wasn't posturing, but his natural carriage.

"Eventually, I hope Carlo will suffice, at least when we are in private." He gestured toward the garden's center, where several benches offered views of the fountain. "Why don't we sit?"

She nodded, then walked ahead of him on the narrow path. At the far end of the garden, she could see the princess's back as she knelt with a pair of clippers, snipped a flower, then placed it in a bucket.

"I had an appointment with Sophia marked on my calendar," the king said as Lina chose a bench and sat. He took a spot at the far end, a distance that allowed for easy conversation without crowding her. "She'll remain out of earshot. She's curious about you, but understands it might be best to meet another time."

"Umberto mentioned the appointment." She resisted the urge to take another peek at the princess. "Rocco thinks highly of her."

"He stayed for dinner with the family following the press conference. I imagine we were a bit much, though he handled it well." The king's gaze flicked to Sophia, then returned to Lina. "Today, however, is about you. I'm glad you decided to visit, though I suspect my wife twisted your arm. I doubt it was a coincidence she needed to fly to New York precisely when you were there."

Lina's surprise must have registered on her face, because he laughed. "Ah, yes. I suspected as much. She's stubborn once she sets her mind to a task, and her tasks often revolve around what she believes is best for me."

"She loves you very much," Lina observed. It seemed the safest thing to say.

"I'm a fortunate man." He folded his hands in his lap and angled his head, his expression growing more serious as he regarded her. "When I met Rocco in Croatia before the press conference, he told me about the letters your mother left you. He had a lot of questions. I assume you do, as well. I'm happy to answer anything you wish to know. However, first, I must express my condolences on your loss. Your mother and I had a complicated history. Despite that, I wished her a long and happy life. I was saddened to hear of her illness. Sadder still for you and your brothers. She loved you to the depths of her soul."

"Thank you." Lina felt she should say more. Not because she owed him anything, but because something in his demeanor invited it.

It was odd. She didn't know this man at all, yet she felt a connection with him. It took her a moment to realize why. Though she'd seen him hundreds of times on television, it never occurred to her how incredibly like Rocco he looked. Or, she supposed, Rocco looked like the king. She'd noticed their coloring before, and the similarities between their noses and their jawline were readily apparent. Even the royal watchers commented on it after Rocco appeared at the press conference. But there was more. Looking at King Carlo felt like looking into Rocco's future, once gray entered his dark hair and the lines at his brow and the corners of his eyes deepened. Their voices were similar. Their hands moved the same way when they spoke. They even smiled the same way. She found it both eerie and comforting.

Finally, she said, "I feel like I should apologize to you. For what she did to you."

He waved off the statement. "She did nothing to me. What happened, we did together."

"You were a teenager."

"A teenager who knew what I was doing was wrong." His gaze warmed as he spoke. "It was a long time ago. I can't change it. I can only change my perspective on it. I regret that I hurt my wife. I regret the hurt it's caused you, your brothers, and my children with Fabrizia. But I don't regret the lessons I've learned. And I certainly don't regret that you or your brothers exist."

There was a note in the king's voice that convinced Lina of his honesty. He'd said something similar to Rocco.

"You have a good attitude about it," she said. "I can't imagine it fades with time, the anger you feel if someone gets pregnant to trap you into marriage. Or when that person leaves with the children."

"I've had years to develop it." He lifted a hand as if he wanted to touch her, but let it fall to his lap. "It never would have worked. Not even if I'd married Teresa when she became pregnant with Rocco. Your mother figured that out eventually, too. She understood that I loved Fabrizia. In the end, she found a better man for her. She loved Jack Cornaro in a way she never loved me, and I was glad of it."

Carlo shifted on the bench. He flashed a look past Lina, toward Sophia. Apparently satisfied that his daughter was out of hearing range, he said, "If anything, I owe an apology to you. It takes two people to create a child. Two people to take responsibility. Your mother denied me access to you, but that was due to our actions—hers and mine—not yours. I deeply regret that I wasn't able to raise you.

My children have been the great joy of my life and having you under my roof would have made my life richer. However, I also knew that Jack Cornaro was a good father to you. I chose not to fight your mother because I knew you were better off." The king raked a hand over his head. It was a gesture Rocco did when he was deep in thought, trying to work through a problem. She'd seen King Carlo do it once before, during a television interview. It seemed he did it when he'd come to a realization and was about to make an important point. "Fabrizia told me once that the best thing a human being can do when faced with a difficult choice is to choose love. Letting you go without a fight was my way of choosing love. If your mother hadn't raised you well, if she'd gone on to marry a man without the qualities Jack Cornaro possessed, I'd have stepped in. No matter the damage to my reputation. The only way to be true to myself would be to choose love."

Lina bit her bottom lip. Hadn't Fabrizia said something similar when she'd come to New York? She'd come for love. *Always love.*

"What matters to me is the here and now," Carlo continued. "Not what happened decades ago. I know that in your heart, Jack Cornaro will always be your father. That is as it should be. But in my heart" — he tapped his fist to his chest— "you will always be my daughter. From the moment I knew of your existence, I knew I would do anything for you. I hope you can understand that, even though you are an adult and not a child in need of guidance."

She resisted the urge to cover her abdomen. Even now, she knew she loved the child growing there. She hadn't thought it possible to feel so deeply connected to a human being she'd never seen and didn't know, but she did.

"I'm not sure what to say."

"You don't need to say anything." He smiled. "I want my children —all my children—to be happy. If I can facilitate that in any way, it would be my pleasure."

Lina couldn't help but return Carlo's smile. "That's very kind of you."

"And selfish. It allows me to get to know you better." Lina heard a low hum. The king checked his watch, then said, "We only have a few more minutes before I'm expected inside the palace."

Lina knew their meeting wouldn't be a long one, given that they'd wanted to keep it private. When the arrangements were made, she'd assured Daniela—and Fabrizia—that a brief meeting was fine. Now, however, she wished they had more time. Seeing this man in person felt surreal. She needed time to absorb the experience, to process how she felt separate from what she'd seen of the king on television and separate from what she'd been raised to believe.

Then Carlo said something Lina wasn't expecting at all.

"I also have news from Belgium."

CHAPTER 27

"Belgium?"

Lina couldn't keep the shock from her voice. Unruffled by her reaction, Carlo rose from the bench, then offered Lina his hand to assist her. She felt awkward accepting it, but the king either didn't notice or had a lifetime of negotiating such niceties and had become adept at pretending not to notice. When he released her hand and gestured toward the gap in the evergreens, he explained, "Ivo Zanardi had a successful qualifying run for the Belgian Grand Prix. He has the pole position in tomorrow's race."

She stopped walking, torn between elation for Ivo and the burning question of how the king would have such information. And why he'd know of her interest.

"I had an alert sent to my watch," he explained, accurately reading her hesitation. He looked beyond her, noted that Sophia had seen their movement toward the exit, and raised his hand in an indication he and Lina were nearly finished. "I'm not as up on Formula One as I should be, but I've seen interviews with Ivo Zanardi. He strikes me as a man who does what he wants. Who calculates his moves before he makes them."

She swallowed, certain the king had a point. He was like his wife in that regard. "Yes."

"I've met a few F1 drivers. Without fail, they are men who like control. If they don't have it, they take it. But what stood out to me about Ivo was something he said during an interview that aired last year here in Sarcaccia. He said he left his modeling career to race because he so loved the sport, he had to do it to remain true to himself. He did it even though fame would have come more easily for him if he'd remained a model." The king tipped his head as they reached the evergreens. "I admire that conviction. That passion. He's a risk taker when he believes in the potential payoff. A good example for us all, isn't it?"

"You're making a point?"

"An observation." He smiled, but it faded as he aimed a discreet look toward the princess. "Sophia has been pursued by men from the time she was young. Men who crave the title, rather than the woman. My wish for her is that she finds her place as one man's princess. A choice of conviction and his passion rather than the choice of his ego. A man who chooses her for the same reasons Ivo Zanardi chose F1... strictly a choice of the heart." His gaze intensified as he added, "I suspect Jack Cornaro wished the same for you. That you be one man's princess. His heart. It is the way of all fathers who love their daughters."

The king's watch let out a beep before Lina could respond. In her mind, she could hear Ivo's words the night they'd gone to the theater, when she'd said she was no one's princess.

You're mine. Always will be. But I'll call you something else.

And he had. He'd been about to call her princess the other night on the phone, she was certain. Then he'd substituted *tesoro*.

She watched, transfixed, as King Carlo bent, glanced through the evergreens, and gave a whistle. "Umberto will escort you to the car and ensure you are taken to the airport without incident. Should you wish to visit again, please do. Hopefully we can enjoy a more leisurely get together, perhaps over dinner?"

"I'd like that." Lina had to admit that she was more curious than ever about the monarch and his children. It would take time, but she sensed they'd become important to her life.

"Keep in touch."

"I will." She hesitated, then said, "I definitely will."

Neither of them said anything, but she knew he wanted to hug her. It was undoubtedly a breach of etiquette, but she moved first, opening her arms to embrace the king.

"Be true to yourself, little butterfly," he said as he held her. "And good luck to Ivo tomorrow. I suspect that is where your heart is at the moment."

She thanked him, then ducked through the gap in the evergreens to see Umberto waiting. She tried to ignore the fact she'd spotted moisture in the king's eyes when he let her go.

As Umberto took her along twisty roads, glancing in the mirror as if he were James Bond attempting to shake a tail, she considered King Carlo's words. Ivo did calculate moves before he made them. And he did fight for what he wanted, even if it was a risk to do so. It was what drove him to essentially kidnap her and take her to the Park Hyatt. To convince her to stay for dinner and a bath, of all things. To insist on walking her to the condo.

Then again, he'd stepped back so she could decide for herself about having him run interference with reporters at some of her launch events.

He liked control. He also respected her wishes. He respected her career.

Then she thought of Marcello, who'd felt compelled to warn her about Ivo, saying that while he was a nice man, he was never home.

Lina pressed her fingers to the bridge of her nose when she took her seat aboard the plane that would carry her to Milan. Ivo was everything she ever wanted. Her lover, her friend. He inspired her. He thrilled her every time he walked into a room. He made her laugh. He expanded her world.

She loved him with all her heart.

Her phone lit with a text.

Pole tomorrow, 1 min to press conf. Will call tonight. All good there?

What a wonderful, wonderful man. Her heart filled for him as she typed.

Congratulations!

Ivo was a role model to so many that his press conferences always generated interest. This one, however, would be insane. No one snagged the pole the first race after a career-threatening injury. She blew out a hard breath, then added to her message.

Look fwd to hearing more. Just boarded flight. All good.

His response appeared in seconds.

After India we'll celebrate in person. Can't wait. I love you.

She stared at the last three words. He was killing her.

She needed to choose love. To let Ivo pursue his dream, to see what heights he could achieve. And she could only do that by letting Ivo be Ivo.

Her fingers shook, but she typed furiously, hoping he'd see her text before the press conference. That he'd walk to the microphones with fire in his veins, take his seat, and own the room, just as he had before his accident.

Better.

Once upon a time, you sold shirts on the street. You told me how you felt holding those first coins in your hand. You were on top of the world. Go win tomorrow. Grab that feeling. Own it. And know I have your back.

"I love you, Ivo Zanardi," she whispered, then clicked send.

LINA ROLLED her carry-on suitcase up the jet bridge and into the terminal, where the passengers from her plane merged into the throng exiting a plane at an adjacent gate. En masse, they followed the multilingual signs toward passport control and customs. She bit back a groan at the sea of people in front of her. Some jockeyed to get ahead while others struggled with bags and children or moved with the assistance of canes.

She had plenty of time to make her connection to Milan, but imagining the wait made her legs ache. Tomasina had apologized for the routing, knowing Heathrow had long lines, but the last-minute changes to her itinerary had proven challenging. While previous flights home from Mumbai took Lina through Istanbul or Abu Dhabi, the only flight via Istanbul today was sold out and Abu Dhabi would've necessitated a seven-hour layover.

Heathrow it was.

Moving the flight to accommodate her Frankfurt meeting was well worth it, though. The Germans had taken their time to commit to Isola, but once they made their offer, they were all in. The CEO had treated Lina like a VIP from the moment she'd landed in Frankfurt, giving her a personal tour of their largest location while talking about his hopes for their partnership. The CEO's enthusiasm gave Lina a boost that carried her through the long flight to Mumbai and hot days spent with her fabric suppliers.

She shifted to the side, allowing an airport employee to push a wheelchair through the crowd. Mumbai in August was a killer. As always in India, the quality and variety of fabric options stunned her, but walking through warehouses and textile markets—none of which had air-conditioning—and sitting through two business dinners on a queasy stomach left her exhausted and craving her own bed.

Only a few more hours, she told herself. Passport control, customs, then the flight to Milan and a car service to take her home.

Bless Tomasina. When she entered Lina's office with the updated travel plans, she'd taken the unusual step of considering how Lina would get home from the airport. "I know you prefer public transportation, but with the changes to the itinerary and a long flight from India, would you like me to book a driver?"

Lina had waffled, not wanting to spend money on what felt like a luxury. Now she was glad she'd decided to indulge.

"This doesn't look promising," a man walking near Lina told his wife. Lina followed the man's line of sight toward the Arrivals sign. A security officer stood underneath and directed passengers to the proper side of a retractable belt barrier, depending on their citizenship. Lina knew from experience there was a long way to go to reach the back of the line once she passed the officer. Then the line itself would snake as far as the eye could see, even for the automated checks.

"It'll be at least an hour before we hand over our passports," the woman said. "I'm going to use the facilities first."

"Good idea."

The couple cut to the right, where a short line extended from the door of the ladies' room. Lina considered following the woman, but opted to forge ahead. An hour she could handle, as long as her stomach didn't betray her. She hadn't vomited since that embarrassing incident at the bus stop near Café San Giorgio, but she imagined it wouldn't be the only occurrence in the months ahead, given how much she'd struggled. A good night's sleep would help.

Her mouth curved at the thought. Ivo promised to meet her at the flat as soon as she arrived. He'd also promised to let her rest. His eyes fairly glittered through her computer screen when she'd called him before checking out of her hotel in Mumbai. "I've waited this long to see you," he'd told her. "I can wait until you've recovered so we can talk. Or do whatever else your heart desires."

She tightened her grip on the handle of her suitcase as she navigated around a woman who'd stopped to search for her passport in the side pocket of her bag. The weeks since she'd seen Ivo stretched forever, even with work to keep her busy. Marcello had been right in his assessment of Ivo that morning she'd been ill: his neighbors adored him and thought he was kind, but he was rarely home during the season.

Racing weeks were intense affairs, involving far more than the race itself. Fan events, team meetings, practice runs, the qualifying run...it was enough to make Lina's head spin. It also made Ivo happy. Energy radiated from him when they'd talked after the Belgian Grand Prix, despite the result not being what Ivo had hoped. An early bump sent him to the middle of the pack, but he'd fought his way to the front. He and Esteban ended up side by side at the approach to the finish, battling for the final spot on the podium.

Esteban beat him out by two-tenths of a second. It only made Ivo more determined. Next weekend was the Italian Grand Prix at Monza, and he was determined to finish in first.

"It is *La Pista Magica*," he'd said. The Magic Track to all Italians. "Monza and San Rimini are the events I want most. I intend to take both. When I do, no one will stop me."

She'd thought back to Carlo's statement about Ivo's determination and passion. While he'd be in Milan all week to prepare for the race, she didn't want to distract him. The lead up to the event, the atmosphere, the planning…all of it fired Ivo's blood. It made him the man she loved.

As Carlo said, racing was a choice Ivo made to be true to himself.

She angled her head to see down the hall, but winced as her hair caught in the shoulder strap of her handbag. She shrugged as she continued walking, attempting to shake the strap to a more comfortable position.

"Allow me."

Her heart slammed into her ribcage at the familiar, gritty voice. She stopped short, nearly causing the businessman on her left to crash into her. "Ivo? What are you doing here? You're in Milan!"

"Obviously not." Gently, he eased her from the flow of foot traffic, nearer the wall, then lifted the bothersome shoulder strap and used his index finger to free the piece of hair that'd been caught.

She gaped at him, shocked to wordlessness. At the same time, she became aware of the stares of people around her and the whispered sounds of his name.

"As to what I'm doing here, it all goes back to this, oddly enough." He indicated her handbag, a glimmer of amusement lighting his face. "The first time I ever saw you, you were approaching passport control. You were ahead of me. Your hair was caught, just like it is now, and I couldn't tear my eyes from it. I had the most perplexing urge to free that poor little tendril."

"Are you all right?" She stared at him, still in disbelief. "Where did you come from? Why are you here?"

"I bribed your assistant." His eyes sparkled as he traced his way down her arm. With his free hand, he pulled her rolling suitcase from her grip and tucked it behind him, against the wall, so he could hold both her hands in his. "Well, bribed isn't the right word. Tomasina is very protective of you. The day we went bike riding in Monza, I called her while you were in the shower and convinced her it was imperative I know your travel schedule, particularly if it took you through Heathrow."

Her mind raced, attempting to keep up.

"I flew to Tunis, then switched and flew to Heathrow. Not exactly a direct path, but it put me at the arrival gate beside yours a half hour ago. It didn't take much to wait for you to arrive and follow you once you emerged from the jet bridge."

"I can't believe you did that. I'd have been just as happy if you met me in Milan." She squeezed his hands. "The last thing you need to do is spend a Sunday flying all over the place. It would have been cheaper, too."

"But it wouldn't be the same. I'm not here simply to meet you. I'm here to propose to you."

CHAPTER 28

Myriad emotions fluttered across Lina's face as she studied him. His pulse thundered in his ears as if he'd just finished an all-out training run. Only this time, he didn't have a proper cooldown routine in place.

Ivo kept her hands wrapped in his. He'd do this. He'd convince her. He had no other goal. "You might not be aware, but when you're trying to convince me that you're being logical or that you're feeling carefree when you really aren't, your voice goes into sales mode."

She blinked. "Sales mode?"

"Bright. Upbeat."

"Upbeat. Upbeat is sales mode."

He laughed. "Let's just say that when something is important to you, when your heart is involved, but you don't want me to know your heart is involved, your voice changes. Like when I passed medical and you asked how long until Ferrari wanted me in the car. Or when I said I was heading to Canada."

"I wanted you to do those things."

"Yes, you did. But you didn't want me to know they worried you. You wanted me to give my career one hundred percent and not worry about you." She opened her mouth to argue, but he shushed her. He needed to get this right. "You also used it to talk about making chicken with hot pepper sauce. You wanted a deeper commitment, at least in your heart, but your brain told you it was wrong."

"I wanted us on the same page."

"We were on the same page. Each of us was too scared to admit it. Just like we were before San Rimini." He raised her hands to his lips and kissed her knuckles, then smiled at her. "You also used that same sales voice when you gave me the big news."

She glanced around, her gaze indicative of the fact they were being watched and possibly listened to. "I told you not to make any big decisions. I meant it, both with my heart and my head."

"The decision was already made. As I said, I called Tomasina after our day in Monza. Before we knew about…about the big news. When I told you during that phone call that I knew what I wanted, it was the truth." He dropped to one knee, fearful of what Lina would say, but gratified by the tears that sprung to her eyes.

"No cameras in the secured area!" he heard a security officer shout. "Read the signs!"

"Lina Cornaro, you are my world. You have been from the moment I saw you walk through this very hallway. From the moment you waved your fingers at a fussy toddler and gave that child's mother a toy from your bag. You cared for me when I didn't deserve it. You give me purpose."

Her hands shook, though her voice remained steady. "You have a purpose. You're going to win the World Drivers' Championship next season."

"I'll win Monza next weekend. And then San Rimini. That's where my plan ends. My purpose is so much bigger than the championship."

"The championship is all you've ever wanted!"

He grinned. His mother challenged him to look long term at what would make him happy. To consider the difficult route. She was right. He told Lina, "When I retire, there are drivers who can take my place. Drivers like Esteban. But there are things only I can do. Growing up in Rome with kids who didn't have much let me see that. Meeting Amira and hearing her story let me see that. I can help those kids in a way few others can."

"You'd miss the track. The atmosphere. Your whole face lights up when you talk about racing."

"There's a track north of Milan that's been for sale for years. It's small and needs renovation, but I could buy it and update it. Use it to train young drivers, have weekend events for disadvantaged kids. And I wouldn't be risking a stint in the hospital to do it." Even as he talked about it, he imagined Lina standing trackside, cheering for kids who got behind the wheel of a kart and felt in control, perhaps for the first time in their lives. "I can do so many things no one else can do. Things that will make me feel accomplished. Things that make a difference in the world. But there's no accomplishment without you."

Tears clung to her lower lashes. "It still feels fast. Like you hurried this decision."

"Do you love me?"

"I do." Her voice was barely above a whisper. "I love you with all my heart, Ivo."

"No cameras!" came the shout from down the hall.

"Can you deal with the press attention that would come with being married to me?"

"You've dealt with it. I'm learning from your example. But for you to give up—"

"Last week, you texted me from Sarcaccia. You reminded me how good it felt when I held those first coins in my hand. How accomplished and proud I felt. For all that feeling, it wasn't the best thing I've ever held. Not those coins, not the steering wheel, not a trophy. You. You're the most valuable, the most exciting, the most humbling. The only thing that could possibly top it would be to hold your child. Our child. It's almost impossible to imagine, because what I already have with you is so overwhelming. I can't let you go, Lina. It would be like living in the shade after experiencing the sun. I want you to marry me. Will you marry me? I wouldn't be giving up anything. I'd be gaining everything."

A single tear topped her lower lashes, then trickled down her cheek.

He resisted the urge to stand and brush it away. Not until he heard her answer.

"You've supported my dreams from the moment we met, Ivo. I want to support yours. You're the best in the world at what you do. What you do *now*. I trust in your doctors. I trust in your ability."

She released a long breath. He waited, his heart in his throat. Then one side of her mouth lifted. Quietly, she said, "You can't renovate and set up a kart track in less than a year. Finish your career on the track the way you want. The way you deserve to finish. The way the world deserves to see you finish. Not just Monza and San Rimini, but next season. I can handle our big news in the meantime. All right?"

There was a gravity in her words that compelled him to nod in agreement. He waited, watched her face. Then a smile blossomed. "Then that's a yes. I'd love to marry you. I can't imagine telling you no."

In one motion, he rose and gathered her into his arms. Cheers erupted around them, but he ignored the noise to whisper in her ear, "You can't imagine telling me no, but you can negotiate the deal."

"The sign of a true partnership."

He held her like that for several long breaths, then gave her a deep, passionate kiss, one that elicited more cheers. For her ears only, he said, "I love you, Lina Cornaro."

"And I love you, Ivo. I'll love you until the day I die. Probably after that."

"Probably?"

"Definitely."

He brushed his lips against hers, then bent to gather her bags. "Let's go home. I promised a celebration tonight and I intend to keep my word."

EPILOGUE

OLD TREES, their limbs gnarled and heavy, surrounded the quiet cemetery just outside Dubrovnik's city walls. On clear days, glimpses of the blue Adriatic sparkled between the trunks, but today an overnight rainstorm left a midmorning fog hanging between the trees and over the headstones. In contrast, bright flowers on several of the graves reminded Lina that spring had arrived.

With it had come the one-year anniversary of her mother's death. And, one year to the day after she, Rocco, and Enzo had buried their mother, Lina gave birth to twins. Healthy, happy, and with heads full of dark hair. She and Ivo chose to call their daughter Cleonice—Cleo, for short—and their son Sergio. They'd gone back and forth for weeks debating names, considering several from their family trees. In the end, they'd opted to take a different route, giving each of the children names unused by family or friends. The two children, they decided, should each forge their own paths.

Lina ran her hand over the slight curve atop her parents' headstone. Despite the damp air and the sound of a baby crying—Cleo, if she had to guess—Lina felt at peace.

"Well, I finally made it," she said to the headstone. "I know Rocco came on the anniversary, but I was occupied. You have grandchildren. Twins."

She couldn't help but smile. In her heart, Lina believed her parents knew all about the twins. But oh, how she would have loved to tell them in person. To see her mother place a hand over her mouth in shock. To watch Jack do a fast blink to hide the fact he'd teared up. The two of them would have loved it.

Lina aimed a look toward the path that meandered from the cemetery and into the hills. "Ivo is taking them for a walk before we visit Rocco and Justine. The babies and I will stay at the villa this weekend while Ivo flies to Sochi for the Russian Grand Prix. I thought Rocco and Justine could get to know their new niece and nephew."

Ignoring the wet grass, she sat. Time stretched as she stared at the names on the headstone. Though only her mother was buried here, Jack's name was added once his ashes were scattered. She felt close to them here. Just as she did at the condo in New York.

Mrs. Metzger had raised her offer on the place, but Lina, Enzo, and Rocco weren't in a hurry to sell. "See how often you'll be in New York for work now that you have product at Mirabeau," Rocco had advised when she informed him of the new offer. "There's no mortgage and Mother left us enough to cover several years of taxes. It might be worthwhile to hang on to it."

So they had.

"Guess I put the cart before the horse with that news," she told the headstone. "I'm married. His name is Ivo Zanardi and he's the best thing that ever happened to me. He races Formula One, but he'll retire after this season. That's a secret, though." She swept her palm over the grass. "He has a huge heart. I suspect he'd like to keep that a secret, too, given that he's in a profession filled with testosterone and swagger, but anyone who's met him knows better. You'd both like him."

She told them about the wedding, which they'd celebrated in the park where she and Ivo had enjoyed their first concert. About meeting Noomi and her partner, Placido, both of whom she admired. About Ivo's work for UNICEF. About Amira, with whom he'd kept in contact. Then about the kart track she and Ivo recently purchased near

Milan. It wasn't much—it desperately needed repair work—but it would give Ivo everything he wanted. A project. A training ground for younger drivers. A place to host events for underprivileged children. "We won't be able to do much with it until Ivo retires, but now that we own it, we can plan."

A female cuckoo flew past, swooping near the Cornaros' headstone before it settled on an adjacent one. Without a care for Lina, the bird released a loud, bubbling call. Lina didn't move or speak until the cuckoo flew away, off to nurture its own dreams.

Jack would've gotten a kick out of the birdsong. Lina wondered if cuckoos visited the cemetery often.

"I moved out of the flat in Milan," she added once the bird was out of sight. "I wasn't keen on doing it while pregnant, but it was easier than trying to do it now, with two babies. Ivo found our new place. It's lovely. A three-bedroom flat only a few blocks from where I was before. The kitchen is small, but it has a bathtub. Can you believe it? In central Milan!" Much as she'd like to think it was for bathing children, as Ivo had pointed out when he showed her the place, she knew better.

She went on to describe her transition at work. She'd taken the title of President and Chief Designer, then hired both a CEO and CFO. "So far, so good. It's only been six weeks. I wasn't sure how I'd adjust. I have to resist the urge to step in all the time, but I'm learning that I need to hire good people and then trust them to do their jobs if I want the company to continue to grow."

She paused. Ivo would return shortly, yet so much was left unsaid. "I've had to learn to let go. I suppose that's part of growing older, but it's difficult. I've also had to learn to forgive. That's been the toughest lesson of all." Emotion clogged her throat. "At the beginning of last year, Ivo ended our relationship. I was angry and hurt, and I had to learn to forgive him. I had to forgive myself for my own role in it."

She blinked, taking a deep breath before she continued, "To move on, I had to forgive you, Mother, both for what happened with Carlo and for lying to us about it. It was hard—so hard—but I had to take a step back and realize that you made a conscious decision to change how you lived afterward. You married a wonderful man. You tried to protect your children from your past. You ensured we had good education and a good home. You taught me how to make lasagna. You even washed the windows of my shop when you knew I was taking a huge financial gamble, opening in central Milan. Ivo helped me realize that. He challenges me to be a better person. A more loving person. He notices when I'm hesitant to share—when I use what he calls my sales voice to gloss over issues—and encourages me to be open, even when it's hard. He treats me as if I'm a princess. *His* princess, the center of his world." She sighed. "Carlo is teaching me to be a better person, too, believe it or not."

She'd spoken with the king on the phone a few times since their initial meeting. With Ivo's encouragement, she'd accepted an invitation to a family dinner at the palace next month. Meeting Carlo and Fabrizia's children both unnerved and intrigued her, but her interactions with the king made her optimistic.

She pressed her lips together and looked to the sky. Low gray clouds hung overhead, but there were blue skies to the west, pushing their way toward the Croatian shore. When she addressed her parents again, it was with a full heart. "You did what you thought was best. You made mistakes. But you taught us to love, and that's the lesson I'll teach my own children. Someday, when they venture out on their own, I hope I'll encourage them the way you encouraged me."

Lina raised her head to see Ivo approach. A cap obscured his face. He wore his favorite leather jacket, one that molded to his body in a way that sent her libido into overdrive. After parking the stroller near the low stone wall of the cemetery, he circled to the front to peek at Cleo and Sergio. He looked at Lina, put a finger to his lips, and smiled.

She couldn't help but smile back. Justine and Rocco offered to watch the babies tonight so she and Ivo could enjoy a romantic dinner at a restaurant overlooking the coast. Afterward, they planned to walk along the water to enjoy the sea and the stars. The wicked look in Ivo's gaze made her heart sing. She knew he was imagining their evening together, too.

"He's a miracle worker. Able to put twins to sleep at the same time." Lina put her palm to the headstone, then rose. "Thank you for all the gifts you've given me. I love my life, and I have it because of you. I promise, I'll be back. I'm sure I'll have more stories to tell."

She bent, placed a kiss on top of the headstone, then turned to join her sexy, wonderful husband and her sleeping children.

Her present. Her future.

Thank you for reading *One Man's Princess*. If you enjoyed this book, please consider leaving a review at your favorite bookseller or book club website.

Learn about Nicole's upcoming releases and receive special insider bonuses by visiting nicoleburnham.com

ALSO BY NICOLE BURNHAM

ROYAL SCANDALS

Christmas With a Prince (prequel novella)

Scandal With a Prince

Honeymoon With a Prince

Christmas on the Royal Yacht (novella)

Slow Tango With a Prince

The Royal Bastard

Christmas With a Palace Thief (novella)

The Wicked Prince

One Man's Princess

ROYAL SCANDALS: SAN RIMINI

Fit for a Queen

Going to the Castle

The Prince's Tutor

The Knight's Kiss

Falling for Prince Federico

To Kiss a King

BOWEN, NEBRASKA

The Bowen Bride

A ROYAL SCANDALS WEDDING

More Royal Scandals titles will be available soon. For updates, please visit nicoleburnham.com, where you can subscribe to Nicole's Newsletter.

Subscribers receive exclusive content, including the short story *A Royal Scandals Wedding*, an inside look at the wedding of Megan Hallberg and Prince Stefano Barrali from the novel Scandal With a Prince.

ABOUT THE AUTHOR

Nicole Burnham is the RITA award-winning author of over twenty novels, including the popular Royal Scandals series.

Readers may visit Nicole's website and subscribe to her newsletter at nicoleburnham.com.

facebook.com/NicoleBurnhamBooks
twitter.com/NicoleBurnham
instagram.com/nicole.burnham

www.ingramcontent.com/pod-product-compliance
Lightning Source LLC
Chambersburg PA
CBHW050336190726
48284CB00007BB/2037